Girl in a Cage

Sandra J. Schurr

Girl in a Cage

A Novel

Sandra J. Schumm

PAPALLONA
BOOKS

Girl in a Cage: A Novel. Copyright © 2020 by Sandra J. Schumm.

Printed in the United States of America.

Literature/Novel

Cover design: Marguerite Schumm

Papallona Books

ISBN: 978 0 578 75316 4

For more information or to contact the author, please visit
www.sandrajschumm.com
or write to
sandrajschummwrites@gmail.com

For Bridget, Madeline, Patrick, Dashiell, Mary, and Henry

Contents

"What is this life? A frenzy, an illusion,
A shadow, a delirium, a fiction.
The greatest good's but little, and this life
Is but a dream, and dreams are only dreams."

—Pedro Calderón de la Barca, *La vida es sueño*

1

Claire de lune

September 2025 and late July 2018

"AU REVOIR! SEE YOU THIS AFTERNOON, Mommy," said my seven-year-old, Andrew, as he climbed onto the school bus. Those two words in perfectly intoned French, uttered so naturally by my son, suddenly jolted me back to July of 2018, before he was born, before I even knew I wanted to have a child. That July was such a pivotal marker in my life, but it was so difficult at that time to distinguish between fiction, reality, and the dream world. I'm a novelist so I definitely recognize the power of fiction but I remember that mystifying time and can hardly believe it was true. It still seems unreal, like a fantasy. So many things happened where the boundaries between reality and fiction, dreams and waking, this world and the world of spirits were so blurred. Those realms that we normally think are distinct seemed to blend together. Did all of that really happen to us?

I truly began to perceive those amorphous dividing lines on that day when I drove past a dilapidated farmhouse on a gravel road near our house. What I saw there echoed what I had dreamed a few days before—or at least I had *thought* the information came to me in a dream. On the day I went by that house, I'd been to an upscale grocery store for chicken breasts, fresh green beans, Dijon mustard, and Romaine lettuce for our dinner that night. Jim had said he'd be home around 7:00, and it was already fairly late in the afternoon—about four—on that sultry summer day—July 27, 2018—when I left the store and headed home. Even in my air-conditioned car, the nape of my neck, my forehead, and upper lip were sweating, so I'm not sure why I decided to turn onto the gravel, county road LL south of our house to see what was in that undeveloped area near us. Well, actually, in what I had concluded was a dream, an alluring guy with a French accent, named Antoine, had suggested to me that something appalling might be going on at a house on a gravel road near to where I lived. He had mentioned my novel *Girl in a Cage* and inferred that, as in my story, there was some nefarious situation involving a juvenile girl living there. But I guess what I'd decided was a dream wasn't really a dream; it was such a strange link into that remarkable realm of spirits.

At any rate, that day I decided it wouldn't hurt to explore more of the area near our home—the area alluded to by the specter, Antoine, who had visited me in that dream that wasn't a dream. My husband, Jim, and I had only lived in our house in Olathe, Kansas just over a week, so I definitely hadn't driven around the underdeveloped areas near there—I was still trying to orient myself toward the places I really needed to go. But on the spur of the moment, I decided to check out a gravel road just south of our housing development. A tangle of dusty trees and undergrowth lined most of both sides of the road, so there wasn't really much to see. But suddenly I slowed almost to a stop when I saw an aging, unpainted farmhouse in disrepair.

A dilapidated brown and tan van was parked in front of the small house and, as I watched, a darkly bearded man dressed in jeans and a black t-shirt pulled a thin girl with long, reddish hair from the house and pushed her into the back seat of the vehicle. She definitely didn't want to go and was yelling something I couldn't understand over my car's air-conditioner fan. Was she about 10? Maybe she was slightly older though and just small for her age; she had the shape of a pre-teen. Suddenly the man looked toward the road and, obviously, saw me creeping along in my car in front of his house. He glared at me with a look that sent chills down my spine. I immediately accelerated, hoping to get out of there as fast as possible and praying that he didn't have time to note my license plate or any other details about my car. My tires skidded on the loose gravel as I sped away and produced a choking cloud of dust in the hot, heavy air behind me.

With my hands and knees trembling so hard I could barely drive, I headed toward my house, looking into the rear view mirror every few seconds to assure myself that the angry man wasn't following me. It was hard to tell with the cloud of dust from the gravel but, after turning onto the paved street, I didn't see that old van behind me. Only when I was convinced that no one was trailing me did I approach our garage and open the automatic door. I drove in and rapidly pushed the button to close it again—safely enclosing myself in our new nest. Still shaking, I sighed with relief and leaned my forehead on the steering wheel. What in the world? How did my dream lead me to that scary situation? Or perhaps it was so frightening because I had already dreamed about it. Anyway, what did it all mean? And how was all this connected to my life in this new place?

The week before, we had just finished unpacking the rest of the moving boxes into our new home. My writing desk was set up with my John Waterhouse print *Destiny*—wearing her red, satin dress and sipping from a cobalt blue bowl—to the right of the table, my books were arranged on the bookshelves, and Jim had just adapted to our abode in Olathe, Kansas and to what we thought then was a temporary move for his job. There was a special vibrancy to our new house though; even on the first day Jim and I had toured it—July 10—I had felt a mysterious resonance there. It couldn't have been just the fact that it was powered totally by solar energy. Or could it? It wasn't a negative, eerie vibration—the kind that would make me want to leave or put me on edge enough to look over my shoulder or absently chew on the cuticle of my thumb nail. No, it had a curious reverberation—the type I feel when I began to write a new novel, and the ideas amazingly begin to reveal themselves even before I know why. Yes, something about the dwelling both perplexed and intrigued me.

The house was basically furnished, which was perfect because we thought we only needed to live there for one year. We were able to rent out our home in Connecticut—without moving all our possessions—to a visiting professor, after Jim's computer company transferred him to manage the Kansas City branch until the following July. Our new domicile in Olathe had all sorts of solar energy appliances and modern features. But it also seemed to have that unique personality of its own. I sensed it in the relatively empty corners and in the varied shades of gray throughout many of the rooms. It reminded me of the mysterious situations I love to write about. The house was like a blank page, begging for words. But there were also bright splashes of sapphire blue—in tiles in the kitchen, in the ceiling of the front hall, and in a few insets in the bedroom windows—that felt like they sparked my sixth sense. I loved this place the minute we entered. Roberta, the chatty realtor who helped us, didn't have to work very hard to persuade us to rent it for a year from Mid-Wester Energy Company, the firm that owned the structure, according to Roberta. In less than a week from when Jim and I viewed the house, we moved to Olathe and into our new home at 1740 Crescent Drive in the outskirts of a new suburb in Olathe—still somewhat in the countryside. I knew from the outset that being in that house with its distinctive, enchanting vibrancy would change me.

Just over a week after we moved in, I had what I thought was that dream that impelled me to drive down the gravel road a few days later. First I had gone to the grocery and then had the frightening encounter in front of the house on the gravel road. That same evening, Jim and I sat at the round table in the kitchen nook with windows overlooking the garden. It was too hot and sticky that night to eat dinner on the screened-in porch. My state of mind was rather heavy and unsettled as well. I wanted to be able to confide in Jim, but was worried about how he would accept what I had seen and the relevance of my dream.

We had been married seven years and were both nearing our late thirties, but lately I'd been feeling that our relationship seemed a bit fragile—like a beloved crystal goblet that has a very small chip on the rim. Could the chip be smoothed? Or would the nick cause the whole glass to break? Or cut someone? Should the whole thing be discarded? Or could it be restored? Jim always seemed to have everything together—almost nothing rubbed his fur the wrong way. But as far as getting into a conversation in depth, it didn't ever seem to happen between us. And so that unruffled air he exhibited had begun to irritate me more and more. Why couldn't we talk about anything significant? Was it his fault? Or mine?

Suddenly though, I decided that I did want to tell him about my scary experience that afternoon and probably about my dream too. I didn't want to worry him too much because I knew he had a business trip coming up and I would be at home alone in this new place. He was sensitive about things like that—always wanting to take care of me—another thing that exasperated me a bit. Did he think I wasn't capable of being responsible for myself? Was it his patriarchal air? Or was it just some sensitivity of my feminism that found it vexing? But I did want to tell him something about what I had witnessed at the old farmhouse because I was still so nervous about the whole thing. So I told him about driving by that house and about the hot-tempered man there who had forced the young girl into his van.

"And why did you decide to drive down that rough, dirty, gravel road?" Jim inquired, looking up at me and interrupting his cut into the Dijon-covered chicken breast I had prepared for our dinner.

"Well, I had a dream that there was something odd going on there and decided to just drive by and see what was there," I said, pushing my hair back behind my ears; I was suddenly hot even in the air-conditioning. There it was again, he probably thought he needed to be there with me. "I feel even more anxious now that I saw that man there with the little girl, as if the dream were real."

"Hmmm. Another dream come true," he chided lovingly, as he reached across the table and stroked my cheek. His fingernail was a bit rough on my skin. "You and your dreams! I would advise you to stay off that road and away from the house and spooky man; I don't want this to turn into a nightmare." Jim looked down at his plate again, and it seemed like he had dropped the subject. But then he added, "I'll check with the county officials though and see who lives on that property. It can't hurt to know who our new neighbors are."

I agreed and looked down at my half-eaten chicken breast. But all I could think about was that curious dream I had two nights ago and the fact that Jim hadn't been as intrigued about it as I was. I attempted to finish my dinner, but the moments that led up to my dream completely absorbed me.

Here's how what I thought was a dream took place. About 2:30 AM a few days earlier, on the 25th of July, I had wakened, itching all over not only from four very swollen mosquito bites but, also, from seemingly innumerable chigger bites around my waist and panty and bra lines. The insects in this area of the country during the summer are dreadful: lots of mosquitos and—even worse—chiggers! I only had to step outside onto the deck or pavement and I'd usually get at least one or two bites, without even having ventured into our well-kept yard. The day before, I had just watered a few flowers in the garden and showered soon after, but in the early hours of the morning I was rudely awakened by this terrible itching. I got up and painted bright red nail polish on the twenty-some bites, to smother the chiggers and to boldly proclaim my agony and protest the bites to anyone who might see my naked trunk and abdomen—most likely only Jim and me.

Afterwards I turned on a tiny book light, hoping to read in bed a while, without waking Jim, and to go back to sleep. Instead I saw two rather large spiders crawling on the ceiling above our bed, probably hoping to devour the rest of my body. Instead of attempting to read or sleep with those potential assailants so near, I grabbed my book and went through the house and out onto the screened-in porch.

That night had also been steaming hot, but there was a strong breeze blowing in through the screens. Looking toward the trees moving in the wind, I had noticed the moon, high in the night sky. It was completely full and brightly illuminated the nocturnal landscape. The air smelled like grasses and flowers—roses and something else I couldn't quite identify. If it weren't for the chiggers, I could have walked outside without the need for a light but, especially because of them, I decided to stay on the relatively safe porch. The moon had been so large and vibrant that it seemed to pulsate in the sky, and a bright star was clearly visible close to it. I set my book down and stood up to look at the beauty of the night, which seemed to palpitate in rhythm with my breath, soothing and calming me; I began to feel more in commune with Nature. After a time though, I perceived that I wasn't alone there on the porch. That impression grew stronger and stronger as I stood there gazing at the moon. Soon I realized that it wasn't just the lunar presence but that there was someone else there behind me. It wasn't a frightening feeling, so I turned to confirm my intuition. And that was when I saw a man standing there.

"*Bonne nuit.* Claire, isn't it?" said the well-built stranger dressed in navy sport shorts and a white athletic shirt. He brushed a strand of auburn hair away from his grayish eyes as he smiled widely and openly at me. He almost glowed.

"Yes, I'm Claire. But who are you?" I answered with my heart in my throat, not knowing how this man had entered our house. But his smile was so entrancing I couldn't help but return it, as if he were the person I most wanted to see. I nearly smile again now, thinking about how unreasonably happy that open expression had made me.

"I'm Antoine Benet. I used to live here. I really hope I'm not scaring you. I feel as if I already know you," he answered, revealing his exotically seductive French accent.

But I didn't know him; I'd never met the previous inhabitant of our house—we rented it from the electrical company—and I couldn't remember hearing about anyone named Antoine Benet. But he seemed so familiar that I felt strangely certain that in some way I did know him

—or at least I wanted to know him. The whole situation reminded me of a novel I had read in my Spanish lit class at university—*The Man in Black* (or was it *The Man Dressed in Black?*) by Carmen Martín Gaite. In that book, the protagonist—Carmen, like the author—doesn't know if she is awake or asleep, but a mysterious man—her interlocutor—appears and begins a conversation with her. I don't know why I remembered the book at that moment, but I realized I wasn't afraid—not at all. Why in the world did I so want to have a deep conversation with this man? Was I myself awake? Or was I dreaming? Instead of any fear, I noticed the same sense of lunar calm that I had felt just before he appeared. Antoine was tall and slim, perhaps about my age, with dark hair that fell languidly onto his high forehead. His cheek bones glimmered in the moonlight. His whole appearance thoroughly intrigued me.

"I've been waiting for the opportunity to talk with you. I really did not want to frighten you and impede any chance to converse with you; I was anticipating the right moment—I hope this is it," Antoine said as he tilted his head to the side with a concerned look on his face.

"What did you want to talk to me about?" I hadn't even asked how he got there—onto my locked porch—because the whole situation fascinated me and even seemed strangely familiar. Maybe I was just imagining myself in that novel.

"Do you mind if we sit down?" Antoine asked, motioning toward the wicker settee that faced the bright night sky.

Carmen, in the novel, asked her visitor if he wanted a cup of tea and went to the kitchen to prepare him one, but I was too captivated to go into the other room. I wondered briefly why it seemed so important to me to be able to talk to him. Then I realized that I felt I could confide in him much more than with Jim—almost as if he were an aspect of me that would help me to understand my own unconscious.

"You know I'm a great fan of your writing," Antoine mentioned after a few moments, "especially *Girl in a Cage*. Where did you get the idea for that novel? I mean, I know that juvenile sex trafficking is a pertinent topic now with all that's going on in world today, but what impelled you to write about it?"

"I really don't know," I answered as I lowered my eyes and gazed into my past. "Ever since a prostitute in Madrid told me she liked my husband as we were walking down the street, I've felt a special empathy for women in that situation, thinking that it is only by chance that I'm in my life and not forced to sell myself like so many other women. It's even more compelling when one thinks about young girls pushed into that role. The idea for the novel just popped into my head after I heard about a Syrian girl who was smuggled into the US in a shipping container and forced into a prostitution ring. I thought about that woman in Madrid again and wondered how she became a prostitute—even if she had been a child when it began. And then I wondered if I had in some way prostituted myself—if I was living in a false or forced life."

"That's intriguing that you empathized with the prostitute. After all, we are all human—she is one of us. I've been guilty of dehumanizing women as well. It's relatively easy to dismiss an adult prostitute as a bad person, but how did she get there?" he asked, shaking his head from side to side.

"I'm afraid I didn't feel the empathy soon enough—I felt fear and repulsion at first, I think. In English, she said to me, 'Hey, laydee, I like you husband.' I wish that I'd looked at her and said, 'Thank you, I do too,' or something like that, and smiled. I don't remember for sure, but I probably just hurried away. Later I chastised myself for not being more humane toward her. I regret that," I added while I wondered what else I needed to recognize about myself from this memory and I looked out again at the moon and stars in that beautiful night sky.

"I'm sure she didn't expect you to be nice to her," Antoine added as he relaxed his arm against the back of the settee.

"No, but her jungle is the same one that I live in too—and it's the same one where my young protagonist, Rima, is sold to men who sexually abuse children in my book."

"*Ah, oui*, I agree," he added and then paused. "Did you know you have moonbeams in your hair?" He traced his finger in the air close to my head.

"Oh, I think they're sun streaks. This Kansas summer sun is so strong," I muttered as I looked toward the night sky, wondering if he could see my cheeks flush or if he knew I'd been putting lemon juice on my hair, hoping for lighter streaks.

Antoine smiled and said, "Not to change the subject—I'm still thinking of sex trafficking—but have you ever explored the uncultivated area with trees to the south of your property?"

"Are you kidding?" I asked with relief; glad to change the conversation from such a flirtatious tone. "I can't even wander into my own yard without getting a million chigger bites! There's no way. But what does that have to do with trafficking?"

"Ha ha. Speaking of the chiggers, it has happened to me too" laughed Antoine. He looked almost as young as a boy when he laughed. "But I was wondering if you had noticed anything strange at that property and was hoping for your assistance, although I really don't recommend that you head that way by yourself—walking or driving. It might be quite dangerous."

I briefly pondered what Antoine might mean by wanting my help, but then the talk drifted to other subjects. He asked if I'd noticed the squirrel with the short tail in the yard and the closet door that madly squeaked even after being oiled, even though it was new. He wondered if the ice maker was still working because he remembered that it was not turning off automatically when the bin was full—just making a clicking noise that was irritating. We chatted about the eccentricities of the house, and it was clear to me that he knew it intimately. As we spoke, I felt like I was reinitiating a conversation with a dear but captivating friend. I eased more comfortably into the settee and rested my head on the back. My eyelids felt heavy despite the compelling dialogue with Antoine.

"Here," he said after a bit, pressing something into my hand. "I know you'll love this flavor."

"Hmmm, thank you," I replied, not bothering to open my eyes or look at what he had put in my hand.

When I awoke there on the porch settee, the sun was high in the sky and my pajama top was dripping with sweat. I looked down and noticed that I was clutching a tea bag in my right hand. Maybe I had actually gone into the kitchen during my dream last night, I thought. But then I remembered that the man in my dream—Antoine? Yes—Antoine—had placed something in my hand and said I'd love the flavor. I looked at the little tag on the tea bag: "*Cerisier vert. Thé de qualité supérieure*," it read on the light green background with an abstract tree and pink cherry blossoms. How odd, I thought; I didn't have any green tea with cherry in my kitchen and definitely not with labels in French. Where had this come from?

After entering the much cooler house from the porch, I found a note from Jim on the kitchen table, explaining that he had looked all over for me when he awoke and had finally found me on the porch. He wrote that he had tried to wake me to say good-bye but, when I didn't even stir, he let me sleep and was headed to work.

"I hope I wasn't snoring," he wrote. "See you tonight, Claire de lune, darling. Love you, Jimbo."

Jimbo is the name I affectionately started calling him when he named me Claire de lune, not only because he likes Debussy's "Clair de Lune," but, also, because he sometimes teases me about my introspective nature—"looney," he often calls it. The Jimbo comes from Dumbo, meaning that he generally ignores any subtle messages he might receive. He suggested it.

I began to think about my dream again and remembered that I had gone onto the porch after the itchy bites woke me. That man in my dream, Antoine—Antoine Benet, he had said—had wanted my help with something near our house. He'd mentioned sex trafficking. I must still be too emotionally involved in my own novel, I thought, if I'm still having dreams about it. I wondered what it all meant—a very curious dream indeed. And it still felt so real. And the tea bag?

Two days after I had the dream was when I drove by that farmhouse and encountered the man and young girl. Was this a sex trafficking situation as Antoine had suggested in my dream? I struggled to sleep again that night, but my brief encounter with the man on that deserted road so close to our house, as well as Antoine's comments in my dream, left me tossing and turning. Finally, around two AM I got up, grabbed my journal and a pen, and headed out to the screened porch. After tuning a violin and piano arrangement of Bizet's *Carmen* to a low volume, I sat looking at the moon again and absorbing the music, not turning on a lamp to write just yet. The now only slightly waning moon still provided plenty of light, and I sat gazing at it, again feeling a sense of calm and connection to the earth. That moment in the night, with the enchanting notes from *Carmen* and the ethereal luminescence, held a sense of peaceful beauty for me. I felt rejuvenated and yet soothed enough that I considered lying on the settee again to sleep instead of trying to write.

The tranquility dissolved a few moments later, however, when I again sensed another's presence and began to realize that what I had dismissed as an odd dream that echoed a novel I loved was not a dream at all: there really was someone in the room with me. Now I was wide awake! I looked around the porch and discerned the shape of a man at the far end near the door. He appeared to be dressed in the same shorts and shirt as the other night.

"*Bonne nuit*, Claire. How are you tonight?" intoned Antoine, sounding just as seductive as he had several nights ago. "Once again, I do not want to startle you."

But tonight I was frightened. I had convinced myself after his first appearance that Antoine had been a dream figure, but I was now quite certain that I wasn't asleep.

"OK. Who are you *really*? *Why* are you here? And *how* did you get inside my porch? Tonight you are totally freaking me out!" I shouted as Bizet's music reached a crescendo at the same time. "After the other night I decided that you had appeared in a dream but now I know that isn't true. Do you still have a key to our house?"

"I would like to be the man of your dreams but, you are right, I am not just a dream," replied Antoine, placing his hands over his chest in the area of his heart. "I'm so, so very sorry to scare you—that's not what I want to do. Please, sit down and let me explain and, please, do not be afraid."

Why did I want to believe him? It was totally irrational. I stood there for a moment, not saying anything, trying to decide what to do. He didn't appear to have a weapon on him, and Jim was just in the other room and would hear if I screamed or yelled loud enough—if he hadn't heard me already.

"I've been trying *not* to frighten you and I really did live in your house. But I don't have a key! I … I don't need those material things anymore. Claire, we've known each other in other life times, and that's why I came to you, to see if you could help."

"What? What do you mean? Why don't you need material objects anymore? Are you … a spirit? A ghost?" I asked with my eyes wide open.

"Would that frighten you more, Claire?"

"No. No, I don't think so."

I did believe that there could possibly be communication between this life and what comes before and after. And I truly preferred to think of Antoine as a spirit rather than a live man with a key to our house who came in and out at will.

"Oddly, I'm definitely more afraid of that man I saw yesterday who lives on the gravel road," I conceded with a slight shiver.

"And you should be! Be very careful!" Antoine admonished as he nodded his head in agreement with my sentiment.

He began to describe how he had often run on that road where the man lived in the badly maintained house. He'd gone past it several times, not only for the exercise but, also, because he was curious about the little girl he'd seen once with that gruff man. The feeling of confidence and camaraderie that I remembered from the first night slowly began to return despite my initial fear. My rational mind still chided me for trusting Antoine again, but my intuition clearly indicated that I needed to. But why had he appeared to me? And how had he died? I did require more information to accept him totally, so I began by inquiring when and how he died.

"I was hit by a vehicle on the gravel road you are talking about while running there in the first part of July—July 2nd, actually," Antoine answered as he stared into the night sky.

"Oh, my God!" I whispered, thinking both of my own anxiety and foreboding as I hurried to leave that road yesterday afternoon and of the fact that we had moved into this house—Antoine's house—very soon after his death. My knees began shaking again, so I sat down on the settee. "Do you know who hit you? How did it happen?"

"I do not remember much about it. I was running that evening and heard a vehicle behind me. I felt it hit me but I don't remember anything else about it. Then I left this world," Antoine explained, as he raised his hands upward and moved them as if smoke were dissipating into the air.

Antoine then began to tell me about the time before his death when he first became suspicious about the man living in the house I had seen when I passed by it. He related that one evening as he was leaving his work at the Olathe branch of Mid-Wester Energy Company rather late, he had seen a man bring a young girl up to a building close to his place of employment that housed a rather raunchy bar.

Antoine had worked for the agency that owned this house, I thought with amazement.

"I asked myself," Antoine explained with a note of furor in his voice, "what kind of parent would bring his child to that awful bar, especially at night? But then I thought perhaps he was lost, so I inquired if he needed help finding something. But he was very rude and angry and told me to mind my own business."

"What did he look like?"

"Tall, dark, with a beard. I do believe he is the same man you saw. Then, while I was working, I happened to drive by that house on the gravel road and saw what appeared to be the same van I'd seen at the bar when the guy got so mad at me. There aren't many cars like that around any more. I guess curiosity impelled me to continue to go down that road and try to observe what was going on."

Antoine told me that when he ran down that road occasionally for exercise he had continued to wonder about the child. He had even had another unpleasant encounter with the bearded man, who he had learned was named Jack.

"It is the same house that I saw then," I interjected suddenly. "And I believe I did see the man and the girl you are talking about."

"Yes, I am quite sure he is the same man. And he is called Jack," Antoine assented and then paused before continuing. "Perhaps because I read your novel, I began to suspect he was sexually abusing that child. I hope that you can either confirm or dispel my suspicions so that we can help the girl if she needs help," he informed me as his gray eyes gazed intently into mine.

We continued talking about possible ways to investigate the situation and how to rescue her if necessary. He also described the second encounter he had with this Jack.

"It's terribly curious that you died on that road," I interjected. "Was he involved?"

"That I do not know for sure—I remember that the night I died I had not arrived yet to the area where his house is and I had not seen him. But I repeat, you must be very careful. I'd like you to look into all that—for the sake of the girl if she needs help—but I really, really don't want you to get hurt, Claire."

Despite the nebulosity of this whole situation, I knew quite certainly that Antoine's concern for my safety was real.

2

Antoine Benet

January–May 2018

"YOU WANT ME TO GO WHERE?" inquired Antoine as he sat in the corporate office of *La Société EE*—the renowned international eco-energy company with its headquarters in Paris.

"To Olathe, Kansas. It is in the central US—part of Kansas City really," explained his boss, Henri Clémence, a man in his early fifties with distinguished-looking gray streaks in his auburn hair, who was very influential at *La Société EE*. "We already have a big wind energy presence in the central and western parts of Kansas, but now there is an opportunity to establish a solar net in some of the more urban areas of the state. It would be a commitment of about three years with excellent benefits for the employee and a wonderful opportunity for advancement."

Antoine had just celebrated his thirty-fifth birthday and had worked for *EE* for almost ten years now. It had been a good profession for him and had supported him well—especially in comparison to the other menial jobs he had held just after graduating from university. Despite his fluency in English, there just hadn't been worthwhile positions until he started at *EE*, but now he was getting a bit bored with his routine. Most of his present responsibilities involved online work or electronic communications that seemed to isolate him even more than he already felt. Ever since the end of his relationship with Elodie, he felt increasingly lonely and culpable. Yes, he could admit it now, it really had been his own fault that she had left. He'd been a real brute. His eyes drifted around this office with its glass conference table where he had had so many meetings with Henri and other members of the board. Through the gigantic windowpanes that occupied most of the wall space on the nineteenth story of this crescent-shaped building, he could see the rain pelting down on the park-like center oasis of this group of super-modern metal and glass buildings in this progressive area of Paris. Several people holding big, black umbrellas were hurriedly crossing the open area, trying to avoid the deluge as they got to wherever they were going—like ants in the rainstorm. This contemporary office park was so different from the intimate Parisian neighborhood where Antoine had grown up.

"Wouldn't you like a chance to take on more responsibilities, Antoine?" Henri asked, bringing Antoine momentarily out of his thoughts and back into the conversation.

Antoine nodded his assent to Henri as he inwardly debated with himself. Well, yes, anything that would change his worn out groove and improve his self-esteem would be nice, Antoine thought. But then again, a change that big would be disconcerting, even frightening. Henri explained all the details of the position, and Antoine asked all the appropriate questions, masking his sudden insecurity about the move. This would be another very influential step for *La Société EE*, to have surpassed American solar companies in their own country and to have a contract like this right in the center of the US. And, explained Henri, it could be an excellent stepping off point for Antoine's career, bringing him the essential international experience that would allow him to progress.

"*Voilà*, Antoine. Do you have any other questions? Your English is excellent, so you would be my first choice, but if you are not interested, there are others who are," Henri said, thumping his fingers on the desk in a gesture of feigned impatience that irritated Antoine's nerves and made him want to bolt out of the room.

But Antoine contained himself, thanked his superior for giving him a couple of days to think about the offer, and left his office in *La Défense*, the ultra-modern business area in the northwest of Paris. It was still raining and quite cold—the wind was biting. He forged through the rain to the metro area below the pedestrian plaza to head back toward his apartment in the 7th *Arrondissement*. Kansas? What a curious destination! He had visited New York and California, but Kansas had never been on his list of travel objectives.

The Paris metro, partially because of the inhospitable weather, was even more packed than it was at the slightly earlier hour when he normally left work. He stood, jammed in the middle of a group of young, tattooed rebels who shouted obscenities back and forth. Most were guys, but there was one dark-haired girl with a pierced nose, red lipstick, and an asymmetrical haircut—long on one side and nearly shaved bare on the other—who seemed to be provoking the whole dispute. She would have been quite beautiful, Antoine thought, if she weren't so extreme. It was hard to tell whose side she was on, but she seemed to delight in the whole fracas. Antoine, however, was soon lost in his own thoughts again and managed to ignore them despite the ruckus they continued and the occasional shove he felt when someone got pushed too far toward him. Maybe he should explore another part of the world.

After he got off the metro and ascended the stairs at his exit at *Invalides*, he paused there in the exit area out of the rain, pulled out his phone, and looked up Olathe, Kansas and then Kansas City. The links kept mentioning that Olathe was part of the Kansas City area—which was both in Kansas and Missouri; that was what he remembered Henri saying as well. Well, going to Kansas was probably better than going to a Latin American or African country though, with all the current political problems he had heard about in those areas. But the US was presently in a sort of governmental affray as well, and with a president who was not eager to have foreigners enter his country. Hopefully that wouldn't be a problem. Then he suddenly thought of a tale from his childhood of someone from Kansas—what was it? What was the name of that story where the little girl got caught in a tornado? Was Kansas still cowboy country? And how would it be to live in such a remote area?

Emerging from the metro exit, Antoine wrapped his scarf around his throat more tightly and walked a bit aimlessly, despite the rain, toward *Rue Cler*, with its brick-patterned streets and rainbow colored awnings, store fronts, and doors. It was such a pleasant change from the cold glass and metal buildings in *La Défense*. Here, despite the evening hour, fruit and vegetable markets, cheese shops, and cafés still opened their doors to customers. He eventually entered *Le Petit Cler*, a small café he often frequented. Ever since Elodie had left him, going home was his last resort. He preferred the animated atmosphere of the little restaurants near his street and often delayed going home until it was time to sleep. He would have an aperitif and dinner, perhaps talk with friends. The warm ambient, the scent of delicious foods, and the lively conversations inside always helped to cheer him even if he didn't know anyone inside. The milieu was so intimate that conversation was easy, even when those seated next to you were strangers. This evening he looked around the tables and, as was more common than not, spotted some friends already seated there.

"*Bonsoir, Antoine,*" voices called from inside the café, nearly at the same time.

"*Bonsoir, Emilie, Marcel. Comment allez-vous?*"

The aroma of grilled *Saint-Marcellin* cheese, *Boeuf Bourguignon*, and lively red wine wafted toward Antoine, immediately comforting him.

"We're fine, Antoine. Come and sit with us. What will you have? *Un kir?*" said Marcel as he jumped up and pulled over another chair. "You look like you've had a difficult day."

Marcel and Emilie were long-time friends who had been close even before Elodie came into and then left his life. Emilie was as blonde and fair as Marcel was brunette and olive-skinned—a good combination of opposites, he thought. He approached them both to *faire la bise*, lightly touching his cheeks to each of theirs and giving Emilie a slightly longer hug. He sat down, agreed to the *kir*, and unwound the scarf from his neck as he pushed back the lock of hair that had fallen down on his forehead. After some preliminary pleasantries, they pressed him on how things were going for him, so Antoine explained the offer his boss had made to him that very afternoon just before closing about him working for three years in the United States.

"Is it a mandatory move for you?" inquired Emilie, looking with concern into his eyes. Hers appeared so clear and intensely blue, besides being beautifully lined with pencil and touched with mascara. Loosely coifed hair framed her slim face, and her soft, black sweater set off her rosy, high cheekbones and shapely lips. Marcel was such a lucky guy, thought Antoine.

"*Alors,* the way that he said there would be others interested in the position if I wasn't made it sound to me like I'd better go or else," conceded Antoine, frowning and looking a bit lost.

Emilie squeezed his hand and looked at Marcel, who patted his friend on the back and proffered some words of encouragement. His friends and he continued to talk during dinner about his new "opportunity," and both tried to booster his mood—to get him to see this as an adventure. They knew his English was excellent, so he would be able to meet new friends, travel to different areas on his vacation days, and try the different food.

"Antoine, I know you've been lonely and unhappy here since you and Elodie broke up. Perhaps this offer would be a good opportunity for you to start a whole new segment of your life. You would be in a totally new environment with the chance to meet different people," Emilie added as she paused delicately between bites with knife and fork in each hand.

"Personally, I'd hate for you to leave," interjected Marcel, pinching his dark eyebrows closer together, "but I also want what is best for you. Maybe this is just what you need."

"Well, I am rather excited about the opportunity to expand our solar technology," Antoine began. However, his voice cracked slightly as he continued. "But Kansas seems so remote—and for three whole years. Also I have a vague negative feeling about it that I can't quite explain." He put down his fork and covered his eyes with his hand momentarily, with the knife still upright in the other.

"Aww, you are just nervous, Antoine. Do not worry. Possibly it would give us a good excuse to visit America, *non*, Marcel?" said Emilie, looking imploringly toward Marcel.

"*Oui, oui, une très bonne possibilité*. A very good chance," added Marcel, eyeing the *brochette de boeuf* Antoine had ordered. "I should have ordered that too—it looks delicious. More wine, Emilie? Antoine?"

Perhaps a change of scenery was what he needed after all, thought Antoine as he continued home later that evening: a new job, a new country, a new life. Now the shops were closed and the pedestrians on the street had thinned out, partially due to the continuing, steady drizzle of rain. Despite the damp, cold atmosphere, Antoine returned to his flat that evening feeling more optimistic than he had in months.

The next day he told his boss he accepted the offer and in the following weeks began to prepare to leave. He sold his little red 2005 *Citroën C2* within a few days, dispensed of many possessions he wouldn't be able to take with him by bringing a box or bagful to area second-hand stores most weekend days when he went out. He rented out his furnished one-bedroom flat, effective at the beginning of March, within two weeks of placing the ad on the internet.

Then he traveled to Aix-en-Provence to visit his mother, Simone, who lived there with her mate, Alain. Antoine hoped to avoid Alain as much as possible but really wanted to see his *maman*. The summer when Antoine was ten, his dad, Georges, had died after being hit by a semi-truck while changing a flat tire on the autoroute heading into Paris. Antoine had been overwhelmed by his dad's unexpected death. Even though he was not a very young child, he had not wanted to leave his mother's side—fearful that he might lose her too. He had followed Simone around their flat, trying not to let her out of his sight, and had gone with her every time she went down to the street, even for a loaf of bread. When school started in the fall, he cried every day when she left him at the door—even though he was supposed to be a big boy by then.

About five years after his *papa*'s death his mother started seeing Alain. Even at fifteen, Antoine had not been ready to share his doting *maman* with someone else. He remembered how rebellious he had become—how once he had even pushed Alain in the chest when he came to take Simone out to dinner. Alain crashed against the door jamb, and Simone had screamed as Antoine burst out the door and didn't return until about 2 in the morning—cold and with no place to go. Simone was so relieved to see her son but she still made him apologize to Alain. Antoine had complied with his mother's wishes, but with no real forgiveness in his heart.

Alain and Simone had been together now for nearly twenty years. Simone, at 58, had unlined skin and the shape a twenty-year-old would envy, and her infectious smile showed how happy she was. How could she have recovered so completely from his father's death while Antoine had felt so much anger for so many years? In fact, he still did not get along with Alain, but he did cherish his mother. She had been a strong anchor for him when he was so tempestuous and adrift. Antoine bid her an anxious farewell. Why did preparing for his new life feel so much like the end of the old one?

Almost two months after he accepted the US position, Antoine found himself crammed into an interior seat of row 23 in the center of the fully booked international flight headed to Newark in route to Kansas City. The large man seated on his left didn't seem to notice that his belly was spilling over the armrest into Antoine's space or that he kept poking his elbow into Antoine's arms and ribs. Also, Antoine was seated in front of a computer screen that did not function at all. The flight attendant said that particular screen had been going on and off, but it wasn't functional at all this afternoon. Now he wouldn't even be able to distract himself from his edgy nervousness by watching a movie. Why hadn't he brought a book in his carryon luggage? And why had he agreed to give up his seat in business class just because the plane was overbooked? The credit the airline had issued him hardly seemed worth it at the moment in this hot, noisy section of the plane. And when the lunch cart got to him the only thing left was the soggy pasta. Antoine got more anxious and irritated by the minute. This journey didn't seem to be starting out well. He wondered now if this might be an indication of how his whole decision to go to Kansas would turn out, with everything working badly and being poked and pushed by the people around him. His breath quickened and became more shallow, and he began to wriggle in his seat.

"Would you like to have this book I just finished?" inquired the older, gray-haired lady dressed in a maroon sweater seated next to him.

She was unmistakably from the US and had just paused the film *Victoria and Abdul* to see if she could make him more comfortable. Obviously his frustration was a little too evident.

"It's really quite good," she said, trying to soothe him. "And I love this author—Claire Schmidt. Have you heard of her? *Girl in a Cage* is her third novel, and the other two are very interesting as well."

No, he hadn't heard of her—and he didn't say that her book probably wasn't one he would have picked—but he was happy to have something to do on this long flight. He thanked his seat mate graciously, and she went back to her movie. It really was quite considerate of her to offer her book. Perhaps many Americans were this compassionate; besides, reading in English would probably be good to boost his vocabulary before arriving in Kansas.

The novel surprised Antoine because it dealt with a twelve-year-old female child being victimized in a sex trafficking scheme. It was subject that Antoine hadn't really thought about much—had never wanted to even contemplate—but the little girl protagonist, Rima, with her soft, dark brown eyes and curly hair, captivated his interest. Even though she had attempted to escape from her hard life in Syria, she had ended up in cheap, rented rooms in the US with men who abused her sexually. The author, in her afterword, informed the reader that, while her work was fictitious, the number of children who were victims of sex crimes like she described was astounding—depending upon which sources one consulted, between one and a half and two million children, mostly girls, worldwide. But in addition to its rather shocking theme and content, the most amazing aspect of the book was that the author's voice seemed so very familiar. Despite his never having thought about child sex trafficking, the writing felt hauntingly intimate—almost like *déjà vu*. Maybe he was just tired, but the presentiment was rather unsettling. At any rate, Antoine promised himself to look up the other novels by Claire Schmidt after he got settled in Kansas and he continued reading throughout the flight.

* * * * *

Antoine was escorted into the president's office at Mid-Wester Energy by the middle-aged secretary, Anne, whose desk was outside the dark wooden door to the president's office. After Anne opened the door, Antoine quickly surveyed the expansive office, which was paneled in darkly stained wood and had green leather chairs around a massive desk cluttered with stacks of papers and a large-screened computer. It looked like a style from the nineties and was in great contrast to the ultra-modern and almost sterile offices where Antoine worked at *La Societé EE* in *La Défense*.

"Hello, Antoine, I'm Fred Woodward, president of Mid-Wester Energy," Fred said as he stood and held out his large, lanky hand, "and this is Cheryl Atkins, our development engineer. We're so happy to have you and your expertise on solar energy here. I hope your flight went smoothly and that you're not too jet lagged."

Fred Woodward was tall, angular, and a bit overweight. He wore a poorly fitted navy suit that seemed too loose around his shoulders and too tight around the belly. In contrast, Cheryl Atkins' light mauve dress and short sweater appeared just right for her well-built body.

"Good day, Mr. Woodward, Ms. Atkins. I am so pleased to meet you. Yes, my flight was fine—long but . . . ," Antoine said as he reached his hand out to Woodward and then hesitated briefly, wondering if he should shake hers too or lean forward for the French greeting.

"Please, call us Fred and Cheryl," said Cheryl, extending her hand and resolving his dilemma. "We aren't that formal here, and it's so nice to meet you as well."

Cheryl smiled warmly as she looked at him, and the corners of her blue eyes smiled too. Antoine hoped his own eyes didn't look too hungry because he had immediately noticed that she was quite attractive and slender, more pleasingly shaped than many of the Americans he had seen so far. Fred, however, looked as if he enjoyed food a lot.

"Have a seat," Fred added, as he pointed toward the chairs surrounding his desk, "and we'll get started. Would you like a cup of coffee? We have some donuts in case you're hungry before our lunch meeting. The three of us will meet until lunch, and then some others will join us at a nearby restaurant. We should be done by 5:00; then Cheryl will show you your house. Later, a few of our staff will accompany you to dinner on the Plaza. They'll take you to some of the nicer evening places in KC."

Antoine helped himself to some coffee. He missed his normal *café au lait*, but the coffee was fresh and fairly strong. He hoped his energy would last through the evening, as he had wakened with the first rays of the sun despite his long journey the day before. Fred pulled up a power point presentation, which he also projected on a large screen behind his desk, beginning with some maps of the area that indicated where they wanted to initiate the solar grid.

"We want to originate the solar connectivity on the outskirts of this area," explained Cheryl, pointing to the overhead with a laser beam, "because it will be easier to accomplish in the more remote areas while we're just getting started. We'll start slowly at first. Then we'll do a more interior neighborhood—this one—as a demonstration and to get people excited about it."

"Yes, we need to sell many of our customers on the idea of solar energy; they tend to be pretty conservative here. Some probably want to go back to coal," joked Fred, laughing a bit too much at what was probably the truth. "And, anyway, we want them to invest in many of your solar products. We'll all profit from that."

Fred explained that the state flower was the sunflower and that, in order to counter resistance to solar power in the area, they had devised a whole marketing plan involving blooming sunflowers to sell the solar energy idea.

"Although we have a lot of wind generators in the more western areas of the state—and there's a lot of wind out there—they haven't caught on completely. Some folks think the windmills destroy the landscape and others say they are dangerous for the birds, so we want our solar scheme to blend perfectly and be very clean— 'Sun Energy for the Sunflower State,'" he explained as he forwarded to the logo and motto on the screen.

Mid-Wester had purchased two houses in a newly developing area just outside the city where Antoine would begin the solar connectivity and help to demonstrate how current customers could boost their solar power usage with a variety of products.

"We thought you could live in one of the houses while you are here, and the other could be set up as a demonstration house for the public," Fred continued, clearing his throat again and looking briefly at the time on his cellphone. "We'll have open houses there to show people in the area how efficient and clean this solar connection will be. We can have your solar tiles installed on the roof areas, have the swimming pool heated by sun energy, solar car ports, water heaters, sun energy to recharge electric cars, phones, computers, etc."

Fred explained that there would be several different solar electrical options in the demonstration home, since most of their customers would be converting items to solar energy in older homes where they already lived. As Fred went on with his explanations, the sugary donut smell in the room, combined with his jet-lag, was starting to make Antoine feel queasy. But then they adjourned to lunch and the afternoon meetings, which continued with power point presentations at the restaurant. More coffee kept Antoine awake and fairly alert.

After the meetings, Fred excused himself to meet his family for dinner, and Cheryl drove Antoine to show him where he would be living. It felt good to get outside—even into the somewhat frigid March air. On the drive there, Antoine was amazed at the open areas covered lightly with snow that surrounded the highway. He felt like he was on an urban route in the countryside with all the stores with gigantic parking lots along the way. He conceded though that the giant grocery chains and superstores near the highway were similar to those that had cropped up outside the major cities in France in recent years. The drive wasn't that long but Antoine's eyes kept blinking shut. He had slept until about 5 AM and then could not go back to sleep even though he had not slept at all on the long flight to Dallas, the two hour wait in the airport there, or the shorter flight to Kansas City. Now he could feel his head nodding, even after all the coffee he had drunk that day. I'm sure

I'm making a great impression on this lady, he thought, as he tried to wake himself up by concentrating on the somewhat boring landscape.

Soon enough though they entered the new suburb where Mid-Wester would be exhibiting homes with solar technology and where Antoine would live. The already furnished house at 1740 Crescent Drive on the periphery of Olathe was innovative and attractive, with neutral gray walls, lots of open spaces, and all sorts of solar powered gadgets. It was the domicile they had set up for Antoine. Then Cheryl drove him by the adjacent, yet unfinished, demonstration house on Crescent Circle that would be open to public viewing and demonstrations. The neighborhood, obviously new, was surrounded by wooded areas and farmland.

"I hope you don't feel too isolated out here," said Cheryl, eyeing him with concern as she pulled back into the driveway of the house where he would be living. "But you will have a car and you're only minutes away from anywhere in Kansas City. You'll see the Plaza area at dinner tonight and then I'll take you back to your hotel this evening. Tomorrow morning, we can pick up your car."

Antoine hoped he wouldn't feel isolated as well, but Cheryl's curly blonde hair tied back into a pony tail, her American but still stylish manner of dress, and her confidence combined with her constant interest in his well-being helped him to feel enthusiastic rather than fearful about his future there. The afternoon meetings had revealed that he would have a rather busy schedule in the next few weeks, and he had met dozens of people he would be working with. In addition to the work challenge, he was eager to see Cheryl regularly at work and was pleased about her role in getting him settled. What luck to have such a beautiful mentor!

Two days later, Antoine was installed in his new home with the meager possessions he had brought from Paris—three suits and a sports jacket, two pairs of shoes, a suitcase full of some shirts and jeans, socks, underwear, and sweaters, his umbrella, a lap-top computer, some family photos, and a few books. It didn't take him much time to unpack, but the house looked nearly as unoccupied after he put things away as it did before. He hung his clothes in the closet that seemed big enough for a whole family and put his personal items in the bathroom—already complete with towels—which adjoined his room. He would just buy things as he needed them—it had seemed too difficult to transport much so far. His kitchen was already furnished with a few plates and glasses—he'd need to buy some decent wine glasses though. Modern IKEA couches, tables and chairs, and a bed that were serviceable and comfortable, but rather nondescript, occupied the mainly grey-painted rooms. It reminded him a bit of his bare, spacious office at *EE*.

The main thing that intrigued him about the house were the bright blue accents of glass or tiles in several of the rooms that echoed the color of the vibrant sea and sky he remembered from August vacations when he was a child. He positioned his lap-top on the efficient desk, along with a framed photo of his parents and him when he was about 8 years old. They were all grinning broadly and seated on the beach at *Saint-Jean-Cap-Ferrat* under a bright yellow umbrella in their swimsuits—his *maman* in dark blue but topless, like nearly all the women in that era, and his dad in a skimpy, red swim brief. They looked so young and vibrant. It brought a smile to his face just thinking of that trip and the secure way he had felt before his *papa* died. That photo was the best he could do for now to make this house feel like his.

After about two weeks, he had settled into a routine and knew his way around the city without getting so lost in his white, hybrid Ford Fusion. He was working long hours trying to get everything set up for the demonstration house so that there would be plenty of visible options of solar energy. Often in the evenings he had meetings with the workers at the Olathe offices. He tried exploring some of the bars and restaurants close to the office afterwards, but so far they were inferior to the ones he had visited on the Plaza or in the Westport area.

One evening, about a month and a half later, after several days of working late, he decided he would like an *apéritif* or at least a congenial glass of wine before he went home. He had noticed a bar in a nondescript, windowless building made of aluminum siding called simply "The Place Bar" in the block next to his Olathe office. The battered sign with florescent letters above the door had a non-functioning "P," so at night it appeared to read "The lace Bar." But nothing about the exterior of the building suggested lace at all, Antoine thought wryly. Even though the outside did not look at all inviting or welcoming to him, the parking lot was always jammed with cars and trucks when he got off work. Evidently it was popular despite its dumpy aspect, so he decided to give it a try.

When Antoine entered the darkened bar that evening in May, he instantly concluded that the warehouse-type appearance of the interior, with its dark, gritty concrete floor, coincided quite well with the bleak outside. The air inside smelled musty, like stale grease and beer with whiffs of unkept urinals, and the hard surfaces of the walls made the dive even louder than it might have been—almost deafening. Antoine grimaced but headed toward the long, cement-block bar. Of course, they had nothing like an apéritif, or even a glass of wine, so he bought a bottled beer and stood there sipping it straight from the bottle as he looked around. The crowd appeared to be the type that his co-workers had described as the "red-necks" who were not open to the advances of solar energy. He listened curiously but even had a hard time distinguishing what they were saying. No one paid much attention to him at first, but then a couple of the patrons, dressed in well-worn jeans and t-shirts and standing near him at the bar, started looking him over and, apparently, even talking about him.

One of them, after he brusquely asked where Antoine was from, loudly jeered, "Oh, you're from France, are ya? I bet ya think ya really know how to French Kiss."

He grabbed a passing waitress—clad in a very short shorts and a sleeveless, pink top that ended well above her waistline—and shoved her toward Antoine. The brute looked at Antoine and said, "Ya better show us how to do it, Frenchie."

The other men around him jeered, "Yeah, show us! Show us!"

"*Mon dieu*," thought Antoine as he excused himself, sat his bottle on the bar, and headed rapidly toward the exit.

"You fuckin, cowardly for'ner. Stay outta our bar," one man yelled, as Antoine hurried outside.

Antoine decided it was definitely the worst locale he had ever entered—full of drunk, belligerent men. No, they didn't have to worry about him going back there; he should have trusted his first impression of it as a pigsty.

So, weeks later, the night Antoine saw a man leading a young girl through the parking lot toward the entrance to "The Place Bar" as he left work, Antoine was convinced it must have been in error: no one in their right mind would bring a child to that crude dump.

3

Black Jack

Late May 2018

"YEAH?" JACK MUTTERED GRUFFLY into his cellphone as he pushed himself up onto one elbow in his rumpled bed.

Jack was still groggy from a late night at the casino boats—a night where he, one more time, squandered everything he had won. He seemed to have lost his lucky streak, and the cards just weren't coming his way. He'd really regressed since the days when he was employed as a dealer at the Isle of Capri Casino—one of the four riverboat casinos in Kansas City. Everyone had started calling him Black Jack there, to go with the card game he dealt. He looked the part too, with his thick black hair and beard and his habitual black attire. Plus, he could out-deal the other dealers and outsmart the players most of the time. He was strutting high in his boots there, and everybody seemed to respect him—even the chicks. But then, again, he'd started drinking a bit too much and got into an altercation with a customer one night. Jack had hit him in the jaw when the guy wouldn't shut up, and his boss fired him on the spot, not even listening to Jack's assurances that it would never happen again.

That didn't stop Jack's love of gambling though, and he still spent almost as much time at the other three boats as when he was employed at one there. Only now he wasn't earning a salary at the game but depending on Lady Luck to fuel his liquor and entertainment, not to mention his living expenses. Except, like all the women he knew, Lady Luck was fickle—she was with you for a while and then she was gone.

Now she'd been gone for a long time with just some teases to keep him playing on. He'd had to move from his apartment near the boats to a rundown old house he'd found near Olathe. He spent more on gas to get back and forth to play at the boats, but his rent was practically nothing, and nobody bothered him out there in the country. Besides, there were some bars nearby where he could always start up a game of black-jack with some blokes who didn't know much about the skills of the game and, hopefully, he could win back a few of the riches he deserved.

"Hey, Black Jack! How ya doin'?" Duke voiced into the phone as Jack threw his legs over the edge of the bed and rubbed his aching forehead with his free hand.

His room was hot already, and he wasn't sure how late it was. His dirty clothes from last night were scattered on the floor.

"Listen, have I got a deal for you! It's a way for some easy money."

Jack definitely needed some cash, so he listened skeptically as his ex-crony, Duke, offered up his "deal." Duke owed Jack some money from when Jack was flush with it with his dealer's job but Duke never had been quite able to pay it all back. Now Jack could really use the money so he waited while Duke explained that he had a girl Jack could use to earn some cash. Jack could hear noise in the background—some people talking. Where was Duke anyway?

"You mean like a pimp?" Jack queried as he ran his fingers through his greasy hair. He definitely needed a shower he decided, sniff-ing at his armpit.

"Well, you'd just own her and you can market her on the comput-er from wherever you are. There are people who'll pay good money for her. She's a real looker—she won't be hard to sell," Duke continued, even though he was interrupted momentarily by some banging noise he could hear going on around Duke.

"Where'd ya get her?" asked Jack, looking at the grimy, grayed paint on the cracked plaster walls of the bedroom in this old place he'd had to move into after he'd lost his job. He did need some more cash coming in after all.

"My buddy Bill in El Paso, Texas and his Mrs., Coreen, tried bein' foster parents to a bunch of Mexic'n kids to collect some pay-ments from the government for keepin' em. But then Coreen left him, and when he tried to take the kids back, the place said they didn't know them and besides they were too full to keep any more kids. So Bill had to bring 'em back home. But he wasn't getting any more money from the government to take care of them either, so he asked me to take a couple," answered Duke.

Duke proceeded to tell Jack about how he and Bill had worked out a way to market the kids, mainly girls, over the internet to get them to pay for their keep and then some. So far the venture had proven quite profitable, he'd make at least $300 a night per girl. There was a website they used to market them—babychicks.com—so he gave Jack the details about that. For the most part, the website sold chicken eggs to hatch and incubators, but there was a special section for "other things."

"A lot of guys really like the young ones, so you can charge more for 'em cause they're hard to find. They're a real cash cow," laughed Duke and made a mooing sound.

"How old is she anyway?" Jack asked as he wondered at the same time whether he brought his wallet home last night. He got up to search for it in his dirty jeans. It was there! He was afraid that it was empty but at least he'd still have his driver's license.

Duke wasn't sure how old—maybe fifteen—but he didn't really have the space for two girls—one could just sleep with him, but two were too many. And it was complicated delivering two different girls and picking them up after their services—one would be easier to manage.

"I don't know how to take care of a kid—especially a girl," protested Jack.

"Just feed her a few times a day and give her a place to sleep—like a dog—; she'll do just fine," answered Duke, obviously trying to convince him. "And she'll earn you some easy dough."

Jack thought back to his own childhood. His mother had left when he was seven and he'd grown up with just his dad. That's about what his dad had done—his dad gave him food a few times a day, and Jack had a place to sleep. His dad drank a lot and, when he did, Jack had learned he had to hide from him. He got mad at everyone and everything when he was drunk and had often beaten Jack, just like he was a disobedient dog. But at least he'd cared for Jack and hadn't abandoned him like his fuckin' mother had. For that Jack loved his dad despite the beatings. His dad always said hitting him would make Jack strong. So if a dog's life had been good enough for him, it was certainly good enough for a stupid Mexican girl. And he really could use the cash.

"Besides," added Duke, "you talk a little Mexic'n—it'll be easier for you to talk to her than it is for me."

Jack's head hurt and still felt muddled from the night before, but he did need money. Yes, his wallet was empty—that's what he was afraid of. He'd spent all of it last night on the games and liquor. And he was pretty sure this offer from Duke was the only way he'd ever get any more back from him on that loan he'd given him; it seemed that this was Duke's final attempt to pay back his debt.

"Okay. Where should I meet you?" Jack asked as he looked at the sunny day outside—a bit too bright for his head right now.

Jack showered—rubbing soap into his hair because he was out of shampoo—then dressed and headed to Peculiar, Missouri where he met Duke at a gas station. His old buddy was already parked there in a slightly rusty, green Chevy Hatchback, waiting impatiently outside the car when Jack arrived. Jack hadn't seen him in about a year and noticed that Duke had packed on a little weight around the middle. Duke hurried over with an outstretched hand as Jack hopped out of his van, hoping to get a peek into the Chevy at his new asset before he agreed. But evidently Duke wanted to shake on the pact right away.

Jack got closer to Duke's car and peeked inside as Duke chattered on about what a great deal this was going to be. In Duke's back seat was a small, skinny, sobbing girl dressed in shorts and a shirt with her head lying on a ripped and worn beige seat. She was so little—no way was she fifteen! Twelve, maybe? Jack really began to have doubts about the whole deal. But Duke immediately opened the back door to the car, scooped up the kid as if she were a bag of potatoes, and hurriedly brought her over to Jack's van. Duke looked around the area nervously as he shut the door with the girl inside. Duke seemed in a big hurry to get back to Branson, so within a matter of minutes after he'd deposited the kid in the back seat, Duke handed Jack a code and password to the special part of the Babychicks website and $50.00—to pay back part of what he owed him in case the girl needed anything at first. There was no luggage or anything. Didn't she have any clothes? Then Duke was gone. And he didn't answer his phone when Jack tried to call just minutes later to pull out of the deal. The girl was still crying.

"Damn him anyway," shouted Jack, pounding his fist on the steering wheel. "Damn him! And you, shut up! Stop cryin' like a baby. *Basta.* That's enough. *Basta. Cállate.* You're making my head hurt."

As if it didn't already hurt! What was he doing anyway? He could get into a lot of trouble because of this kid if he got caught. But all he had was Duke's phone number, and Duke obviously didn't want to talk to him. He'd just have to be careful not to get caught.

"*Necesito encontrar a mi mamá*," whimpered the girl, cowering on the brown bench seat behind Jack. "*Necesito encontrar a mi mamá.*"

"Your mama—well, if ya want to see your mama, ya're going to have to work and earn some money. *Tú—trabajar.* And stop your cryin'," yelled Jack, pounding on the steering wheel again and flooring the gas pedal.

Jack drove a ways in silence, and the girl was quiet too. Then he suddenly pulled over at a MacDonald's drive-up window and bought himself a Big Mac with fries and a giant coke, along with a cheaper kid's meal and a small coke for the girl. He handed the Happy Meal back to her without a word. She actually stopped sniveling in back, and he could see in the rearview mirror that she began to eat hungrily. Without stopping to look up, she gobbled down the burger and then the fries as well. Obviously Duke hadn't fed her in a while. Her eyes met his in the rearview mirror after she finished and seemed to convey gratitude. Maybe he could get her to cooperate if he just fed her.

"*¿Cómo... te llamas?*" queried Jack before he took another mouthful of his burger as he continued along toward Olathe.

"*Soy Anita*," she replied softly, wiping at her eyes.

"Jack here," he mumbled with his mouth full. At least she'd stopped crying for a while.

The first couple of days at Jack's house Anita slept most of the time. He had taken a couple of sofa cushions off an old couch left in the house when rented it and put them on the floor in a corner of the dusty, unused upstairs bedroom. He did have an extra tattered sheet and blanket for her and even loaned her one of his pillows—the flatter one he didn't much like for himself. Her room was smaller than his— probably only big enough for a bed and dresser—which he didn't have for her. But the cracked plaster walls were like the ones in his room. Some of the cracks even showed the little parallel wooden slats beneath the formerly cream-colored paint that now had dark splotches in the corners. The wooden floor boards were rough and dirty with a few holes big enough, perhaps, for a rat to enter. A bare, tall window in the center of one wall, where the sun shined in a little too brightly in the afternoons, overlooked the wooded area surrounding the house. Jack opened the window a crack, with difficulty, to let in some air. Anita gazed absently at the room with a frown, but then she curled up on the cushions and fell asleep—more like a kitten than a dog, he thought. But she woke several times that night and most of the nights that followed, screaming out in her sleep.

"*¡Mamá, mamá! ¡No me dejes! ¡Mamá!*" Or simply, "*¡No, no, NOOOOO!*"

Her blood curdling screams in the night jolted Jack from sleep too, but he didn't know what to do about it. He cursed Duke under his breath and tried to go back to sleep.

That first day he put a padlock on the outside of her door and left her there sleeping several different times to go to buy food and other supplies—toilet paper and shampoo. The first couple of days he brought food up to her room and she ate it sitting on her cushion bed. Every time he fed her she looked at him with her big, pleading brown eyes, conveying something Jack didn't quite know how to interpret. In the meantime, he'd been working on his phone to get into the website and to use the code Duke had given him to set up an ad to market her. On the third day, she was more wide awake, so he took her to Walmart and let her pick out a few articles of clothing—some panties, t-shirts, and another pair of shorts. He also bought some red hair dye, hoping to disguise her appearance somewhat, just in case. After they got home, he read the directions on the box and dyed her hair. Then he took a photo of her with his phone and put it in the ad he'd worked up for the website.

"We'll call ya 'Annie'—tú, Annie," he said, pointing at her.

"*No, me llamo Anita y quiero encontrar a mi mamá,*" Anita replied, looking both scared and defiant at the same time.

"Nope, now ya're Annie. And ya have to start working if ya wanna find your mama. *Tú—trabajar. Yo—ayudar.* But ya've gotta *trabajar*—ya've gotta work. *Dinero—trabajar.* Then we'll find your mama.*"

Of course, Jack had no intention of finding her mother and wouldn't have had the slightest idea where to start even if he'd wanted to. But he did know that he needed money, and fast. Buying her food and clothes had depleted most of the $50.00, and he had practically nothing left—not even enough to try to gamble for more. He was getting some response on the ads though—and she did owe him something now that he was taking care of her. He'd advertised her as being ten years old, but he really wasn't sure how old she was and didn't care to know. He, personally, was no more sexually attracted to a ten-year-old than he was to a dog, but he had to hope lots of guys were. He bargained online with one chap who called himself Romeo and agreed to drop her off at a Days Inn, room 210 at 10:00 PM and pick her up at 11:00.

Anita went with Jack willingly to "*trabajar*" that first time he farmed her out. They left the house with her in the backseat again and drove along the highway until they reached the motel and parked at the far end of the lot. It had just started to sprinkle rain as they emerged from the van, walked across the parking lot, climbed up the exterior stairs, and knocked on the door. A skinny, brown-haired man with a droopy mustache and equally droopy clothes hanging on his body, opened the door to the motel room.

"Romeo?" Jack asked, scowling.

"Romeo, Romeo, that's my name," the man laughed nervously, exposing his brownish-yellow, tobacco-stained teeth as he stepped back so they could enter.

After he closed the door behind them, Romeo handed Jack a few bills, which Jack immediately counted and nodded when he found the amount correct. Jack then confirmed the hour he would return—11:00 —precisely one hour later. The small room with a double bed must have been one of the "smoking rooms" in the motel, because it reeked of stale tobacco, made worse by the lighted cigarette in the ashtray next to the bed. The bed was covered with a rumpled olive green bedspread, partially turned back to reveal the pillows. Anita looked around and evidently had thought she was going to clean the room or something when they talked about going to "*trabajar*," but then she began to look nervously at Jack when she heard he meant to leave. Her eyes widened immensely, and she looked pleadingly at him as he headed toward the door. Jack didn't even want to think about what followed. He returned to his van and pulled out the bottle of bourbon he'd stashed under the seat and took several swigs while he alternately watched the time on his phone and the door of the motel room. This isn't any fun for me either, he thought defensively.

When Jack fetched Anita at 11:00 sharp, she was sobbing and withdrawn. She cried and screamed out in the night and slept fitfully most of the next day. When he fed her that following day, she ate but wouldn't look at him. At least they had a bit of money now though, and he also had more "dates" set up for her to keep the cash coming in. After that first time, he always had to drag, carry, or push her into the van—she was definitely no longer cooperative about her work. Some nights, however, he just locked her in her room to give them both a break and went to the boats by himself, now that he had a bit of cash to work with again. A few bourbons and some games of blackjack bolstered his mood even when he wasn't winning.

One evening Jack decided to take Anita by a bar near his house that he'd hung out in fairly often to see if he could drum up any business for her there. It was just turning dark outside when he pulled up into the crowded parking lot of "The Place Bar." At first Anita probably thought they were going to a store, but he told her it was a bar and maybe they could get her something to eat. Evidently the loud music and boisterous yelling from inside weren't what she was expecting, and she began to act more nervous as they walked toward the establishment. Jack took hold of her shoulder and started to push her across the gravel parking lot toward the entry door. At this point, however, a man he didn't know approached and said something to him. He hadn't heard anyone drive up, so it startled him when he heard the voice behind him.

"Pardon me, sir," the stranger called out in oddly accented words. "Can I help you find something?"

"Mind your own fuckin' business," answered Jack roughly, glaring at Antoine as he pulled Anita to one side. "I just have to pick somethin' up here. Leave me be."

Antoine shrugged, as if, perhaps, he was out of line and headed to his car across the street in the utilities parking lot.

Shit, Jack thought, that could've been a cop. Am I stupid, or what? If not him, someone else in the bar. Any one of those guys could turn me in.

Jack continued to scowl at the man until after he drove away, noting details about Antoine's car and license plate and hoping the other hadn't noticed the same regarding his vehicle. Then Jack pushed Anita back into his van and returned home. That type of encounter at a public bar was way too dangerous—he only could bring her to public places where he could pretend she was his kid or something—not to try to sell her. He'd be in deep, deep trouble if he got caught.

4

Anita

May 2018

THE MAN NAMED DUK SHAKES ME to wake me. His stinky, sour breath blows over my face as he says, "Shhh," for me to keep quiet. He motions for me to come with him, but I don't want to go. He's dressed in a dirty gray t-shirt that says "The Cave" and old jeans—he doesn't smell or look like he has taken a bath though. He takes my arm and pulls me up out of the bed. I can tell it's morning; the sunlight is peeking around the edges of the dark shades in Duk's bedroom, but Lupe is still sleeping on the dirty bed where we all sleep together. I wonder why I have to leave while Lupe still sleeps. Duk pulls me into the hall, pushes me toward the bathroom, and locks Lupe in the bedroom with a padlock he has put on the outside of the door.

"Hurry," he growls as he shuts the bathroom door behind me, "we're leaving in a few minutes." He doesn't say for where.

I use the toilet and slowly wash my hands and face. I clean my teeth with soap on my finger. He knocks on the door and tells me again to hurry. I know if I don't come out soon he will open the door and come in to get me. I still don't want to go with him—I'll be even more afraid without Lupe. Lupe is fourteen—a year older than me—and she came all the way from Guatemala. We don't talk to each other much, but it's still nice to have company. Sometimes she hugs me or I hug her if one of us is crying.

Within minutes Duk and I walk outside the door of his apartment into the hallway. He checks to see if the door is locked and then turns the key in the lock above the doorknob to bolt it, and we head down one flight of stairs. The faded beige, worn out carpet is covered with grass, dried mud, and bits of trash. Soon we walk outside into the fresh air. It smells so much better outside—like leaves and green grass instead of sweaty, rank man-smell. He holds onto my arm and heads me to the back door of his old, green car. He opens it and pushes me inside. The car smells almost as bad as his apartment and has paper trash and boxes on the floor of the back seat. He climbs in very quickly and backs out of the parking place and heads toward the road. He is driving fast.

"We're gonna meet Jack—you're gonna live with Jack now," Duk explains gruffly. "I'm tired of takin' care of both of ya. Jack can have ya now."

I hear him repeat the word "gek" several times but I'm not really sure what that means and I'm not sure what he has said. Even though I took English classes at my school, I can't understand most of what he says. He sounds so different from our English teacher. We are driving farther away than we normally go and going fast on a highway. I am very hungry and thirsty too, but Duk doesn't give me anything for breakfast. Duk usually takes me places at night—places where another man keeps me for a while. Duk sometimes brings me to a small, carpeted room in a little, old motel—where the bed is the main thing in the room—to see a man I don't know. Other times he takes me to old houses where a man lives without his family. The men in these places almost always have shifty eyes and act like I am one of their things—like a shoebox that they put something inside and then stick back into the corner of the closet, out of their sight. While I am there, with a shifty-eyed man, I go in my mind to visit my home in *México*. I miss it so much.

Whenever I have to remain with those *hombres de ojos furtivos*—men who can't look at me honestly—I can't think about it. It's too scary. It feels bad and smells bad and hurts in many ways. Instead, I always think about *Mamá* and *Papá* and the life in our *pueblo* before *Mamá* had to take me to *Estados Unidos*. I think about when *Papá* was with us and when we had happy life. I remember one particular time or another, like when I used to play *Escondidas* outside with my cousins; sometimes I pretended not to find the littlest ones even when they hid in very obvious places. Or like the *fiesta* for my last birthday, when we had a white pillar birthday cake decorated with blue butterflies and pink, purple, and yellow frosting flowers that tasted like *vanilla*. Or when *Abuelita* taught me to make *tortillas*. Or when my cousins and I went swimming in the river. Or lots of other moments when I was smiling. I remember every detail, every sound, every taste and smell—I remember the clean smell of limes, the magic taste of *canela* spice, and the guitars that play music at the fiestas. I remember how I felt on the day of the *Tres Reyes* when I got a little jewel box that played music. Or the *cenas* when Mamá cooked a warm *pozole* soup. Or when I did something with Mamá or Papá for the other one. I remember all the times that I loved, without even letting the darkness of the moment—those yucky, little rooms with shifty-eyed men I don't know—push into my thoughts.

At least I can do this for a while but, even though I escape part of the time by remembering, a vision of me getting hurt usually interrupts me. I can be riding bikes with my cousins or climbing a tree but then I fall out of the tree or off the bicycle and I crash to the ground with a pain that pulls me into another world. Or sometimes someone throws a rock at me, and it hits my body. Sometimes I even bleed. I try to go back into my beautiful memory, but the pain from the blow stays with me. I feel confused and hurt and I'm crying. And it's so sad when I realize that I'm not really back with my family; instead, I'm in the creepy room with the shifty eyes.

And then Duk comes and brings me back to his place. Sometimes Lupe is already in the car waiting for me, and sometimes we have to stop at a little house or a motel to pick her up before we go back to the place where Duk lives. I wonder if she tries to escape from those shifty eyes the way I do. We don't ever talk about that though. After Duk picks us both up we go to his place, with his dirty bed where we all sleep. Sometimes I have to visit my old life in my mind even there in the bed of Duk.

Lots of times when I sleep though, I guess I remember that dirty bed in Duk's house or the ones of the men with shifty eyes and I have scary nightmares. I wake up screaming. Lupe hugs me, murmuring, "*Tranquila, tranquílate,*" and Duk yells at me. I'm so glad Lupe is there. I think Duk would hit me if he were next to me in the bed.

Usually when I dream it begins with a fiesta or a dinner at the house of my *abuelita*, and all of a sudden I am in a room by myself trying to keep someone from opening the door. It is often a dark-haired man, or a monster, yelling or yowling and banging on the door. I pull chairs and furniture in front of the door, but the creature or person starts pounding on the door, sometimes with a big log, and breaks the door. Or sometimes he pokes a knife through the glass in the window or breaks in through the wall. Then I wake up terrified—crying and shrieking for *Mamá*. In order to go back to sleep I have to calm myself by putting myself into the nice memories of my *pueblo* and *familia* again.

I try not to think of the last few days at my home though. I try to forget the night when I woke up and heard *Mamá* crying and screaming, and *Papá* and some other men were yelling. There were several loud bangs; then I heard the men yelling again and their heavy footsteps running across the floor. A moment later, the door crashed closed.

Mamá began to sob and called out, "*¡Ay, Dios! Diego, Diego, ¡no me dejes! ¡No me dejes!—por favor.*"

Did *Papá* leave with those men? Did they take him with them? Just a few minutes later, *Mamá* rushed into my room and grabbed my shoes and some clothes for me. She told me to dress as fast as I could and took me out of the house. We ran all the way to where my *tía* Elena lives. *Mamá* kept looking behind us and telling me to hurry, but she was still crying so hard she couldn't even answer my questions. I never saw my *Papá* after that. I'm afraid those men hurt him and I worry that I'll never see him again. *Mamá* and *tía* Elena decided that we needed to leave for *Estados Unidos* right away that very night. We stayed one night in a town in the North, then we crossed the river in a boat to go into *Estados Unidos*.

We were trying to go to stay with my *tía* Rosa; she works in Arizona. *Tía* Elena made me memorize and repeat again and again the phone number of my *tía* Rosa. I say it now in my head to myself to be sure I remember, just as I do many times every day. *Tía* Elena helped me to think of a game to remember the number: 1 (to begin), 4 (my mother, Ana, and her three sisters, Elena, María, and Rosa), 8 (the four sisters and four brothers), 0 (no problems), 6 (my birthday), 1 (me), 7 (my lucky number), 13 (my age), 8 (my mother and her siblings), 9 (the siblings and my *abuelita*). 1-480-617-1389. Now this number may be my only hope to find my *tía* and *Mamá*. I wish I could use a phone to call it, but Duk guards his phone and won't let me near it.

"Ok, kid, we're here," Duk says suddenly as he pulls into a gas station and stops. He gets out of the car, but I get really nervous and lie down on the back seat crying.

After a few moments, Duk pulls me out of the car and carries me to a brown van where a bearded man with dark hair and pale skin, wearing a black t-shirt and jeans, is standing. Duk calls him "Gek." Gek is this man! Duk opens the sliding door and pushes me into the back seat of Gek's van. I can't help but cry—I'm scared, and this Gek will probably take me even farther from *Mamá*, wherever she is. Then Duk gets back into his own car and drives away. And Gek and I leave in the opposite direction.

"*Basta, cállate*," Gek yells, telling me to shut up. But he says it in Spanish. He also asks me my name.

I wonder if I should have any hope—at least he speaks some Spanish, but this brings me to the memories of how I got to *Estados Unidos*, and I start to sob more.

I remember how *tía* Elena drove *Mamá* and me to the countryside to find the man who took us to his little boat the next night to cross the river. *Mamá* was afraid that the men that came for my *Papá* would come back for us like they told her they would. I wonder what has really happened to *Papá* and if he is hurt—or worse. If not, why didn't he come with us? The man who took us to the river told us we should lie down in his fishy, wet dinghy so that no one would see us in case they shined lights on us while he motored us across. The man, called Jesuito, pretended he was fishing even while he slowly drove the boat until we got to the other side. Then we crawled in the mud after reaching the shore under a steep cliff, and Jesuito helped us up the cliff and told us to keep crawling during the night and to hide in the bushes during the day so the border guards would not see us.

Mamá said *tía* Rosa was driving to Tornillo, Tejas from Arizona and would pick us up at the *Dolar General* parking lot—we just had to get to Tornillo and it should not be very far away. Jesuito gave *Mamá* a compass and a map, but it was dark outside, and we were wet, muddy, and scared. We kept crawling as fast as possible from the place where we had climbed up the cliff, even though we were very, very tired.

"*Ven, Anita, un poquito más,*" *Mamá* encouraged. "Just a little farther. We can rest when the sun rises."

When the sun came up, we were in a field of alfalfa near some trees, and *Mamá* said we could sleep for a while in the shade among the plants where we wouldn't be seen. My hands and knees hurt and were crusty with blood and dirt. We still had a little water and some *tacos de carne seca* that *tía* Elena had packed for us, so we ate them and then fell asleep on the soil, hidden in the alfalfa.

I woke up to loud voices with the sun shining brightly.

"Stand up slowly and raise your hands in the air. *Levantarse.* You are under arrest," said one of the two men standing over us.

Mamá began to scream, "*No, no—por Dios. ¡No!*"

The men showed us badges and said they were "*policía,*" then they put plastic ties on our wrists and pushed us toward a van. They opened the back doors and put us inside the cages in the back. I heard them talking about Tornillo and El Paso before they started up.

"*¿Estás bien, Anita?*" questioned *Mamá.*

"*Sí, pero tengo miedo,*" I whispered. I was very scared but I tried not to cry so I wouldn't upset *Mamá* even more.

In a little while the van stopped, and the men took us out and into a big building with more cages inside. Lots of the people in the cages also spoke Spanish—I could hear them talking and shouting. The policemen brought us to a desk and kept asking for our "*documentos.*" Of course, we didn't have the "*documentos*" that they wanted, so they led *Mamá* to one of the cages.

A woman in a uniform took my arm and said to *Mamá*, "*Voy a bañarla,*" pulling me aside and supposedly taking me to have a bath.

"*¡No, no! ¡No me la quiten!*" screamed *Mamá*, begging them not to take me away. "*Anita, Anita.*"

"*¡Mamá, mamá! No quiero dejar a mi Mamá!*" I screeched too, struggling to stay with her.

But nobody paid any attention to us. They easily pulled me away and took me to another van with a cage inside and drove me to a separate building—this one completely filled with children. The officers locked me in a small pen with about twenty other girls before they cut the ties off my wrists. I fell down onto the floor, crying hysterically. They handed me a blanket made of shiny aluminum and left me there. The other girls tried to comfort me. After a while, the officers brought bags with a sandwich, some grapes, and a bottle of water for each of the girls, but instead of eating mine, I remember that I vomited into the bag.

Now Gek suddenly pulls off the road—interrupting my thoughts of how I got to where I am now—and stops at a drive-by restaurant. He buys some food and drinks, and the whole car is filled with the odor of food. I smell meat and fried food, and this time I am so, so hungry. I don't remember exactly when Duk fed us last. I begin to greedily eat the hamburger and *papas fritas* that Gek passes to me and to drink the cool, sugary *coca cola*. He even hands me some of his *papas fritas* after I eat all of mine. They are still warm and practically melt in my mouth. I gaze forward into the rearview mirror, seeking his gaze, and trying to thank him with my eyes—and to see if his eyes are shifty like Duk's and those other men we visit. I can't tell. He only looks at me for a second, but he is driving too. Maybe, maybe he will help me find *Mamá*. He tells me I have to work—*trabajar*. I will gladly work hard to earn money to find her.

Finally, we get to the house where Gek lives. It is surrounded by a green *bosque*, with trees and a thick growth of vines and leaves all around. I shiver when I see it—it looks scary with no people around it, like the middle of a jungle. There is only a gritty dirt road in front of the house.

When we get inside I ask for the *baño* and he takes me upstairs to a dirty bathroom that *Mamá* would never have permitted or believed and he waits outside. Then he shows me an empty room and tells me to stay there and shuts the door. I look out the window and only see the green woods, tall grass in the yard, and a long drop to the ground from the window I am looking out.

Gek comes back in and puts some thick cushions on the floor where I can sleep and gives me a rumpled sheet. I am so thankful not to have to sleep with him like I had to do with Duk and so very tired that I fall asleep right away. Gek wakes me later with more food—pizza and another *coca cola*. The next morning, he wakes me again and feeds me cereal with milk and a banana. I feel hopeful but still very tired. The third night though, when I wake after my nightmare in the night, I try to leave the room to go to the bathroom, but the door is locked from the outside. That is not a good sign.

I go to the window and look out toward the woods. I can see the full moon high in the sky and imagine that *Mamá* is also looking at the moon and thinking of me. I lie down in the moonlit room, listening to the insects chirping outside, wondering if I will ever see my family again and wishing I could use the bathroom.

The next day I feel better though, and Gek takes me to Walmart for food and to buy me some clothes, he says. The store is gigantic. After we pick out some food, he even buys me a toothbrush and some toothpaste. That makes me happy. Then we find the section for clothes for girls. I pick out two pairs of shorts and three shirts packaged together (pink, lavender, and blue) as well as a package of underpants, also in different colors. The clothes I am wearing are very dirty and torn. When we get back home, he lets me take a shower and then dyes my hair red. I like it—it looks very dramatic. But he starts to call me *En-ni* instead of Anita. I wonder if I'm still me.

Later, when it's already dark outside, he says that I'm going to work—*trabajar*.

"*¿En la oscuridad?*" I question, at first fearing the worst, since I would need to work after it's already so late and dark. It reminds me of the nights when Duk took me to the places with the men with shifty eyes. But I am still hopeful that Gek has another plan for us, because he was so kind to buy me new clothes.

"They need workers at night here too," he reassures me, as he runs his fingers through his hair and then glances up at me in the mirror.

It's dark in the car though, so I can't see his eyes, causing me to worry a bit more. After driving on several wide roads, like highways, he turns into a place that I'm sure is a motel. Am I going to clean here? We climb the stairs outside, and Gek knocks on the door. A man he calls Rómio opens, and Gek and I go inside. Rómio gives Gek some money, and now I am scared. I think this will be like what Duk made me do. Gek leaves me there alone with that Rómio—I never should have trusted Gek, even though he bought me nice things. Rómio has those same shifty eyes as the others, and within minutes I must escape the only way I can—in my memories and imagination. I remember times that I loved with my family or with the imaginary friends I had as a little girl—like fairies and butterflies.

This time my memory is when I am with my cousins, going house to house singing *posadas*, asking for room in the inn before Christmas.

One aunt and uncle are dressed like María and José, and some children are angels or shepherds, and many carry poinsettias. We knock on a door, and when the neighbors answer, we sing:

En nombre del cielo
os pido posada,
pues no puede andar
mi esposa amada.

In the name of heaven, we ask for room in the inn because our beloved María cannot walk any further. The neighbors answer back in song, and then, singing, we plead again revealing more details. We all continue in this way through the whole song, and then at last the neighbors invite us in and bring us to a table, laden with rich foods and give us cups of warm chocolate. The atmosphere is hospitable with the smell of candle wax and fragrant, warm cinnamon. And then we take turns hitting a star-shaped *piñata* with a stick until it breaks and candy spills everywhere. We all rush to gather up as much as we can. We all know we will repeat this same ritual for the next several nights, visiting a different house every evening until the night that Jésus is born and we go to Christmas Eve mass.

I stay here with my cousins and friends in my mind, talking, laughing, eating and drinking our traditional advent treats, but then the scene in my mind changes again. Now this scene is different from the posadas I remember. Instead of enjoying time with my friends and family, I am riding on the donkey with María. But the donkey begins to buck and jump. I fall off his back and crash onto the ground. I scream as I fall. There are rocks beneath me and the fall hurts so much that I can't remember what happens for a while. What happened to María? Did she fall too?

I feel quite confused until Gek comes to pick me up there. As we leave I don't even look at Rómio. When we get back into the van, I do not look at Gek or speak to him either. I know he has betrayed me.

5

Ana López de Domínguez

May 2018

THE ANTISEPTIC SMELL IN THE ROOM woke her. Ana struggled to open her eyes—they did not want to open. She faded back into that in-between space—neither here nor there—neither awake nor asleep. That insistent odor, however, brought her back to here again. But where was here? A wave of nausea overcame her, and Ana let herself slip back into the medial, lost space. She didn't really want to know where she was and she couldn't think about why. Queasiness again flooded over her and she retched violently, but there was nothing in her stomach to heave out.

"*Está bien*. You're okay. Just relax. *Tranquílate*," said a woman's voice.

Ana slowly opened her eyes. She was in a bed, with tubes attached to her, and the woman standing next to her was dressed in a pale blue top and pants with a stethoscope hanging around her neck.

"*¿Dónde estoy?*" Ana asked her.

"You're in the clinic of the *Casa del Migrante en Ciudad Juárez, México*," the woman replied in Spanish. "I'm your nurse, Pilar, as well as theirs," she motioned to the many other beds in the room—some partially screened from her view—all filled with patients.

Now Ana noticed the other noises in the room—a few people in different beds throughout were snoring; one woman was sobbing; another person was talking to himself; others were just breathing. She wasn't alone there—all the others there were in similar circumstances to hers. Ana felt strangely united to them.

"*¿Hace cuánto tiempo?*" Ana asked as she brought her thoughts back to the moment.

"You've been here two and a half days," Pilar answered. "We've been feeding you intravenously. You were extremely dehydrated and malnourished when you arrived."

Ana began to remember now—to remember what she wanted to forget—what she couldn't think about. They had sent her back to Ciudad Juárez. The border control in El Paso had deported her back to Mexico. But Anita! Where was her little girl now? Tears sprang to her eyes.

"Anita, ¿dónde estás, mi vida?"

With both her loving husband, Diego, and her little girl taken from her, what did she have to live for? No, she could not think of Diego now, she had to find Anita. Ana never had told Anita what had happened to her father that night. She couldn't. She couldn't stop crying enough to be able to talk, even if she had had the time to explain it all to her. Instead, she had needed to get Anita out of the house and out of danger's path immediately. Besides, how do you explain to an innocent child that—in the space of an instant—her life will never, ever be the same as it was? Ana just couldn't do it. So she had avoided that conversation, leaving Anita scared and confused—not that knowing the details would have alleviated either of those feelings. Besides, all Ana could do was shake and cry.

Instead of explaining anything that night, she had hurried Anita to her sister Elena's house. She and Anita had run the whole way, with Ana constantly looking back over her shoulder to see if anyone was following them. Juan Pablo, Elena's husband, answered the door in a t-shirt and gym shorts and had obviously been asleep. He could evidently see the anguish in their faces.

"¿Qué pasó, Ana? Ay, Dios. Come inside and I'll get Elena," he said as he pulled them inside the door.

Ana couldn't tell them everything—she couldn't explain it all in front of Anita and couldn't even face it herself. But Elena and Juan Pablo understood; Ana and Diego had talked in the past with Elena and Juan Pablo about the dangerous potential that existed in their community—they'd considered all the possible alternatives.

"You need to leave here. In fact, you need to leave *México,*" Juan Pablo had asserted while Elena got on the phone.

Elena then made arrangements for Ana and Anita to cross the border with the aid of a *coyote.* She would drive her sister and niece to

Ahumada that night, and then the *coyote* would meet them tomorrow afternoon. Juan Pablo would stay with their children and let Elena take Ana and Anita since he was expected at work the next day—it could arouse suspicion if he did not show up.

"*Tengan mucho cuidado,*" he told them after they had packed up some food to take with them and had gone out the back door to their car. "Be very careful. *Les quiero a todas mucho.*"

The next day, after spending the night in Ahumada, the *coyote,* Jesuito, successfully got them across the border. Ana had felt an enormous surge of relief and believed she had surmounted the majority of the dangers to get her child to safety. They had made it safely into *los Estados Unidos*—the country that promised sanctuary and shelter to "the tired, the poor, the huddled masses...." What a falsification! How had whole generations of people been led to believe this lie? She herself, as a teacher, had helped to perpetuate it. Ana remembered the classes of eleven- and twelve-year-olds that she taught before she became director of the school. They had studied the history and government of Mexico and the United States. The book they used had a beautiful picture of the Statue of Liberty and included part of the poem written by the New York woman Emma Lazarus in 1883 that gave voice to the statue, welcoming the "huddled masses," saying, "I lift my lamp beside the golden door!" What had happened to that warm, bright welcome? What had happened to the idea of democratic liberty and the nation of immigrants? Their reception into the United States of America had been nothing like Ana had suggested to her students.

In contrast, even though she and Anita had fled to the US in fear for their lives from the criminals in Mexico who had overrun their town and even their government, they had been not been protected. The criminals in her own country had taken her loving husband from her and had threatened both her and her little daughter. And how had the United States welcomed them as a sanctuary? It had not! Instead they had been harassed in the worst way—locked up like criminals. Not only had she not been believed, she and Anita had had their rights abused. Was what the border control in the US had done to Anita unlike kidnapping? To Ana it did not seem any different, and she felt completely betrayed by the country she had always held up as a model. She and Anita had been so close to connecting with Rosa at the *Dolar General* outside of El Paso. What else could she have done to have prevented being intercepted? Not fallen asleep in the field? But both Anita and she were so completely exhausted—both physically and emotionally.

Ana relived the frightful detention by the border patrol that was so unlike the imagined welcome she would receive in *los Estados Unidos*. Instead of greeting her or helping her, the border agents had made her feel like a criminal—worse than a criminal. In addition to locking her in a cage, they had robbed her of her only child. Was there anything she could have done? But no; it wasn't her fault. How could they—those government officials—not only have doubted them so much—a frightened woman and her young daughter—but, also, how could they have been so heartless? If she and Anita had been wild animals—put in cages and then separated—it could not have been worse. Those so-called officials had abducted her daughter from her. Nausea flooded over Ana again, but then her rage came back to the forefront, and she knew that she had to be strong. In order to find her Anita she was going to have to be tough and think calmly. She needed to get well and get out of this hospital bed. Was Anita here in *México* or still in *Estados Unidos*?

"*¿Estás bien, Ana?*" asked Pilar as she touched Ana gently on the arm. "I've been with you during the days and part of the evenings, but this is the first time you have answered me when I've talked to you."

"*Sí, creo que sí…*, Pilar. I think I'm okay. At least I am awake now."

Ana glanced around at all the other patients in the room. On the wall was a large picture of Pope Francis.

"Yes, you were unconscious most of the time since you got here," said Pilar. "I don't know what condition you were in while in *Estados Unidos*, but I can imagine."

Ana rubbed her forearms to try to make herself more alert. That tactile sensation would help her to stay aware. And she did need to bring herself into attentiveness if she was going to find her daughter.

"Pilar, do you know if my little daughter was deported with me?"

"Let me check your chart. I haven't seen her, but I've been mainly in this clinic. I'll be right back."

Ana prayed that Anita was there or at least that the chart gave some indication of where she was. Anita was her only child, and she loved her so much. God had not blessed her with other children, not that any other child could compensate for losing Anita.

Ana thought back to when she met Diego—and then to Anita's birth. Ana and Diego had married late—at least for Mexico. After Ana had attended university and became a teacher, she had worked on a higher degree and eventually became an official of the school system in her *pueblo, Luis Aldama*. Because of her serious nature and her dedication to her profession, she had never been that interested in any man until she met Diego when she was thirty-eight. Diego was slightly younger, but not so much that it was unseemly. And he thought the world of her! Most men she knew were afraid of women with her level of education, but not Diego. He took pride in her accomplishments and even bragged about having *una mujer super inteligente*. Ana smiled as she thought of him, and then tears came into her eyes.

After they had been married three years, Ana discovered she was pregnant—she never thought she would have a child because of her age. Then Anita was born, and Ana felt like her life was truly fulfilled and rich. She had a career, a loving husband, and now a child who was so enchanting and caring; she loved her more each day of her life. Following Anita's birth though, Ana never had her menses again, so she knew Anita was meant to be a special gift from God for her to care for. And now she didn't even know where her daughter was. What was happening to her own country that it wasn't even safe to raise a family anymore? And she had always thought that *Estados Unidos* would be a secure haven if they ever needed to migrate from their home. What a misconception that was!

Pilar returned after a few minutes.

"Ana, this chart says that you were deported alone. It says nothing about your child. How old is she?"

"*Ay Dios. ¿Dónde está mi Anita?*" Ana sobbed. But then she made herself get control, "Pilar, are there legal representatives here? The border agents took my child from me, and I don't have any idea where she is or even, at this point, how long she has been away from me."

6

Claire de lune

July 29–31, 2018

A CAR DROVE DOWN MY STREET, and its headlights briefly shone into the screened-in porch. Suddenly Antoine was gone. That night, after he told me he was a ghost, I was even less inclined to sleep than I had been before he appeared. My mind was jumping all over the place.

How, exactly, did Antoine die? Was he correct to suspect that the girl in the house near ours was being abused? I wondered. Should I tell Jim that Antoine was not a dream but a ghost? Would he believe me or just think I was crazy? Did he believe that ghosts could appear to the living or even that they existed at all?

These questions and others raced through my mind. One consideration was that Jim was leaving the day after tomorrow for Montreal on a business trip. Perhaps it would be better to have a conversation about all this after he returned. He would be even more worried about me if he thought I was being haunted by a ghost—whatever he might think that meant. He might think I had totally lost my mind.

I tried to read out there on the porch, hoping either that it would distract me enough to go to sleep or that Antoine would return and continue his discussion with me. Neither thing happened. I tried to write, but my mind felt like mud—thick, dark, and sticky. I finally climbed back into bed with Jim, exhausted, as daylight started entering the room. Foggily, I heard Jim get up for work and felt him kiss me goodbye. With a sudden jerk, I finally woke after ten.

The sun was shining brightly, and already it was quite hot. I heard the recycling truck stop outside our house and knew that the trash truck had already come earlier while I was sound asleep. I dressed quickly in stretchy grey leggings and a loose, sleeveless, navy tunic, just whipping a comb through my now Kansas-sun-streaked hair and pulling it back into a pony tail at the nape of my neck. Jim had prepared coffee earlier, so I just stuck a cup of it into the microwave to warm, grabbed my laptop, and then went into the living area. Jim had signed us up for an online subscription to *The Kansas City Star*, and that was the only area newspaper I was familiar with. So I began searching on Google to find out the best source of news for the Olathe area. Under "Olathe KS newspaper" Google directed me to several sites, and most lead to kansascity.com the website for *The Kansas City Star*. Good; it included Olathe news, so I clicked on the *Star* site and began to search for anything related to a runner's death nearly a month ago.

"Bingo," I shouted out loud after just a few minutes of searching.

"Olathe Runner Killed in Hit and Run," proclaimed the title.

The article went on to explain that Antoine Benet, a French employee of *La Societé EE* working in Olathe with Mid-Wester Energy had been struck by a vehicle while running on a county road near Olathe and had died of his injuries. Benet's body had been discovered on a desolate part of county road LL around eleven in the morning on July 6 by a telephone service employee. The body appeared to have been there more than several days, according to the county coroner. Police said that no suspects had been named and that they were still investigating the death. Benet was dressed in running attire and lived in a newly annexed area close to the road where he was found.

Also, there were pictures of the road where his body was found and—Oh, my God!—a passport picture of Antoine Benet. The photo actually looked like the ghost Antoine who had visited me. My hand on the computer mouse began to shake uncontrollably, so I sat on both hands and continued staring at the computer screen. His hair was shorter in the picture, but it had to be the same person. Another wave of terror and fear swept through my body. This was too eerie to be real, but there was his picture. Was he murdered? Was he intentionally hit by someone? I had to remind myself to breathe and not to panic. So Antoine was telling the truth, I thought—not that I had really doubted it. I glanced up and out of the window, briefly distracted from my fear and horror by the male and female cardinals flying in and out of the flower bed where we had put a bird feeder. I got up and walked toward the window to calm myself by watching the birds there in the sunlight— they were undoubtedly real and live.

I went to the sink and filled a glass with water then downed it before returning to my computer. After staring for several minutes more at Antoine's picture, I reread the article two more times before I continued my search and found another piece published the following day. This second article quoted the president of Mid-Wester Energy, Fred Woodward, regarding the outstanding character of Antoine Benet. Woodward explained that Benet had been living alone in a new house owned by Mid-Wester Energy—*now our house*—while he worked with Mid-Wester on a solar energy project. The police chief added that the investigation was ongoing and invited any possible witnesses to contact law authorities regarding the accident or the last time Benet was seen or heard from.

"We believe Benet may have been running near sunset or after dark the evening of July 2 or after," the paper quoted the police chief in the article. "The cell phone he was wearing was cracked and had stopped at 9:04 PM on July 2, so we believe that was when he was hit. It's hard to imagine that the driver who hit him didn't realize someone or something had been hit, but it is very dark on these county roads at night. Benet was last seen on July 2, 2018 at work at Mid-Wester Energy, according to other employees who knew him."

Later articles were quite brief and offered no new information about what had happened. Amazing. It seemed like they had dropped the case. What could I do? Didn't *I* have further information about the case? But who was going to believe my ghost story? I was living in Antoine's house, and it might make sense to some that his ghost could be haunting his old house, but the more likely scenario was that the police would think I was a total nut case. I looked out the window again at the birds. Was I crazy? Was this really happening? I went to the cupboard where I had put the French tea bag Antoine had placed in my hand. This was real and I had not imagined it, and I'd never had this type of tea before. I had to do something—perhaps I could get some more information from the president of the energy company who was mentioned in the article. After all, that company owned our house

After looking up the phone number on their website, I contacted Mid-Wester Energy and asked to speak with Mr. Woodward, explaining that my husband and I were the new tenants of the house owned by their energy company where Antoine Benet had lived. The receptionist who answered said he was busy but that I could try again later. I tried two more times during the day before she said she would try to connect me. After a brief delay, I was actually connected with Woodward.

"Fred Woodward, President of Mid-Wester Energy. How can I help you?" he blared into the phone.

I explained that I was the new tenant of the house where Antoine Benet had lived and wondered if he knew anything more about the investigation into his death. But Woodward said he'd not heard of anything new. He also asked how I liked the house and explained that Antoine had directed the installation of the many solar features in the residence.

"Did you know Antoine?" queried Woodward.

"Well, yes. I have…had met him," I stumbled over my words and hoping he didn't ask anything about how I had met him.

"Well, we really hated to lose him—especially in that way. He was a real boon to our solar connectivity here," he boasted. "A really great guy too!"

Later I attempted to call the police chief quoted in the article, but was connected instead to one of his subordinates who said he couldn't divulge anything about the case.

When Jim returned home that evening, he proudly told me he had obtained some information for me about the property on County Road LL. It seemed like I hadn't seen him in days, since he kept leaving before I woke. He was dressed in a lavender long-sleeved shirt with the sleeves rolled up and had already removed the tie he had worn to work. The shirt color looked good on him, and his curly light brown hair practically begged to be touched. I felt a sudden pang of affection toward him for going to the trouble to do that research; obviously he was concerned about me. He had a printed copy of the information the county registrar of deeds had discovered for him. The house was an old farmhouse that had belonged to the Anderson family since it was built in the early 1930s. They had raised poultry back in the day. Members of the family had lived in the house until 1995, when Paul Anderson and his wife and children moved to Wichita.

"The registrar told me that the house was vacant for about twenty years, even though the family had listed it for sale with a local real estate company," Jim said, pouring over the papers.

"It must have been in very poor condition after being vacant for that long," I commented. "I wouldn't have wanted it. It looked rather dilapidated."

"Yes, you're right. The clerk knew the property and said it was pretty sad, especially after the family of raccoons moved in," added Jim. "They had quite a bit of cleanup to do after that."

"Yuck, that sounds awful."

Apparently the family decided to clean it up a bit several years ago, Jim had discovered, in order to try to either sell or rent it. The price had been lowered as well. Then about two years ago, they found a renter, but they could only charge only a very minimal rent. The county clerk didn't know the name of the renter, but he suggested that Jim call the real estate company to find out who was on the rental contract and who was paying the rent, which Jim had done.

"The guy's name is Jack Collins," said Jim, consulting the notes he had made. "They didn't have much more information about him there, except that he had mostly paid the rent on time."

"Did they know if he was married or had kids?" I asked, totally absorbed in this new information.

"Nobody I talked to knew that information," said Jim apologetically as he got up to get a bubbly water from the refrigerator. "He was the only one on the contract."

"I saw a little girl with him when I drove by, and…," I stopped abruptly before I mentioned that Antoine had too.

Now was not the time to get into a discussion with Jim about Antoine. He was leaving the next day and I still wasn't sure how or if I should broach the subject of ghosts with him.

"It really pained me to see a little child with a man who looked so mean," I stressed, looking into Jim's eyes.

"Claire, you can't worry about that. You don't even know anything about the situation except that he gave you a dirty look."

"Jim, you weren't there. It was the most threatening look I've ever seen. That poor child!"

I was truly and surprisingly distressed, Jim noted. He commented that this was unlike me—I was normally so calm.

"Let's change the subject now," said Jim, returning his can of La Croix to the refrigerator and taking out a bottle of rosé wine instead.

"I'd rather talk about something more cheerful before I leave tomorrow," he added, opening the rosé and pouring each of us a glass.

"How long did you say you would be gone?" I asked as I took my glass and then glanced out at our mowed lawn and remembered how close that uncultivated area with the old farmhouse was to our house.

"Five days. Why don't we go out to dinner tonight and have some time to enjoy each other before I leave."

He silently raised his glass in a toast and looked into my eyes.

"That sounds lovely." I toasted him as well. "I'll miss you tons but I hope to write a lot. Also, I may meet with some acquaintances of my friend Anne. She says they are quite nice and live in Leawood—which isn't that far from here."

We freshened up quickly, and I even put on my new black, sexy dress. Jim whistled and raised his eyebrows when he saw me and commented about how beautiful I looked, even noticing the sun streaks in my normally brown hair.

"Did you get your hair highlighted? You look stunning," he said, smiling.

"No, I actually just put a little lemon juice on it last week. I read that would make it lighter. I'm glad you like it. You look very dashing as well," I answered, returning his compliment and touching his gray silk, short-sleeve shirt but also remembering Antoine's comment about my hair.

He took my hand and led me to the car, and then we drove about twenty-five minutes to a little French restaurant, La Bouche, close to Westport. The owner was a lady from France who treated us to her beautiful accent and friendly attitude, as well as an amazingly tasty little cheese and watercress puff as she took our orders. Each dish she brought us was exquisite. We shared a plate of sautéed mussels, then I had a salad of beets and goat cheese followed by sea bass with rice and tarragon scented carrots, and Jim, in addition to a salad of greens and radishes, had the steak *au poivre*, of course, and gave me a bite.

Although the food and wine were as wonderful as Jim's complete attention, I couldn't help but think of Antoine. In fact, it felt as if I could sense his presence there in the restaurant and could hear him whispering in my ear as I ate.

"Claire, try the *mousse de chocolate. C'est délicieuse!*" I could hear his voice even above the conversation in the restaurant. How could that be?

It also seemed like I could feel his breath in my ear and sometimes hovering around my mouth and eyes, almost like a kiss. Was it just my imagination? Was he there as a spirit? Had he been there before? I felt certain that he had and perceived Antoine accompanying me as I ate my dinner, and that sensation was rather intrusive on my romantic dinner with Jim.

"Are you tired, Claire?" asked Jim, looking very concerned as he reached across the table for my hand. "You seem very distracted. I wanted this to be a lovely and intimate dinner for us before I leave."

"I'm so sorry, Jim. I'm not sure what is the matter with me. I *am* enjoying being with you for this lovely evening—I just feel … odd. It's not your fault though."

"I hope you aren't coming down with something."

My uncontrollable inattentiveness continued even after we returned home and made me feel incredibly guilty. While Jim was making love to me I could sense another presence, spooning my back and blowing softly in my ear. And, worst of all, I actually enjoyed the attentions of both of them.

Despite my chagrin regarding my distraction from Jim, that night I slept very soundly until I was awakened by a dream just before Jim's alarm went off. I dreamed I was running through the woods on a narrow path at dusk with a full, reddish moon ahead of me. Suddenly an enormous raccoon jumped out onto the path in front of me, arching its back, showing its teeth, and growling at me. In the next moment I was in an unknown house, wandering through the empty rooms and wondering where the front door was and if the raccoon was also inside with me. I awoke when I began to panic that I couldn't get out.

7

Antoine Benet

May 2018

"ANTOINE, DO YOU EVER RUN?" asked Mark, one of Antoine's assistants from Mid-Wester Energy, with whom he'd been working a lot.

"Run? You mean like a sport?" Antoine asked while he finished organizing some papers in the office.

Antoine's desk, like Mark's, was in a compartmentalized group space. Each individual unit had partial walls that formed a cubicle around the desk area but left open space so the employees could interact without going into separated rooms. The area was carpeted and had other kinds of sound buffers to keep the noise down. In Antoine's area, there were six cubicles in a larger room, while some rooms in the office building had as many as ten cubicles. Within the individual cubicles, the desks could be raised or lowered so that the employee could work either sitting or standing or could change positions during the day. Some had regular chairs, some kneeling chairs, and others ergonomic or ball chairs at the desks. Employees also normally decorated the walls of their own spaces to reflect their personal tastes. After Karen—one of the long-time employees in their shared space who had decorated her cubicle with family photos and personal mementos—had commented that his was bare and sterile looking, Antoine framed two colorful photos he had taken on *Rue Cler* and hung them there. One was a picture of an outdoor fruit market and the other of a flower shop with a bicycle parked in front. Karen had enthusiastically approved and now stopped by his desk often—"to see those beautiful scenes," she said. Antoine glanced up at the photos now and smiled nostalgically. He did miss Paris even though he was getting along fairly well here.

"Sort of," Mark said as he looked up over the pony wall where he was straightening up his own desk in preparation to leave for the day. "I mean running for exercise, basically."

"Well, in Paris, we walk so much that I never much felt the need to run. I like it though and participated a lot in sports, usually tennis and football—I think you call it soccer—when I was attending the *lycée* and *université.*"

Antoine remembered that his *maman* had wanted him to join a sport's club when he was thirteen, in his second year of *collège*, but Antoine was still hurting so much from the death of his *papa* that he would not participate in anything. He simply refused to go, even after Simone had pointed out that most of his school friends were playing in it. He still didn't want to leave her side and was hurt that she was trying to separate herself even that much from him. But after he entered *lycée* at fifteen, he was so angry with Simone for spending time with Alain that he began to participate in a football club just to get away from them on weekends. It turned out that the activity actually helped him to dispel some of his indignation about Alain, but he tried not to let Simone know he was less enraged. He still wanted to dominate her attention and feared having her share her affection with another.

"Then how about going with us after work on Thursday? Three or four of us like to run together at least once a week; we usually work out for about an hour. It would be great if you would join us."

"I'd love to," replied Antoine. "I'm feeling like I am inside too much lately. It would be *fantastique* to be outside with some exercise. I need to get some new trainer shoes and running clothes, but I can do that before Thursday."

"Great! We look forward to having you join us!" affirmed Mark as he headed for the door. "See you tomorrow!"

Antoine got his shoes and shorts the next day and practiced running after he got home. The first practice run was hard. Even though it was nearing sunset, the temperature was still stifling. His legs and lungs ached, and he was covered with sweat from the humid weather and exertion. But after joining Mark and his buddies on the first few Thursdays, he couldn't believe how much better he felt. Granted, at first his legs were painfully sore, but then he started running several times a week, either with Mark or some of the others or even by himself sometimes, after he got home in the evenings. Not only did he feel better physically, but he enjoyed the camaraderie with the others. Soon he was convinced he couldn't live without his run. He was sleeping better and perceived himself as powerful and alive again—something he hadn't felt since Elodie had left him.

In addition to regularly running with his group of co-workers, Antoine began to jog most of the other evenings around the neighborhood near his house. Since the area was still partly undeveloped, he also used his run as a way to orient himself and explore the surroundings. Many of the roads, instead of being concrete streets like in his new development area, were dirt or gravel county roads without curbs or street names. Sometimes he preferred those rough, dusty gravel roads to the hard concrete of the new city streets; it felt better on his ankles and knees. Also, the undeveloped countryside interested him. Once, he even saw a soft brown, white tailed doe run across the road in front of him one evening at dusk as the sun was lowering itself in the sky. He stopped in his tracks, watching until he could no longer see her.

"*Phénoménal!*" he yelled out loud after the doe had passed.

There were also always rabbits, squirrels, birds, and other animals—one evening he saw a red fox—that surprised and intrigued him as he ran. And amazing pink and red sunsets on the horizon, varied cloud shapes, and early evening moons and stars presented themselves in the wide theatre of the sky. He'd hardly ever had such amazing access to Nature from day to day—certainly not in Paris. That closeness to the earth was as invigorating as the run itself.

One evening, as he was running the county roads, he saw an old van that immediately brought back his encounter with the rude man and little girl in front of the seedy bar near Olathe's Mid-Wester office. He nearly tripped as he suddenly attempted to slow down and take a closer look. He bent forward and put his hands on his knees, looking toward the van and panting to catch his breath. It most assuredly did look like the same brown and tan vehicle and it was old enough that there couldn't be a lot like that around. *He* certainly hadn't seen another like it.

Antoine stared curiously at it and at the older farmhouse behind it that definitely could have used a paint job. It was plainly in an isolated area—totally surrounded by trees and dense undergrowth on both sides of the sparsely graveled road. The space adjacent to the house was also overgrown and unkempt, with a trampled path to the door and an unpaved drive. And the house itself was not in the greatest shape, perhaps even more rundown than the yard and van. He didn't see any movement around the dwelling, but he stayed on the road because he really didn't want another encounter with that jerk he'd seen outside the bar, especially with what he had heard about Americans and their guns. His curiosity was definitely aroused though, and he worked that route into his jogging schedule fairly often, hoping to have a safe confirmation of whether or not the house belonged to the guy he had seen before. Once the van even passed him on the road at some distance from the house, but Antoine couldn't see the driver because of the dust the vehicle raised behind it.

Sometime after he started running regularly, Antoine ran into Cheryl at work. She had been at some conferences and then on vacation, so he hadn't seen her in nearly a month and was really missing her presence. She almost radiated in her red sheath dress and cropped jacked, with her skin glowing a bronze color from her vacation.

"Antoine, how are you?" greeted Cheryl that morning with a big smile. "You look great!"

"*Bonjour*, Cheryl. You are looking *très, très magnifique* yourself! It has been a long time since I last saw you. Was your holiday good?"

Cheryl explained that after going to a couple of conferences about energy use, she'd had area meetings at other offices and then had left for vacation in Colorado. Antoine wondered if she was glad to see him or was hoping to avoid him.

"I've missed seeing you," said Antoine. "The days are much less filled with sunny energy without you here. What did you do in Colorado?"

Did she flush slightly when he said that?

"Well, I was hiking with my sister and her family mostly. She lives in Denver. The weather was cool but beautiful, and I love being in the mountains. It was a good break from work," she replied with a sigh, squeezing the folders she was carrying to her chest.

Cheryl asked Antoine about the latest developments in his work and told him a bit about some of the new ideas she had heard about in the conferences. They decided they needed to keep their conversation brief because they both had appointments later in the morning.

"By the way, Cheryl," Antoine said as he turned back toward her, "I was wondering if you might be free to go to dinner with me some evening. I have found an authentic little French restaurant. Do you know La Bouche?"

"I've heard of it but I've yet to try it," said Cheryl, smiling softly, "I'd love to. What night did you have in mind?"

After Antoine checked online for a reservation, they agreed that he would pick her up on Friday at seven.

That Friday was pleasantly warm with a soft breeze. Peonies and irises were in bloom everywhere. Precisely at seven, Antoine pulled up at Cheryl's condo, strode up to the door, and knocked. Cheryl opened quickly, wearing a form-fitting sapphire, long sleeved dress, dangly earrings, and high, block-heeled sandals. She had a small bag and a silky, print scarf in one hand.

"*Mon dieu*. I feel like I'm back in *Paris*. You look *fantastiquement* stylish, Cheryl," Antoine affirmed as he kissed Cheryl on both cheeks in the typical French greeting.

"Thank you, Antoine. You look quite stunning yourself. Look at that beautiful striped shirt you are wearing," she said as she touched the fabric on his sleeve. Looking directly at his eyes, she continued, "I'm very excited to go out to dinner with you this evening. Would you like to come in for a moment?"

Cheryl gave Antoine a quick tour of her one-bedroom condo. Antoine admired the modular, plum colored sofa she had in her living area with its contrasting blue pillows and upholstered table in front. The space was small but very organized and decorated with tall glass vases of long-stemmed, tiny dried flowers, also in blue. The kitchen opened into the living area, and the walls were all painted white, making it seem quite spacious. He stopped for a moment to notice her bookcase with the books arranged by color, which amazed him. He would have liked more time to explore the titles. After she quickly showed him her bedroom and bath areas, they headed for the restaurant so as not to be late for their 7:30 reservation.

At first, Antoine was amazed that he felt rather nervous being there in the car with Cheryl on their first personal outing and he didn't know what to say next. He didn't want to blow his chances with her by saying or doing the wrong thing. But the cool evening breeze and soft light, as well as Cheryl's presence there in his car, began to comfort and animate him—he could faintly smell her intriguing perfume—so, minute by minute, he began to relax. Soon their conversation began to flow more naturally.

"I hope you like French cooking," said Antoine as he opened the car door for Cheryl in front of La Bouche. "I think this restaurant is quite good."

"Oh, I love it! I'm a very adventuresome eater. And I really have been dying to try this place," she continued as she struggled to exit the car gracefully in her slim skirt.

Antoine glanced discreetly at her shapely legs, then took her arm and steered her into the doorway of La Bouche.

"*Bonsoir, Antoine,*" greeted Madame Lautrec, the owner of the small, intimate restaurant, kissing Antoine on both cheeks. Madame Lautrec was a short and sturdily built woman of an undeterminable age, who demonstrated her determination in every movement.

"*Bonsoir, Madame Lautrec. Comment allez-vous?*" Antoine greeted. "I'd like to present you to my colleague and friend Cheryl Atkins. She's been wanting to try your restaurant."

"*Enchantée, Mademoiselle,*" she replied and kissed Cheryl's cheeks as well.

Madame Lautrec led them to a small secluded table near the window, lighted the candle on their table, and handed them each a menu. Antoine asked Cheryl about her preferences and then ordered for both of them, requesting two *Kirs* and some small bites to begin and then a special bottle of wine to go with the dinner. He ordered everything in French, so Cheryl asked for some translations about what they were getting. He told her that parts of it were a surprise. The mood at their table felt as cozy and upbeat as the ambience of the place. They went from one subject to the next in their conversation, interspersed with fragrant plates of delicious foods, including *Escargots de Bourgogne,* a sautéed Dover Sole in *Meunière* sauce, rack of lamb with lemon thyme *jus,* and exquisitely prepared vegetables, in a variety of courses. They traded plates back and forth so they both could try each item.

"*Alors,* Cheryl, tell me more about yourself," asked Antoine as they sampled the *escargots.* "It appears that you are not married, but I must be mistaken about that. You have surely been snatched up by some rival of mine."

"Ha," laughed Cheryl as she blotted her lips with her napkin. "I was snatched up but I discovered right away that it really wasn't going to work out for me. I've been divorced now for five years. And how about you, Antoine? Do you have a wife and children back in France?"

Antoine told her briefly about Elodie and their break-up and then they went on to other topics: family, hobbies, childhood, travels, colleagues at work, and even reading preferences. Cheryl said she loved reading and, particularly, novels.

"I'm trying to think of the French novels I've read. Oh, let's see— Camus's *The Stranger*, a couple by Sartre, one called *Second Thoughts* by Butor. Yes, and I loved Flaubert's *Madame Bovary*," said Cheryl as her gaze continued to be magnetized toward Antoine.

"*Second Thoughts*? Is that *La Modification*? About a man on a train with a second-person narrator?"

"Yes, exactly," said Cheryl. "I loved the effect of that second-person narrator. It feels so personal."

"Wow! I'm impressed," he said with his eyes open wide in admiration. "You should read it in French too. Would you like another bite of my lamb?"

Cheryl did want another taste but said she doubted if her high school French would let her read a novel that long and asked Antoine if he had ever read Mario Vargas Llosa's book about *Madame Bovary*.

"The Peruvian author? No, I did not know he had written about it. What is it called?" asked Antoine.

"Ummm, I think it's *Perpetual Orgy: Madame Bovary and Flaubert* or *Flaubert and Madame Bovary*. It's also about how the novel changed Vargas Llosa's life and inspired him as an author. You should read it," Cheryl nodded as she took another bite of her fish.

"Yes, I will do that. Didn't he run for President of Peru? By the way, speaking of political situations, I have a novel you might like from an American author. Have you read *Girl in a Cage* by Claire Schmidt? A woman on my flight over from Paris gave it to me. It's indirectly about the immigrant situation in the US right now—and more obviously about the abuse of immigrant children."

Their conversation continued throughout the meal. After they had finished the entrees, they split a strawberry-raspberry tart with home-made, vanilla ice cream that they ate to the very last crumb, even though their hunger was already satisfied from the dinner. Neither Cheryl nor Antoine were ready to call the evening to a close, so they drove to the Plaza and walked around, looking at the fountains and statues and sitting for a while at an outdoor cafe to have coffee—decaffeinated for Cheryl. It seemed that neither of them wanted their time together to end.

Later, as Antoine pulled up in front of Cheryl's condo, he pulled her over for a quick kiss—on the mouth this time. It was a kiss that lingered longer than either of them had intended. They both agreed they wanted to see each other again outside of work.

8

Black Jack

June 2018

JACK DECIDED TO SPEND THE EVENING, or at least have a couple of drinks, at an upscale bar in a new shopping area not too far from his house. He was sick of carting Annie around in the evenings to different locales to put her to work. That meant he had to drop her off and then wait nearby until the customer was serviced to pick her up. He couldn't even trust the clients not to take her away from him, so he had to carefully keep watching the customer's whereabouts and the clock. He couldn't afford to have her stolen from him or risk that some authority would find out about her. All that was not the least bit enjoyable for him. And, even though he was making a decent amount of money off the kid, it wasn't a very satisfying occupation for him. He was getting damn lonely with only a Spanish-speaking girl to talk to.

So tonight he decided to take the evening off for his own enjoyment. Tonight he had hoped to have some luck on his own with something—women, new friends, a new hangout—anything. Something needed to change in his life.

Jack trimmed his beard, showered, and dressed in his swankiest black jeans and only white shirt, which he'd had freshly laundered so he would look smart.

"Ya look pretty good, man," he said to himself in the mirror.

Annie was reading a book in the living room, where she was seated on the couch. Jack went into the kitchen and quickly prepared her a turkey sandwich, got out an apple, a coke, and an extra bottle of water for her dinner. Then he told her to go up to her room. Her room still only contained the two sofa cushions for her bed, but she had arranged her new books and clothes in boxes and bags and had made it all very tidy. She had also hung some pictures she had drawn with pencil on her walls—one of a butterfly and the other two of flowers he didn't recognize. They looked nice—the only really nice thing in that shabby room, he thought. He told her she needed to stay in her room because he was going out and gave her the sandwich and other things he'd gotten out for her supper. He also handed her an old pan in case she needed to pee before he got back. She'd already complained about the lack of access to the bathroom when he was gone, and once he found her screaming and crying because she'd had to pee on the floor. Well, now she wouldn't have to worry about that, he told her. He shut the door to her room, took another peek at himself in the bathroom mirror and headed out the door. After locking the outside door of his house, he pulled away in his van while the evening was still early and took the highway toward a new place he'd seen last time he went to buy groceries.

"Did I bolt the door to Annie's room?" he asked himself out loud after he got onto the highway. "Man, stop bein' paranoid. Sure ya did."

Jack pulled into the parking lot of Score Sports Bar in a newish retail complex and parked his van at a far edge of the lot. He got out and sauntered casually toward the door, checking out the cars and types of customers. Not bad—the few cars in the lot were all newish and some were even fancy—a Mercedes among Subaru Outbacks, Toyotas, Nissans.

When he entered into the softly lit, fashionably furnished bar, there weren't many people, but it was still early. The high top tables with tall chairs as well as the leathery, upholstered booths were all new —in various shades of greens and bronze—and made the place look pretty fancy. The shelves with liquor behind the bar were lighted, and the bottles of liquor shone in the mirror behind them, almost like Christmas tree lights. And there were at least ten beers on tap. Modern paintings of sports figures hung on some of the walls, and big-screen TVs were placed throughout the room so that customers could have a great view wherever they were seated. A few people were already having drinks and chatting over the background TV noise.

"Hey, man. How ya doing?" Jack asked the bartender, as he sidled up to the marble-top bar and eased onto one of the light olive green, leathery bar stools.

"Well, I've been better," said the clean-shaven bartender in a green polo shirt stamped with the word "Score!" in gold letters on the upper-left chest. "What'll you have?"

"How 'bout a beer to start—Bud Lite."

"You got it," replied the bartender, grabbing and opening the beer with one smooth movement.

Jack sipped at his beer and looked around and up at the sports screen.

"What's the problem, man? Ya said ya'd been better," queried Jack good-naturedly as he sized up the spiffy bartender with his leopard-speckled eyeglass frames—or were they called tortoise?

"Awww. It's fine so far, but my other bartender hasn't showed. This place usually fills to the brim in about another half hour. I'm gonna be running like a mad man if he doesn't get here pretty quick. The ball game's gonna start soon—the Royals play the Tigers in Detroit this evening."

"Well, let me know if I can help," offered Jack, taking another slow sip on his beer. "I worked down at the boats for years and have filled many a drink."

"Seriously? What's your name? I'm Evan Greene. I'm part owner and the manager of this place," said Evan, holding his hand out to Jack.

"Hey, Evan. Jack Collins here. Yeah, I'd be glad to help ya."

Jack shook Evan's hand and then continued sipping at his beer while Evan cut lemons and arranged items for drink preparation. As Jack struck up a casual conversation with a couple of other patrons, Evan began to scurry back and forth tending the bar and also filling waitress orders. The evening crowd was beginning to file in like clockwork, keeping the three waitresses busy—and Evan too busy. About a half an hour later, Evan turned back toward Jack. The Score was hopping now.

"Were you serious about helping me out tonight, Jack?" Evan asked with a line of sweat on his forehead and upper lip.

"You bet. I'd love to," said Jack, trying not to sound too eager.

"Great, come on back. I'll pay you $17.50 an hour tonight if you're willing."

Jack hopped up and joined Evan behind the bar, and the two of them worked nonstop. Jack, having sat at many a bar drinking and observing, caught on very rapidly where things were located. And he and Evan worked quite smoothly together, bantering back and forth as they served drink after drink to an animated sports crowd watching their team win.

"You're a mean bartender, Jack. Very fast and efficient," Evan shouted over to him as they worked.

"Hey, who are ya callin' mean?" joked Jack, smiling widely.

Jack's good mood about his productive evening passed over into his interactions with the customers as well. He conversed with many of them and even flirted with the women customers. He hadn't been in such a positive frame of mind in months, maybe not even since his beginning days as a dealer at the Casino. He began to regain self-confidence in his interactions with other people. Several of the women didn't seem to be as interested in the game and responded favorably to his attentions, not that he had a lot of time with them; everything was moving fast tonight. It was about time something good happened to him, Jack thought.

He and Evan worked steadily until about 1:00 AM, when Evan shouted out, "Last call!"

After that all the patrons finally started trickling out. When they had left, Evan offered Jack a burger with a whiskey on the rocks and paid him $150.00 in cash.

"Great job, Jack! I don't know what I would have done without you tonight. And you fitted right in. Any chance I could hire you to work some more for me on a more permanent basis? I'm terminating that guy that didn't show up tonight," Evan said, banging his fist on the bar.

"Well, let me think a minute," replied Jack with feigned hesitation. "My other job has been a little slow lately, so I might consider it. I think I'd like working for you though."

"What are you doing now?" asked Evan discreetly, without looking directly at Jack.

"Oh, it's just a service business I started with some others, but it's not very satisfying for me—sort of lonely as well as slow."

Jack didn't want to appear too excited about it, but he was really jumping at the chance to have a real job again.

"This job could be part time at first if you like. And it would definitely be more socially interactive, from what you say. What do you think? Do you want to give it a try?" pressed Evan.

"Well, sure, I'd like to give it a try," Jack said with a shrug to hide his eagerness.

"Great!" said Evan. "Would tomorrow evening work to start?"

They worked out the details, and Evan said he'd have the Social Security forms, etc., ready before the shift started at 4:30 the next afternoon. Jack would help do the prep work for happy hour, but Evan didn't expect that there would be quite as large a crowd as they had served tonight. All the same, any down time could be used to show Jack more about how the bar ran. Evan was excited for Jack to begin and told him he needed to have a dependable worker again and wanted Jack to learn as much about the business as possible in a short time. He also gave Jack a Score green polo shirt in size large to wear to work the next day.

"I'm sure you'll like working here," assured Evan, nodding his head. "I can tell by the way you interacted with everyone tonight. Also, I'll order another shirt or two for you."

It was about 2:45 AM when Jack finally headed home. The streets were empty and the night was peaceful and quiet, except for the sound of crickets chirping in the dark. The humid air caressed his face through the open van window as he drove. He relived the whole evening in his mind on the drive home, smiling and repeating some of his banter with the customers and with Evan. Jack literally gave himself a pat on the back.

"Good job, man! It's about time somethin' started going right for ya!" he said out loud.

But then he started to think about Annie and how she would work into all of this. For the first time since she came, he'd be making plenty of money, and she didn't fit into the picture. He wasn't quite sure what to do with her—he couldn't just leave her locked up in that room hours on end. He could earn his own living again, and she was suddenly a fifth wheel. He didn't need her any more.

After he got home, he walked into the kitchen to get a drink of water before going to bed and did a double take. The kitchen looked as if a cleaning service had taken over and shined it from top to bottom. All the dirty dishes he'd left piled in the sink were put away in the cupboards, sparkling clean. The floor had been thoroughly scrubbed, and the chairs were arranged neatly around the table, which was emptied of its normal clutter.

"What in the hell? Shit! I must have forgotten to lock the damn door."

He rushed up the stairs, glancing in at the ultra-clean bathroom as he passed. It, too, gleamed as he had never seen it, with the polished tub and sink glowing from the reflection of the hall light. And, sure enough, on her door the padlock was hanging loose and unfastened from the loop. He quietly opened the door and walked over to Annie's bed of cushions, where he found her curled up and sound asleep.

"Well, I'll be damned. She didn't escape, and she cleaned the whole fuckin' house as well! Maybe I should let her outta her cage more often," he chuckled and headed toward his own room—but not before he bolted and locked her door.

After he got in bed, however, his mood became more serious, and his thoughts tumbled over and over about exactly what to do about the kid now that he had a job in the evenings. He really didn't relish the lonely life of carting her off to serve those jerks who fucked kids while he sat alone outside guarding his property. But if she got away, escaped, or even went to live with someone else, he could still get into deep trouble. He could also get caught by simply hanging onto her though. But how could he get rid of her and the potential problems she might cause him?

Duke still wasn't answering his calls—he obviously had washed his hands of him and the kid completely. And giving her to anyone else could get him into just as much trouble as if she just ran away. Jack punched his pillow, turned over and over in his bed, and finally got up and went back downstairs. He poured himself what was left in a nearly empty bottle of bourbon in the cupboard. He took a deep breath and then a big gulp of the booze.

"Calm down man! You just had a great night; you got a new job; and you have proof that Annie wants to cooperate with you. She needs you and she's not going to run off and tell the cops about you. You'll work it out."

Jack savored the warmth of the rest of his whiskey, downed the last few amber drops, and went up and fell into his bed, totally exhausted. He was asleep almost as soon as his head hit the pillow.

9

Anita

June 2018

I LOOK WITH DISGUST at the rusty, old pan Gek brings in with my meal when he tells me I can use it to pee into. I make a terrible face, but he just turns away. I know that means he is leaving for the evening—but at least he won't be taking me anywhere tonight. Gek is all cleaned up and *guapo*—with his hair clean, beard neat, and a crisp, white shirt for a change. As I chew absently on my sandwich I hear Gek leave in the van, the gravel spattering as he pulls out of the driveway and speeds away. Listening to that sound though, I suddenly realize that I don't remember hearing him bolt the door. But he probably did; I hadn't really been paying that much attention because I'm so used to being locked in. I was caught between the humiliation of having to pee in a pan and the partial relief that at least I wouldn't be forced to hold it for hours—or the even greater embarrassment of not being able to hold it any more and having another accident on the floor. Did he lock the door though? Surely he did—or else he would be back in a minute.

I finish my sandwich of sliced turkey meat from a little plastic package that Gek put on stale, white bread. It's so dry I can barely swallow it. I think all the while of *Mamá's* tasty *frijoles y arroz con tortillas*, with spicy salsas of tomatillos and peppers, and her warm and heavenly smelling pumpkin soup with a little ball of soft, fresh cheese and *pepitas* on top. My thoughts about *Mamá's* cooking help me to escape for a few minutes from the empty, lifeless room where I am confined. Instead, I relive the warm, hearty smells and flavors of those familiar, everyday dishes that seem so special now. The memory of the warmth of the food and the spiciness of the *salsa picante*, along with *Mamá's* loving hugs and kisses as I helped her clean up after the meal, bring me to a different time and place where I am safe and loved.

"*Gracias por ayudarme, mi hijita,*" *Mamá* would thank me and then would hug me tightly and plant a kiss on my cheek. For a moment I can even smell *Mamá*, with her faint aroma of cinnamon. I can feel her squeeze my body against hers and I remember how safe and loved I always felt. Tears come into my eyes and suddenly I am shaking and sobbing as I remember that I'm really locked in this awful room, so far away from my loving parents and relatives. And they don't even have any idea where I am. Where is *Mamá* now anyway? Is she still in *Tejas*? Or did they send her back home? I hope that at least she is back with *Papá*. And what happened to *Papá* that night? I wish and wish that I could be free to find them! Suddenly I think about when Gek was getting ready to leave and that I didn't remember hearing him lock the door. I hold my breath as I get up and rush to the door—just in case it isn't really locked like I know it must be.

Gek se olvidó; puedo escapar, I think when I, amazingly, can open the door. This means I have a chance to escape and find my parents. I can't believe my luck that Gek has forgotten to lock me in this room.

I hurriedly tiptoe down the stairs, still not believing my good fortune and halfway expecting Gek to reappear any second. He surely will come back any moment to lock me in. I open the back door and step out into the sunlight that shows signs of disappearing any minute. Where should I go? I am afraid to walk on the road in case Gek returns. It would probably be better to head into the woods for a while, and I immediately wish I'd left earlier. But at least I am free! I enter into the quiet, wooded area I have watched so many times from the window in my room. From that window, the area within the trees had looked welcoming and free. But now I feel the bushes and vines grab at my arms and legs, and low twigs and branches pull and tangle my hair. The uneven ground is covered with roots and vines, and I trip again and again as I go farther into the tangled woods. Those vines and branches seem eager to chase and catch me. I can see less and less as I head into the dark, darker forest and I don't know at all which way to go. What is left of the dying sunbeams is even harder to see as I wander through the wooded tangle, which does not seem friendly now.

"*U-u, u-u, u-u,*" I suddenly hear above my head and I nearly jump out of my skin. I realize that it is a very big owl and I can hear it flying through the leaves.

Then I hear another animal that frightens me even more.

"*Un coyote,*" I whisper in my fear; I feel less and less certain about my plan. "*Necesito escapar por día,*" I say to myself as I realize that escaping in the dark without a light and without some idea about where I am going will not work.

The coyote yelps again, louder this time. I hate to give in to fear but I am scared, so scared, and—in that moment—I feel even more trapped and frightened in the woods than I had in Gek's house. I turn around, hoping that I am headed in the right direction to get back to the house. It is so dark now. I need a flashlight at least. Several times I stumble over the grasses and rocks and once I fall down on my knees. I scrape one of them badly on a rock and can feel the blood oozing out of the wound. With the back of my hand, I wipe the tears that come into my eyes and promise myself not to cry or scream. I tell myself I *will* find my way out of the woods and I *will* find my mother—just not yet. Finally I see the clearing around the house in front of me. I run across the more open yard, not stopping until I enter back into the house and slam the door behind me.

Necesito un plan, I think as I sink onto the floor. I am shaking and crying and my heart is beating hard. I finally realize that I really hadn't had a plan and that dashing off into the woods in the dark was not a good idea. I need to work out a better way to get out of Gek's house and find my family. Once again I repeat *Tía* Rosa's phone number in my mind: 1 (to begin), 4 (my mother and her three sisters), 8 (the four sisters and four brothers), 0 (no problems), 6 (my birthday), 1 (me), 7 (my lucky number), 13 (my age), 8 (my mother and her siblings), 9 (the siblings and my *abuelita*). 1-480-617-1389. I *will* get out of here and I *will* find everyone again.

I look around at Gek's depressingly dirty house and have an idea. Maybe if I clean up the house instead of just running away because Gek forgot to lock me in my room he will start to leave the door unlocked more often. *Abuela* always told me that I could do more by helping out and cooperating than by being difficult. And that had always worked when *Mamá* was upset with me, or when my younger cousins were being mischievous, and even with my teachers at school.

Cleaning Gek's kitchen and bathroom becomes my project. If he comes back and finds me doing that, how could he be upset with me for that? It just might work, and if I have more freedom I could work out a better plan to escape and find some supplies to help me—like a flashlight, perhaps. I start looking around for cleaning supplies—Gek doesn't have much of anything—but I finally find some vinegar and an old box of *bicarbonato* that looks about a hundred years old. I begin to scour and polish like I've seen *Mamá* do—as if she were fighting against a demon. I imagine that demon too and vow to conquer it. I begin to feel happier and more confident—stronger—as I scrub all that grime from the sinks, toilet, and floors. I start to feel like I am organizing and renewing myself as well.

By 11:30 I have finished cleaning those two rooms and I am so tired. Gek has not returned yet, but I am starving after working so hard, so I hunt around in the kitchen, eating chips, crackers, cheese, and a little of whatever I can find. I don't want Gek to be mad that I am eating up all his food, but I need something else to eat besides the sandwich he gave me earlier. I continue to eat small bits of different things I find and then I go back upstairs, climb onto my cushion bed, and fall asleep as soon as I lie down.

When I awake the next morning, the sun is high in the sky. I climb off my bed and hurry to check the door of my room. I am very disappointed to find it locked after I did all that work. That means Gek came home and probably noticed at least the bathroom and definitely realized that he had left my door unlocked. I wait to see what will happen. Hours pass, but Gek still doesn't come to my door. Finally I begin to knock on my door and call to him because I really, really need to pee. When he doesn't come, and I can't wait any longer, I decide to use the pan he brought me the afternoon before. I feel better but I am really hungry again. I look out the window at the wood and have second thoughts about leaving it the evening before to return to this prison house. Why was I such a scaredy cat? I should have stayed the night in the woods and then found another way out during the day. At least it wasn't cold outside at night since it is summer. Where is Gek? Is he never going to get up? Or did he leave again after he locked me in my room? I wonder if I should try breaking the screen in the window and climbing outside. I am on the second story, but maybe I could make it. I can tell by the sunlight that it is already well past noon.

Finally I hear Gek in the bathroom. Soon after he opens my door.

"*Hola.* Do you want some breakfast? *¿Quieres comer?*" Gek asks. He sounds like he is in a good mood.

I tell him that I do—that I'm very hungry—and after stopping in the bathroom, and also emptying and rinsing that awful pan, I hurry downstairs.

"*Gracias—todo limpio*"—he says, gesturing at the whole, sparkling-clean kitchen.

"*De nada*. I work. Door open—I work."

"Okay. We'll make a deal. Open door—*tú trabajas. Pero no puedes salir.* You can't leave."

"No, no. I no leave," I reassure him.

Gek asks if I want to go to the store with him, and we head to Walmart. On the way, I look at all the street signs and also signs of stores. I see that our road is LL, but the nicer streets have names, and many are numbers—I see 157 and 154. Also, there is a big highway, I-35, that we go on to get to Walmart. Jack buys a bunch of food there —chicken, hamburger, beans, cheese, cereal—more that he usually does. We work out that I can cook for us and I will clean up the house. I ask for some books so I can read and learn English, so he buys me a couple in the kids' book area, as well as a watercolor set and some color books.

While we are driving home, I watch carefully again, trying to re-member things on the way and to recognize familiar things. We get off the big highway before we get to a place called Gardner. I think that word is *jardinero* in Spanish. Usually it is dark when I have ridden in the car though, so I haven't seen what is near to Gek's house. But this time, as we get closer, I see a gas station with a Quik Shop and then a bunch of houses on a street that looks new pretty close to where we turn onto the rougher road by Gek's house. I notice that the trees behind Gek's house prevent me from seeing those houses from my window. I also observe where the afternoon sun is in relation to everything. Gek is looking at me, so I begin to talk to him. I tell him I want to go to school and to learn English.

"There's no school now. It's summer—*vacación*," he explains.

"*¿Más tarde?*" I ask.

"We'll see. *Vamos a ver*," Gek replies.

"*Y quiero encontrar a mi mamá.*"

"*Sí, sí*, we'll find her." He sounds a little impatient now.

I tell Gek that I have my Aunt Rosa's phone number in Arizona and that we could call her to help find my mother. Gek immediately stops smiling and looks at me almost like he is frightened or something. His eyes get wide and his eyebrows bunch together like black fuzzy caterpillars crawling toward each other. Then he looks back at the road.

"*Es imposible*," Jack tells me. He sounds mad. "*Mi teléfono no* calls *Arizona*. It won't work. I'll ask someone how we can call. Later—*más tarde*."

After we return home, Gek tells me that he has to leave for work, and at first I think he means he is going to take me out to work. I begin to cry. But Gek gets all cleaned up and *guapo* again—he is wearing a shirt that says "Score"—and says he is leaving soon. He also tells me to make some dinner and that he will eat before he leaves. He shows me how to work the TV and makes me promise I won't leave the house. If I do, he makes clear, he will never leave my door unlocked again and he won't let me call my aunt.

10

Claire de lune

August 1–2, 2018

THE DAY AFTER JIM LEFT for Montreal, I drove around my neighborhood and some of the little roads around it, avoiding County Road LL. I was trying to get a better idea of exactly where our house was in relation to the house I'd passed where the dark-bearded man had pushed the little girl toward his van. I used the map feature on my car screen to help plot out exactly where our house lay in relationship to the other one. Since it was a new area, some of the roads didn't even appear as streets on the navigation app. But I drove on the surrounding county roads, except for the dangerous one, back and forth until I knew where all the roads around that house led; a few turned into paved streets, while others—in various conditions of repair—were loose gravel with ditches along the edges. Some roads were lined with fields and farmland or with dense overgrowth, while others had apparently just been cleared and surveyed for upcoming development.

After circling around the area for nearly an hour—with its combination of dusty roads and barren new streets—I returned home. On my computer, I pulled up a street map of the area, printed off several sheets that I taped together, and began to plot out where everything was that I'd seen. I even looked up the satellite map of Olathe and found where we lived, where County Road LL was, and also where the infamous house was located. By zooming in on the house, I confirmed that the wooded area behind it was not too far from our residence. After studying the aerial view of the house and the wood even more closely, I had a plan.

That afternoon I drove to Target and Dick's Sporting Goods and, between the two, bought hiking boots, lightweight hiking pants, a backpack with water reservoir, insect repellant, sunscreen, and an airy baseball cap. At Dick's I also bought a mosquito repellant shirt, binoculars, and a compass.

"Is there anything that repels chiggers?" I asked the lady attendant with brashly-dyed, auburn hair who was helping me at Dick's. "They seem to love me—I can get eaten up just walking down our sidewalk."

"Oh, you poor dear," said the lady, lightly touching my arm. "The only thing I know of that really works is sulfur powder. It smells awful but it helps. We don't carry it here, but Lowes has it."

I thanked her, went to pay for my purchases, and headed toward Lowes, where I picked up a one pound container of Lilly Miller Sulfur Dust. The smell of sulfur penetrated even through the packaging.

Following all that, I headed home and fixed myself a salad to accompany my left-over sea bass from La Bouche from the previous night's dinner. After pouring myself a glass of Chardonnay, I studied my maps while eating. On the maps, I marked the best spot to park my car in order to approach the wooded area behind the house I knew Antoine had been talking about. The point I marked was where, according to the satellite maps, I would have the shortest trajectory to walk through the overgrowth I needed to traverse to come within viewing distance of the back of the old farmhouse. I couldn't be sure if there were fences or other obstacles that might block my path, but that was what I would discover on the trek I planned to undertake through the woods the next morning. I decided to bring work gloves and some cutters in my backpack that could work for branches or even wire, just in case, and I retrieved those items from the workbench in the garage.

After it got dark, I put on a comfortable pair of light blue knit pants and t-shirt that I could sleep in, turned on a Consort of London's recording of Handel's *Water Music,* and ventured out onto the screened-in porch, hoping, wishing that Antoine might appear again. I stretched out on the sofa, exhausted from my busy day and so many nights of interrupted sleep. Although it was still only shortly after nine, I fell asleep almost as soon as I lay down. I don't know how much later it was, but I awoke, sensing a movement of air and realizing that I was no longer hearing music. Instead, there was an active quietness to the pneuma, a sense of enchantment.

"*Bonne nuit*, Claire. Are you awake?"

"Antoine? I was hoping you would return. I have a plan to help that little girl, but I may need your assistance to help keep me safe," I replied as I quickly sat up on the sofa and tried to arrange my hair a little after falling asleep there.

"*Bien sûr*. Of course I will do whatever I can to aide you," Antoine said in a soft but confident voice. He was wearing the same running clothes as on the other two nights—perhaps ghosts don't have a wardrobe selection. "I have begun to understand how to use *mes pouvoirs fantômes;* how do you say? Ghost powers, yes? I can use them better now. At first I could not even control where I was."

I snickered for a second, imagining a ghost who couldn't control where he appeared or when, and Antoine grinned too and shrugged with a funny gesture. Then he sat down on the sofa with me again. A soft waft of cool air coincided with his movement. Only the ethereal glow of the moon coming in through the screens lit the room—even the light was other-worldly. A chorus of cicadas and the fragrance of roses from outside in the garden accompanied us there. After a moment of quiet, when we were both appreciating the atmosphere, I told Antoine about my plan to hike into the woods toward the back of the house and then showed him my maps and binoculars I had laid out there next to the porch sofa with a flashlight, in hopes of showing them to him.

"You will do this even with the … chiiggers?" he questioned wide-eyed with his palms turned up in query. "But how will this help?"

"After I find the house, I'll use binoculars to see if I can observe the child. Then I'll contact the police and, perhaps, some federal authorities. School hasn't started yet, so perhaps I'll see her outside or something," I explained as I tried to convince him that I really had planned this out.

"Ah, and how shall I help you?" asked Antoine.

"Just warn me if I am in danger of him spotting me, and I'll get out of there. Perhaps you could be with me there tomorrow?"

"I can do that," he affirmed.

Antoine then proceeded to tell me about another encounter he'd had with the man evidently named Jack that we didn't trust.

"One night I brought one of my supervisors, a woman named Cheryl that I liked a lot, to a nice sports bar near here. We were sitting at the bar, and I recognized him working as a bartender."

"Which bar?" I queried, wondering momentarily if I should find that place too.

"I think you call it Score Bar, or something like that. Anyway, I watched him for a while as he worked. He evidently had not recognized me. So after a moment I asked him how was his little girl. His expression changed from *aimable* to *horrifiée* in a half second, and he propelled a martini he just made, with the glass, toward me," he said, imitating the action of hurling the drink.

"Oh my god! Then what happened?" I asked as I involuntarily tensed up just thinking of the potential danger Jack might cause either to me or to the little girl.

"The glass hit the pillar right next to me. Cheryl screamed, and the manager came. She explained what happened as I cleaned martini off my face. There was broken glass all on the bar and floor," Antoine gestured toward his face and then the floor as he spoke. "The manager fired him in the moment."

Antoine went on to explain that Jack had dashed out from behind the bar, left through the closest door, slamming it behind him, and then they could hear him squealing out of the parking lot.

"That was an extremely severe reaction to your simple question," I observed, absorbed in his story.

"*Exactement*! This supported my feeling that the girl was probably in a dangerous situation."

We both agreed that Jack's behavior was very suspicious and that something had to be done, and then Antoine conceded that my plan was our best option at the moment. We both feared that Jack's explosive temper and whatever he was hiding about the girl could be dangerous—perhaps it had already been more than dangerous to Antoine, I observed. Had Jack actually caused his death? Had he intended to do so?

Then I felt Antoine's spirit surround me like an embrace, and tears filled my eyes. I really didn't want to cry, but my anxieties about the whole situation as well as my personal situation overcame me. Had I been trying to pretend that I wasn't alienating myself from Jim? Now that possibility was the first thing that came to my mind when I felt so much comfort from Antoine. Finally I voiced some of my concern.

"I'm worried, Antoine, that I feel closer and more attracted to you —even as a ghost— than I do to Jim. And I am committed to him and don't want to hurt him," I said as I wiped the tears off my face.

"Do not worry about this, Claire. I am mostly in a different world now and soon I must completely surrender myself to that realm. In certain ways I will be with you always, but you must live your life in this world—and I—I am no longer part of it," he said as I felt a caress of air along my cheek.

"Why have you come to me?" I asked, shaking my head in wonder.

"We knew each other in other life times, and now—in this one—I need your help. Do not worry, we will see each other again in other lives."

"That's funny. I've always felt like I was born in 1887 and that I lived in some artist community in Europe," I told him.

"Really? That is truly amazing. I think it might be correct."

We sat there in silence for several moments, breathing in the night air and watching the fireflies.

"But, returning to why I have come to you, I am quite certain something is amiss with that child. She would be very lucky to have you and Jim as her permanent or even temporary guardians—I do not know why she would be with that rude man. Truly though, I would envy any child who could live with you and Jim. I see you two as very loving parents. I wish I could have grown up with both of you."

"Oh," Claire interjected abruptly, adamantly shaking her head, "We aren't going to have children! I am glad to help the girl if I can but I don't want to be a parent."

Antoine looked at me quizzically but he stayed there with me, seated on the wicker sofa, listening to the sounds of Nature outside, hearing an occasional car in the distance, looking out at the moonlit leaves blowing in the breeze, and breathing that soft air of the night. Antoine's presence was cooling and calming—he actually made the hot summer night feel cooler. Also, even without words, his presence distracted me from the upcoming harrowing project I had planned for the next morning. I curled my legs up onto the sofa cushion, calmed down again, and drifted off to sleep.

The chirping of birds and bright rays of sunlight awakened me, still outside on the porch sofa. I glanced at my phone lying on the floor next to me: 6:15. Perfect. I immediately got up, went inside, through the kitchen-living area, and back to our bedroom, where our bed was still made up since I hadn't used it last night. I asked myself if Antoine would visit me this morning or wait until I got into the woods. I really hoped I could get dressed and everything alone. After entering the walk-in closet dressing area, lighted by an amazing solar panel skylight, I dusted myself liberally, especially around the ankles and waist, with Lilly Miller's Sulfur Dust before putting on my new hiking apparel. Lilly Miller—what a pretty name for such an ugly smell!

"Whew! I can see why the chiggers won't like this" I commented, wrinkling my nose, as the odor of sulfur filled the air. I regretted having applied this power in my beautiful closet and hoped it wouldn't continue to smell of sulfur; I turned on the exhaust fan. I doubt if Antoine would like it either—can ghosts smell?

I returned to the kitchen to down a cup of coffee with almond milk, a protein bar, and an orange, before filling my water reservoir and putting on sunscreen. I also sprayed myself with insect repellant and checked to see if the binoculars and other supplies and my cell phone were all in my pack. Then I grabbed my hat, sunglasses, and keys and headed for the garage.

As I drove away from the house, the morning was bright and still cool. With the car window open, I breathed in the still verdant summer air—luckily I'm not allergic to ragweed—as I drove several blocks away and then parked my car on a suburban street of a new development. Then I walked through the dirt-covered lot of a nearly finished house under construction—no workers had arrived yet—toward the un-cleared, brushy area behind it. Tangled vines and leaves crowned the trees and overgrowth in the shady, cooler area behind the houses being built nearby. I foraged deeper into the entwined thicket, checking my compass from time to time to be sure I was headed in the right direction. The chirping of birds enjoying the morning and the ever-present sound of cicadas all around accompanied me along my route. One kind of creeping plant with pointed oval leaves had fine, hair-like thorns on its thin but strong stems that kept catching on my clothes. As I bent to free them from my pants, I noticed the compound, emerald leaves composed of three leaflets I knew was poison ivy. Jim had discovered that plant the hard way in our own yard, suffering almost as much from what I had discovered was *Toxicodendron radicans* as I had from chiggers.

Here in the woodlot it grew lushly, with some of its leaves nearly as big as my hand. Luckily, I thought, I had already covered most all of my skin to avoid insects—and that served against this poison ivy as well.

After about ten minutes, I knew I should be approaching the cleared area surrounding the house. I wanted to get close enough to be able to observe the house but still stay camouflaged in the wood. Then, presently, I could see the house; it was 7:26. I scanned the back of the domicile with my binoculars and then skirted the yard a bit—still hidden by the native cedars, red oaks, and assorted other trees, bushes, and vines—without seeing any signs of movement. A loudly buzzing insect flew around my head but didn't light. When I ventured a bit more to the West, I recognized the van I'd seen when I drove by the house a few days ago. A wave of adrenalin surged through my body; this meant that at least Jack was home.

"Antoine?" I whispered, as the surge of fear and nervousness hit me, "Are you here?"

"*Oui, oui*, Claire. I am with you," he answered with his cool presence.

I back-tracked a bit to the East, where I could observe the back of the building again and could still see if the parked vehicle were to leave. I made sure that I was blocked from easy view from the inside and took out my binoculars again to study the windows and door at the back of the house.

On the first floor, I identified what I thought was the kitchen because of the slightly higher window, which was probably over the sink. There was a door with a screen in the center of the house and another longer window on the other side of the door. Neither window had any curtains or shades. On the second story, one window was smaller and higher, so I assumed it was the bathroom. It was flanked by two larger windows, one with a dark shade inside covering it, but the other equal-sized window on the other side had no covering.

After some time, I intuited some movement inside and redirected my binoculars to the uncovered upstairs window. In a moment, a little girl stood before the window, looking out into the woods.

"Claire, do you see?" whispered Antoine.

"Yes, I see her. She's just looking out here toward us."

I observed the child standing in front of the window, leaning on the sill and gazing in my direction for several hours. She looked like a pre-teen, with a very slight build, and was dressed in a large T-shirt. Her eyes were dark and almond shaped, and her skin, although more olive than mine, had a certain pallor to it, as if she'd not been outside in the sunlight very much. Also, her reddish hair did not seem natural with her skin tone, eyebrows, and eyes. Could it be dyed? And, if so, why? The girl continued to gaze toward the wood, as if enchanted. 10:20. She didn't appear to be in a hurry to do anything.

It was now after 11:00, and I was getting really, really tired of standing in the woods, but I just couldn't leave while the little girl was still standing in the window looking out. I took yet another sip of water from the CamelBak reservoir in my backpack and was trying to decide what to do next when the shade in the other upstairs room flew open. The girl left briefly and came back wearing a shirt and shorts and had combed and fastened her hair into a ponytail. She peered toward the woods again. I began to wonder if she knew I was out here observing her. Could she have seen me? Presently she left her space in front of the window and eventually appeared briefly in front of what I had imagined as the kitchen window downstairs. Then my hands holding the binoculars began to tremble as I saw that Jack was also standing now in front of that same window.

11

Antoine Benet

Late June 2018

CUSTOMERS AT THE SCORE SPORTS BAR, after hearing the martini glass hit the pillar near the bar and Cheryl's scream, stopped their conversations and directed their attention toward the bar. Then Jack, with a look of furor on his face, dashed out from behind the bar heading toward the front door. Just before he reached the door, he ripped off his Score polo shirt, threw in onto the floor with an expletive, and rapidly exited—bare-chested. He slammed the door so hard that the canvas reproduction of an abstract Kobe Bryant painting—showing two basketball players vying for the ball on a shot into the basket—fell off the wall near the doorway and onto the floor. A woman seated near there screamed and jumped out of her chair when the painting fell next to her. A general murmur of concern buzzed throughout the locale. Then several tables of people got up and appeared to be heading toward the door, obviously frightened by all of this.

"Don't worry, folks. There was just a little misunderstanding and a glass got broken. Everything is okay now," Evan worriedly reassured his customers as he walked to the front side of the bar with a broom and dustpan to sweep up the broken glass. He was wearing a green Score polo shirt identical to Jack's discarded one, which he picked up as he walked past.

At the same time, he was apologizing profusely to Antoine and Cheryl; his facial expression clearly communicated his concern as well. Then, wide-eyed, he noticed a small trickle of blood on Antoine's face. Evan grabbed a clean napkin to hand to him and then offered to call an ambulance and pay for it. But Antoine completely refused that suggestion, as well as Evan's offer of complementary drinks. Evan kept asking if Antoine was all right, even though there was only a small cut on his face. Then Evan directed a nearby waitress—wearing a v-neck, feminine version of the Score shirt—to pick up the painting and organize the other wait staff to rapidly go to each table. They were to offer a drink on the house for all the customers.

"You know, I need to call the police about this incident," Evan told Antoine and Cheryl. "Jack has been a great employee for me, but I can't just let this go. Won't you sit down and have a drink on me so you can be here to make a statement to them? I'm sure they will have questions for both of you."

"We really do not want to stay right now," Antoine answered, dabbing his face with the napkin and then setting it down after he saw there was only a minimal amount of blood on it. "I'm okay. But we just need to leave and calm down. Do you agree, Cheryl?"

Cheryl nodded and murmured her assent, wondering what in the world had just happened. Antoine and Cheryl exchanged business cards with Evan, and they decided to talk again the next day. Evan repeated that the police would probably want to interview them.

"I really need to find out more about what happened here tonight," explained Evan, shoving his glasses up onto his head and rubbing his forehead. "Jack has really been a most competent employee. I can't believe that he did that to you—and that he just walked out. Not that I'm blaming you—not at all—I'm just totally perplexed."

"I don't really know any more," Antoine explained, shaking his head in confusion. "I just asked about his little girl—how she was."

"Do you know him?" asked Evan as he glanced around at other customers in the bar. At least the waitresses seemed to have calmed them down.

"*Non, non.* I just saw him once outside a bar with a little girl. That night I asked if he needed directions, and he cursed at me."

They agreed that Evan would also call Antoine at 10 AM the next morning. Evan explained that he'd like to have Antoine's perspective about what had happened for his employment insurance if nothing else, but he hoped to make a little more sense of the whole incident. He also assured Antoine that he wanted to make right whatever injustice he and Cheryl had suffered in his place. Evan stressed that his name and personal phone number were on the business card from the bar too and that they should call him if they had any questions or concerns.

Antoine took Cheryl's arm and led her to the main door, where Jack had exited just a few minutes earlier. The night air was light but quite hot, but it still was a relief to get out of that bar. Cheryl and Antoine were still both visibly upset by the shocking incident with Jack. Cheryl looked at Antoine's face and then gave him a big hug.

"Perhaps we should stop by an emergency clinic to be sure you don't have any glass still embedded in your skin," she suggested.

"*Non*, I think I am fine. I just need to get away from there and think about this a little bit."

"Do you think we should call the police too?" she queried. "This is really like an assault."

"Well, the glass did not hit me directly. I assume he was trying to throw it at me, but I don't really know. I think the police will say there is nothing to do. I don't know how are the police here, but they could think it is an accident. I really would like to calm down a little before I have to talk with them."

Cheryl suggested they go back to her condo and offered to drive, so she got behind the wheel and headed toward her condo while Antoine held a handkerchief against his bleeding cut. He was feeling horrible that he had brought Cheryl into such a dramatic and potentially dangerous situation. The evening was beautiful but unseasonably hot, so being inside the air conditioned car felt good even though it was after eight o'clock. The trees in Cheryl's neighborhood were leafed out in the lush, verdant foliage of early summer, but seemed to beg for a breeze of cooler air. Pink and purple hydrangeas, yellow day lilies, and all colors of roses were in bloom in the yards surrounding her complex of condominiums but were also beginning to look strained and wilted from the heat. The landscaping, too, with its crimson barberry and variegated light and dark green euonymus bushes, added splashes of strained color that nearly begged for a temperature break. Everything was stressed. As they pulled up outside of Cheryl's condo and got out of the car, they lingered a few moments, appreciating the tranquility and beauty of the evening despite the heat. At least it wasn't as humid as some of the days earlier in the heat wave. The soft rose hues of the almost setting sun were a beautiful contrast to the tensions they had undergone in what was supposed to be an enjoyable evening out.

It was still stiflingly hot though, and the heat reminded Antoine of Jack's fiery outburst. Actually, Jack's anger was not so very different from what had happened to Antoine himself. He too had thrown something in rage; his fury was directed at Elodie when she had flirted with another man at a party. When they got home, Antoine had begun yelling at Elodie, and when she shouted back at him, he picked up a book and threw it at her. It hit her in the shoulder, and she left immediately, telling him she would not stay in an abusive relationship. He had yelled at her several times before, when he thought she was paying too much attention to other men, but never had tried to strike her. Where did his anger come from? It was mainly from fear, Antoine had realized—fear that he would lose another person he loved. Fear that she would leave him as his father had left—even though his father's parting was through death. He still had his mother, but he was so afraid of losing her too. And when Alain came along, he did lose part of her attention. Antoine was still so angry and fearful about separation from his beloved father that he could not tolerate the possibility that Elodie might leave him too. His anger was definitely motivated by fear. Was Jack's anger also fear? If so, what was he afraid of?

"Antoine, are you okay?" asked Cheryl, taking his arm. "You still look upset—and very distracted. Shall we go inside where it is cooler?"

So they entered into Cheryl's serene, cool, and orderly living room with its plum and blue hued furniture and collapsed onto the couch, not saying anything for a moment. Then Cheryl got up to get them glasses of cold water. She also retrieved bandaids and sterile cotton pads and cleaned off the dried blood from Antoine's face with a few of the wetted pads and then patted it dry.

"They say nowadays not to put antiseptic on cuts like this—just to clean them with soap and water. It really doesn't look that bad," she reassured him as she gingerly and gently cared for his wound. "It's just a surface cut—not so deep that it would require stitches. I think it will be fine. I'll just put a small bandaid on it in case it bleeds a little more tonight."

"*Merci beaucoup, ma belle docteur*. I'm quite sure I'll be fine. It is nothing. I never did get to take you for dinner tonight though," Antoine apologized as he held onto her arm and looked into her eyes. "I am so sorry."

"That doesn't matter at all," she replied, looking back at him tenderly. "Why don't we just have some of that wine you brought? I'll find something simple for us to eat so we can relax a bit. I would really like to hear what this was all about though. It was quite frightening to witness."

Cheryl got the bottle of Sancerre and some snacks from the refrigerator, as well as plates and two wine glasses. While Antoine uncorked the bottle and poured each of them a glass, she brought in cheese, olives, salami, and crackers. They sat on her sofa and lifted the glasses to toast to each other and then savored the first few sips without saying anything—both slowly relaxing and enjoying the peaceful atmosphere of Cheryl's apartment and the refreshingly crisp wine. After a bit, as they snacked on the appetizers, Antoine began to tell her about the evening he had seen the bartender Jack the first time.

"Do you know the bar they call 'The Place' near to our office?" Antoine asked. "Have you ever seen the people who go into that bar?"

"I've never been inside but I know where it is and I've seen the type of clientele they entertain. Other people have also told me what a dump it is and have told me not to go there," Cheryl answered, wondering why this was important in Antoine's story and wishing he could explain the incident at the Score Bar more rapidly.

"Yes, you should not go there. One night when you were on vacation, I was working late and stopped by there after work, not realizing what an uninviting place it was. The patrons harassed me for being French, so I was leaving."

Antoine explained a bit more about the rude encounter. He told how the men were trying to get him to demonstrate a French kiss on the scantily-clad waitress. Tonight the absurdity of the whole incident became rather funny to him, so he began to explain it in a humorous way.

"I can't believe this, Antoine! A French kiss—what a bunch of jerks," she laughed, relieving some the tension they had both been feeling.

"Yes, well, perhaps I should have stayed and demonstrated—the famous French kisser such as I am," he teased with a quick smile. "But a few days later," he continued more seriously, "as I was leaving work, I saw the bartender from tonight, Jack, pushing a little girl with red hair toward the entrance of The Place. I thought he must have been confused—this was not a locale for a child—so I asked if I could help him find something."

"And what did he say?" she asked, still anxiously trying to understand the situation better.

"*Alors*, he told me to mind my own business, but in dirtier words—I think you call it the 'f-word.' And he gave me a look like he wanted to kill me—like tonight." As he spoke, Antoine thought again about the possible element of fear connected to anger.

"So what did you do?" Cheryl kicked off her heeled sandals and pulled her legs up onto the couch to make herself more comfortable. Obviously Antoine was still trying to understand everything as well.

"I just left. I had recently read the book I was telling you about—*Girl in a Cage,*" he said, trying to remember his exact reaction at the moment, "—and I started thinking that maybe my imagination was running too fast."

"Do you mean your imagination was too active?" Cheryl asked.

"Yes, maybe it was too active," he laughed at his erroneous word choice and noticed that Cheryl was smiling too. "I wondered if she might be a sex slave to him. Maybe I just imagined a situation that wasn't there at all."

They both considered this option and several others for a few moments. Was his imagination in error? Or did he need to worry more about what he had seen and about this new development? And what else could he do about it all?

"So tonight all I did was to ask how was his little girl," Antoine continued, "and you saw what happened. Maybe my imagination was right. Why would he react that way? There is something wrong regarding the girl—I can feel it. I even have evidence on my face." He touched the bandage and remembered how close the glass had come to his head. Jack's fear was definitely connected to the child.

"Perhaps talking with the police is a good idea," agreed Cheryl somberly.

He sighed and then decided to let all that out of his mind for a moment. He didn't want to waste his whole evening with Cheryl reliving those negative moments. She was too lovely in her so very stylish black and white paisley top and fitted, white pants; he still wanted to enjoy their time together and really wanted her to enjoy it too. He turned on his charm and changed the whole mood.

"And perhaps demonstrating my French kiss is a good idea too," he laughed as he moved closer to Cheryl. "Tonight I am not so eager to talk with the police—it's not really the plan I had for this evening with you—but I suppose we will have no choice. In the meantime, we have some moments together before we are interrupted."

Antoine's phone, conceivably responding to this cue, began to ring. It was the police.

12

Black Jack

Late June 2018

"WHAT A STUPID, STUPID ASS I AM!" shouted Jack as he pounded repeatedly on the steering wheel and drove away from the Score Sports Bar.

Well, no! No! It wasn't really *his* fault—that jerk shouldn't have been prying into his business; that guy was an even bigger ass. And Evan should have been more supportive; he should have kept that nitwit from harassing him. Jack stepped on the gas and speeded down the street until he suddenly screeched to a stop for a red light. Damn, it just wasn't fair! He'd just started doing well again. He had a job and was earning money instead of gambling so much. Now what? What could he do now? That jerk had ruined him!

Or maybe it was partly his own fault; could he have done something else? Maybe he could have denied it instead of acting so guilty. Maybe he didn't need to get mad right away.

"Why couldn't I just have said, 'What girl? You mistook me for someone.' Or 'Fine. She's my niece' or anything except throwin' a drink at the guy," he shouted out as he drove.

But, after all, that dimwit didn't need to pry. Maybe Jack needed to throw something to show he was serious. Or maybe that just looked really suspicious—like he'd been doing something wrong. Even after he threw the glass, he could've apologized and said he did it by accident or something—anything but what he did. How was he going to fix that now? Jack drove around rather erratically, not knowing where to go next, not knowing what to do next. He'd probably blown it with his job by rushing out like that, unless he could get Evan to agree to take him back. And why did he yank his stupid shirt off like that? Evan probably thought he was quitting. Should he just quit and get out of there? That idiot who asked about his kid knew where he worked now—he'd probably be tailing him, trying to get even or to get him into trouble. But if he quit, he'd lose that good job and he'd be back in the situation he was before he started working there.

Maybe Evan still wanted him back—he'd liked his work after all. Jack had been a real help to Evan in a pinch. Maybe he'd better straighten it out with Evan right away. Maybe he'd better call him—call him now. Jack pulled over to the side of the street, took out his phone, and found the bar number in his contacts. After several rings, Evan answered.

"Score Sports Bar, Evan speaking."

"Hey, Evan. Jack here. I'm really sorry about tonight…," Jack hesitated—perhaps he shouldn't admit to too much—it wasn't all his fault, after all.

"Listen, Jack, I don't know what happened, but I can't risk that type of behavior with my customers. You're terminated. I've called the police, so you can talk to them about it—you don't need to come back here. I've got to go now."

Evan hung up. That dummy! He said he'd called the police! The police! Jack started driving again—still not knowing what to do or where to go. Maybe he should go back there and try to convince Evan not to let him go. Maybe Evan could call the police back and tell them it was all a misunderstanding. Should he go back and try to talk to Evan? He could go reason with him in person and…

Suddenly a car from a cross street screeched to one side, and the driver blared on his horn. Jack realized that he had just run a red light, and the near accident left his heart beating rapidly and his hands shaking. After another block or so, he pulled to the side of the street and parked. He put his head into his hands and leaned onto the steering wheel. His head was not very clear. Now he regretted having downed those whiskeys before heading to work. Maybe without them he would have been able to respond without hurling that drink at the jerk who asked him about his "little girl." Why did he so automatically propel the glass at him? He was acting more and more like his dad did when he drank. Now Jack suddenly remembered that the guy was the same one who'd encountered him outside The Place. Maybe he was a cop or an undercover agent tailing him. Anyway, Evan had already called the cops because of what had happened. Jack needed to think. He'd had to give Evan his address when he got hired at the Score, so the cops would know where to find him if they wanted to question him. How could he be so stupid? He couldn't let them get there before he did; Annie was not locked in her room and she might answer the door. He needed to get home quick.

After pulling up at his house, Jack entered rapidly and found Annie watching TV in the front room. She jumped up rapidly, startled to see him home way earlier than she had expected him.

"Take your stuff and get up in your room," he shouted. "I'm locking your door and you'd better be quiet—*Cállate*. Go! Now!"

"What I do?" she asked. "What *problema?*"

"Shut up! If you say anything ya'll be spending all your time locked in your room. Don't make any noise or ya'll be sorry!"

Jack grabbed her arm, and pulled her toward the stairs with a look of utter desperation in his eyes; he hurried her into her room and locked the door. After going into his own room to grab a shirt and pull it on, he headed downstairs to check for any signs that a child had been there. He stashed a book she'd left in the kitchen in an envelope of junk mail and combed through the rest of the downstairs to see if there were other traces of her. Then he drank a mug of cold coffee to sober himself and tried to think about what he would do when the police came.

After a couple of long, agonizing hours, two cop cars with flashing lights pulled into his driveway. He peered from the edge of the front window at the two policemen as they communicated over a car radio. When they begin to walk toward the house he sat down again in a stuffed chair in front of the TV; he pretended he was watching it when their knock sounded at the door.

Jack cautiously opened the front door and peered out through the fastened screen with the TV still blaring inside.

"Good evening," said one of the cops—both of whom had an imposing physical, muscular presence. "I'm Officer Gerney and this is Officer O'Connell from the Olathe Police Department," Gerney stated as they pulled out leather-encased, official police identification cards to verify themselves. "Are you Jack Collins?"

Jack peered at each ID and then up at the man holding it, as if he wondered if they were really police officers. Gerney appeared to be more than six feet tall and was broad through the shoulders with brown short-cut hair and a clean-shaven, ruddy face. O'Connell was even taller, but thinner through the mid-section, and had lighter skin with freckles, darker hair, and piercingly blue eyes. After putting away their IDs, O'Connell kept his right hand on his belt, resting near his holster. They didn't look like they'd be easy to get around if he needed to. He'd better cooperate—or at least act like he was.

"Yeah," Jack answered hanging onto the door handle in case they tried to pull it open, since the door was only latched with a small, metal hook-and-eye screwed into the wood.

"Well, we need to talk with you about an incident at the Score Sports Bar this evening," Gerney explained. "Can we come inside?"

"I don't think ya need to come in. We can talk here," Jack replied.

Gerney pulled a small spiral notebook and pen out of the pocket of his dark gray uniform shirt, flipped through the pages, and then asked Jack his full name, birth date, and if he had been employed at the Score Sports Bar. Jack answered his questions and complied with their request that he show his driver's license as official identification by holding it up to the screen door. Gerney peered closely at it and notated what he needed on the pad of paper.

"Can you tell us about what happened there tonight?" O'Connell asked. "One of the customers reported that you threw a drink at a patron there. We just need to get it straight."

"Well, I didn't throw it at him—I accidentally pushed it toward him. He kept harassin' me and I was getting mad," Jack retorted.

"What was he harassing you about?" Gerney asked, looking up from his notebook.

"He kept askin' me about my little girl. I don't even have kids. I don't know what he was talkin' about. Maybe he's some sort of pervert."

"The gentleman near the bar says he saw you before with a little girl," O'Connell added while Gerney continued to make notations.

"Well, maybe it was when my niece was visitin' or maybe he just saw someone else. He didn't need to keep buggin' me about it. I don't know him, and he just got on my nerves. I know it was a stupid thing to do—I lost my job over it. My dad and me both have sort of short fuses—well, my dad's gone, but I still have his short fuse."

The officers asked more questions, but Jack seemed contrite and kept assuring them that he just flew off the handle but hadn't intentionally thrown anything at the customer. The glass had accidentally flown out of his hand when he just meant to shoo the guy away; it had hit the pillar, after all, not the guy. It was an accident.

"Okay, Mr. Collins. Thank you for your time. We'll just be outside for a few minutes to write up our report. If you think of anything else you want to tell us, just give us a call," Officer Gerney said as he wedged his business card in between the screen and the door jam. "Have a nice evening."

As Jack shut the door, the two officers turned to leave. Jack watched through the window while they sauntered toward the black squad cars with white doors that had "Police" painted across them in gold letters. They both got in the front seat of the closest car and left the doors open while they supposedly wrote their report. Jack wondered if they still were really just observing him. He left the living room lights on and went between the couch in front of the TV and the window to peek out to see if they were still there, pretending he was just getting something from the kitchen or doing something in the house.

Inside the squad car, the two officers shared their observations as Gerney wrote up the report on his small computer pad. The night was quiet and rather dark without streetlights so, in addition to the interior car lights, O'Connor held a flashlight when Gerney needed it.

"Let's see; 9:35 pm, June 21, 2018, name—Jack Collins. Followup of incident at Score Sports Bar. Uhh, he said the glass flew out of his hand accidentally, right?" asked Gerney as he looked up from his iPad with a sardonic expression, visible despite the low illumination.

"Right on, that's what he said," shrugged O'Connor.

Gerney kept writing and pulled out his notepad to verify Jack's date of birth.

"I don't know, O'Connor; what do you think of this guy?" asked Gerney, running his hand through his short cropped hair after he had entered all the pertinent details required in the report.

"Well, we'd better research his background for sure. We don't have grounds for a search warrant at the moment or even to bring him into the station, but he's hiding something. I can just smell it. Somehow he stinks," O'Connell said, pinching his nose to emphasize his point.

"I agree," said Gerney. "Let's get out of here for now but we ought to keep him in our radar."

13

Anita

Early June 2018

IT IS WORKING! AFTER I CLEAN Gek's house and cook his meals, he starts to leave my door unlocked almost all the time. He even leaves it unlocked most nights when he goes to work. He is so much happier when he works at night. And I am much happier too because I don't have do the other work. But he also warns me always that if I leave the house ever he will lock me in my room again and he won't help me call my *tía*. So for a while I do what he says. I watch TV a lot so I learn very much English. I read too and see many words I hear on TV.

But I am lonely and bored sometimes. And Gek always says he will get the long distance calls soon but he never does it. I think he could if he tried. I try to watch when he uses his phone to see his secret code. I know it is four times the same number but I'm not sure which number. Usually I mind him but, since he hasn't tried to help me find my mother, I don't trust him. So sometimes right after he goes to work I go outside into woods, just a little bit. I want to see how far the woods go but I usually get scared that I will get lost or that Gek will come back before me. And I don't want to get lost there again when it's dark.

One morning when I get up, I see that Gek is still sleeping and his phone is on the table in the kitchen. I still think he is lying to me about not being able to call my *tía*, and I really want to try to phone her. It is my best chance to see my family. He never leaves his phone in the kitchen, so I think it is my perfect chance. I am very nervous but I pick it up and try number 5 four times, then number 4, then 6. Finally with 7, I see that it works and opens to the starter screen. I am just trying to touch the numbers to call my *tía* in Arizona when I hear a noise up-stairs. I jump and put the phone face down on the table and then touch it again to turn off the light button. Then I hurry into the other room and sit down with a book. I pretend to read but my heart is pounding so hard that I cannot really read. Gek is coming down the stairs. I am lucky I put his phone back then. My heart beats hard and fast like the *tambores* in a fast song. I can hardly breathe.

"Hey Annie," Gek mutters as he walks to the kitchen. "Can't find my phone." Then, "Oh, here."

I see him look at the phone and wonder if I should have left it face up, but probably he doesn't remember that. Luckily he has to use his code like normal. I am almost sick and want to breathe faster but my breath is stuck. I am glad that he goes back upstairs again. I lie down on sofa and try to make my heart slower, try to breathe. At least I know his code now, I think. I also wonder if he will ever leave his phone downstairs again. Maybe next time I will have to go in his room while he sleeps to find the phone. Where does he put it in his room? I wonder as I lie there on the sofa.

Maybe Gek has gone back to bed; when he works late he usually sleeps late too. But I hear him in the shower, so maybe he has other plans today. I hope he will take me to Walmart so we can buy more groceries. I need more food to cook for him and, also, that is the only time I see other people. Soon he comes downstairs and drinks some coffee and makes some toast. I can smell it cooking and hear the toaster pop it up, but I have already eaten breakfast.

"Hey, Annie, let's go to the store," he says after he finishes eating.

"What store?" I ask in English; TV is really helping me.

I am happy when he says Walmart.

"When does school start, Gek?"

"Not yet. Later," Gek answers.

I know that is true because I saw on TV that school is out, but I still don't trust him about calling my *tía*. I don't say anything though because today I hope he will buy me new books at Walmart. Also I have a plan that I saw on the news on TV. Another girl *sequestrada*—I think it's called kidnapped—with her mouth shaped the words "Help me!" to the attendant, also in a Walmart, and he called the police for her. I want to try this too but I am nervous now because my phone call did not work.

We drive toward the Walmart, and I keep looking at the things around Gek's house as we leave. Today is so hot! The wind blows into Gek's car windows, but it isn't cool. I'm sweating and sticking to the seat. But when we go into the Walmart it's freezing! I wish I had a jacket or something.

"What else do ya know how to cook?" asks Gek after we get inside. "I'm kinda tired of rice and beans."

"I can make soup of these," I say in the vegetable area holding up a *calabacita* and wondering how to say this in English. There are so many vegetables here, and this store is so big. I doubt that I'll ever learn all the names but I really want to.

"Zucchini? Soup from zucchini? Sounds weird," Gek puts some in the giant sized cart but he wrinkles up his nose and doesn't look convinced that he will like it. "Is it any good?"

"It is very good," I say, nodding my head yes and thinking of the so delicious soup *Mamá* made of … zucchini. I repeat zucchini to myself as I see the sign now that spells out its name and the price—$.79/lb.—it says. I'm not sure if that is expensive or not, but I start looking at the prices on other things and their names as well.

"Well, let's get some hamburger or pork chops to go with it," he says quickly. "We can't just eat soup."

We go through the store and Gek buys lots of food. I start to get hungry. He's being very nice to me though and asks me what kind of food I want and even what *sabor*—flavor, he says—of ice cream. I choose chocolate, and Gek says he likes it best too. Then he gets me new books; he lets me pick three from the table on sale. One is *Pippi Longstocking* and the others are two Harry Potter books I have already read—but not in English. He also buys me a mandala coloring book. He's being so nice I almost don't want to try my plan, but I have to find my family, and he is not letting me call my *tía*.

When we go to the cashier, Gek jokes with him and makes him laugh and then he even calls me his "little girl" when they talk about my new books. Gek pays with lots of money. Then while Gek is putting the bags in the cart I watch the cashier. I wish and wish that he will look at me. Finally he does, and I shape my mouth to say "Help me!" without making a sound. But the cashier just looks at me like he doesn't understand or maybe he thinks I'm crazy. Or maybe I don't shape my mouth right. Anyway, I don't think my plan worked, so I get sad again.

"Why're ya cryin'?" Gek asks me in the car. "I got ya books and chocolate ice cream."

I tell him again that I want to call my *tía* and my *madre* and to go to school, but then he starts to be mad, so I get quiet again.

"*Gracias por los libros*," I say finally, because I am thankful for the new books. They help my English a lot and give me something to do.

After we get home and put away all the food, I make the soup, and Gek cooks the pork chops outside on a fire in an old round grill. Our meal is good, and Gek has a good mood again. It almost feels like a family—almost. Then Gek gets ready for work. Now he doesn't lock me in my room, but he has put new locks on the doors to outside so he can lock me inside the house when he leaves. He even put nails in the windows so they don't open very wide.

When he leaves, I stare out into the woods, searching for a path and praying that the *Virgen* will help me find a way out.

"*Ayúdame, Santa María, Madre de Dios*," I pray again and again.

Finally I go downstairs and watch a little TV, then read my book, but I can't concentrate. I eat a bit more of the chocolate ice cream, but even that creamy, sweet flavor does not cheer me up. Then I go to bed on my cushions, crying myself to sleep.

Two nights later I am still awake very late—until after Gek comes home. I know he falls asleep soon because I hear him snore. The sound seems louder and closer than normal. I wonder if the door to his room must be open a little bit. I walk quietly into the hall and peek into Gek's room. The moon is shining bright, and Gek has not closed his door or the window shade, so I can see him sleeping on the bed. He lying on his back with his arms and legs spread wide and his mouth open, snoring loudly. His room stinks from the liquor on his breath—*borracho*, I think.

Papá explained to me years ago what happens when people drink too much of the drinks children are not allowed to have—*cerveza, tequila, mezcal*, and others. I have seen *borrachos* in *México* as well, even at parties with my family. Sometimes, after drinking a lot of that stuff, one of my *tíos* would start yelling or acting sort of crazy. *Mamá* would tell me that he had been *borracho*. Once it might have even happened to Luisa and me when my cousin Raúl gave us some *tequila* at a family fiesta and dared us to drink a little glass of it. He drank a whole glass of it, and Luisa and I looked at each other; both of us knew we didn't want to be bested by a boy. Not only did it burn my throat when I swallowed it but it left a burning, dizzy feeling in my head. I had a headache even the next day so I told *Papá* about it. That was when he told me about the dangers of drinking those things. Raúl got in trouble for giving it to us and wouldn't even speak to Luisa and me for a long time.

I wonder if those drinks will make Gek sleep harder or if he will just be madder at me when he's drunk. He has left his clothes scattered on the floor near the bed. Also I see his phone lying on there on the floor; it's not too far from me. I must try to call my *tía* in Arizona. Without making noise, I walk very slowly on my toes, getting closer to the phone. One part of the floor makes a noise though, and Gek coughs and turns over in the bed. I bend down quickly so he will not see me. My breath stops. I can hear him breathe but I think that he might see me there. I do not move. Crouching there on the floor, I wait.

"*Santa María, ayúdame*," I say in my mind.

14

Ana López de Domínguez

May 2018

AFTER WAITING SEVERAL HOURS for her turn in line, Ana entered the closet-sized room to talk with the lawyer. Three days ago her nurse, Pilar, had arranged for Ana to meet with one of the lawyers who volunteers several times a month at the *Casa del Migrante*, providing the endless wave of migrants with legal help. Approximately 250-300 migrants end up at the Ciudad Juárez *Casa del Migrante* each month, she learned. And Father Javier Calvillo acts as a very proactive director for the center and consistently succeeds in getting help of all kinds from the community to help the nearly 10,000 migrants who have passed through the center. Some of the volunteers are lawyers, nurses, and doctors. Even so, everyone at the center is overworked and more than slightly stressed by the new United States practice of returning even the migrants who claim political asylum back to Mexico to wait.

Ana was lucky that a lawyer could see her after what seemed to her like an endless three days wait. And the line outside the door that day had moved painstakingly slow. Finally, a man opened the door to her and invited her inside to have a chair in the hot, stuffy office. Ana looked curiously at the lawyer, who appeared to be about 40 or 45. He was definitely *moreno*—with bronzed olive skin, slightly curly auburn hair with a high forehead, and dark brown eyes. His most compelling feature though was his deeply dimpled cheeks that dipped inward each time he smiled and even when he talked. He was obviously overly warm despite his friendly smile, as his forehead and upper lip were slick with sweat, even though he was wearing a short-sleeved, white shirt—also ringed with sweat under the armpits.

"*Buenas tardes, señora. Soy Rafael Gómez*. I'm trained in migrant law and I help out quite often here at the *Casa del Migrante*. How can I help you?" He smiled and offered her his damp hand to shake.

Ana began to explain how and why she had crossed the border illegally, making Rafael aware of the danger she felt from the gang members who had assassinated her husband and threatened both her and her daughter. Even though she finally had admitted that Diego had been murdered, she still could not allow herself to think of how that all transpired. She quickly changed the subject to the fact that her sister had found a *coyote* who helped them cross the *Río Grande* and then aided them up the bank of the river.

"And then what happened after you got across the border?" the lawyer asked as he took a few more notes about what she was telling him.

"After we slept for a few hours in a field, we were apprehended by some officers and taken to a detention center. Just after arriving there, a woman officer took my Anita and said they were going to give her a bath."

"And did you ever see her again after that?" Rafael asked as he paused and looked up from his notes and into her eyes.

"*¡Nunca!*" Ana sobbed. "I never saw her again."

"I'm sure you are desperate with worry, Ana. Yes, I've heard from both other lawyers and other migrants that the US has begun to separate children from their parents at their border. The US officials claim there's a safety issue if children are kept in the same facility as adults."

"What?!? Safety? How is it safe for little children if they are taken from their own parents?" Ana nearly screamed.

"Oh, I agree," said Rafael. "It's totally abusive to separate children from their parents. I'll do whatever I can to help you, Ana."

Rafael explained that relations had become very tense now between the government officials of Mexico and the US, but that Father Calvillo of the *Casa del Migrante* there in Ciudad Juárez had an excellent relationship with the priests across the border in El Paso. Because of the amicable associations with El Paso clergy, Rafael thought they could arrange for Ana to cross back into the US—just for a day—to visit the detention centers for children there, accompanied by a priest from each country. He added that the Trump administration was getting into trouble, both legal and political, for separating children from their parents. Therefore, just to help resolve the problem, there were some loopholes, especially through certain trusted officials in the Church, to try to reunite as many parents with their children as possible.

"When could this happen?" asked Ana. "I've already been here at least three days and I'm worried sick about my daughter."

"Yes, I know you are. But I'm thinking about tomorrow. Let me check to be sure it can happen, but I'm pretty sure it can."

"*¿Mañana? ¡Ay, gracias a Dios! Gracias, Rafael.*" Ana's eyes began to tear up again as she thought about the possibility of seeing her daughter the very next day.

Rafael made a few phone calls and then confirmed that a priest, Padre Manuel, would accompany Ana tomorrow to the border, and then an American priest would go with them to the different facilities for immigrant children.

Ana could barely sleep that night she was so excited. She tossed and turned in the bed, able to hear all the other migrants breathing, snoring, and moving—both in waking and sleeping states. Even the air felt stagnant and heavy around her. Finally she rose about four AM. She could not—and didn't even want to—try to sleep again at that hour. It was the day she hoped to be able to see her darling daughter again. Instead, she went into the shower facility at the center, then dressed in the same yellow blouse and khaki slacks she had worn since she left home. She headed toward the center's little chapel and quietly entered, closing the door behind her. She knelt there before an almost life-sized statue of the Virgin Mary and prayed fervently to find Anita that day.

At six-thirty, Padre Manuel arrived in a battered white Ford on the *Calle Neptuno* to pick up Ana in front of the *Casa del Migrante*. Pilar directed Ana to the car and introduced her to Padre Manuel, a small, thin priest with receding gray-streaked hair and wire rimmed glasses—probably in his sixties, thought Ana. He was wearing the traditional black short-sleeved shirt and clerical collar with frayed black trousers.

"*Muy buenos días, señora,*" greeted Padre Manuel rather hoarsely as he cleared his throat several times.

"*Sí, muy buenos y mucho gusto, Padre Manuel,*" replied Ana, taking his hand.

After she got into the car, Padre Manuel handed Ana a small waxed paper bag filled with two warm *gorditas*—small, thick, flour tortillas filled with potato and sausage—and a small bottle of orange juice.

"I doubt that you have eaten breakfast yet and I think you will need the energy," he said.

Ana had begun to recuperate her appetite after so many days without eating and she truly was hungry and grateful for the meal. Padre Manuel and she talked about her dilemma on their short drive to the heavily guarded border crossing.

"Several of the priests in the US have a good relationship with some of the border guards. So we have been able to reintroduce migrants into the US for very brief periods of time to resolve emergencies like yours, where migrants are separated from their children, or in cases of extreme illness or a death where a family member must help or even identify the afflicted person," he cleared his throat again. "As for us today though, we must leave the US again by five PM."

"Will it take us that long?"

"We never know. They have opened so many new holdings areas for children, and most are very crowded and quite disorganized. I hope we can find your daughter quickly, but I do not know."

"*Espero que sí, querido Jesús,*" murmured Ana in a continuation of her prayers.

"Father Bill will meet us at the border and guide us to the detention areas for migrant children in the El Paso area" explained Padre Manuel.

Then he pulled up to the control station number two—the second one on the right—where a tall man with salt-and-pepper graying hair, also dressed in the typical shirt with Roman collar and black trousers, was talking with the guards. Father Bill strode over to the car, shook hands with Padre Manuel, reached over and took Ana's hand, and after a few minutes of conversation between him and the border guards, Padre Manuel climbed into the back seat, and Father Bill took control of the car. He greeted Ana more warmly now that he had time to do so and then pulled away from the border control, heading into the light, early morning traffic of El Paso toward the first compound for immigrant children just outside the city.

Father Bill spoke in slightly broken Spanish with an American accent as he drove and chatted freely with Ana and Padre Manuel. Ana liked his warm smile, the way his eyes crinkled at the corners when he did so, and his wry sense of humor. She began to like the US more again just because of these few moments with one pleasant, welcoming person.

Ana knew from the imposing fence surrounding the property when they approached Clint, the main immigrant detention center for children, located in the town of Clint, in a desert area outside of El Paso. Armed guards stood at the entrance gate and came toward the car as it pulled near. Father Bill obviously knew the guards and conversed amicably with them for a few moments, pointing toward Ana as he explained in English. The guards peered into the car and checked the trunk before permitting them to enter and park the car near the cement block building, which had other fences around parts of it.

Ana and the two priests got out of the car and entered the building. After Father Bill spoke with the guards, again with his winsome, smiling manner, one woman guard led them to a locked door, which she opened to let them enter. Inside, there were various cages that separated the groups of children instead of housing them in different rooms. Although some children had cots, most were sleeping on the floor, either on rough army blankets or shiny, spaceship-like aluminum ones. The florescent lights burned brightly even though most of the children were still trying to sleep. Ana's eyes filled with tears as she gazed at the dozens of children, confined like animals in these cages. Some of the children were crying and wailing loudly as the others tried to sleep. A nauseating whiff of unwashed clothes and unbathed bodies assaulted Ana. One very dirty, little boy about three years old stood gripping the wire caging, sobbing hysterically while thick mucus dripped from his nose and onto his shirt. The noise in the large building with cages was irritating and distracting as it echoed from one corner to another. Even with many children asleep, it was still disturbingly loud. The thin aluminum blankets given to the children rustled and crackled endlessly. How comforting could a semi-rigid, noisy, thin aluminum blanket be? Ana's heart literally ached as she surveyed these orphaned children.

When the female guard, Shiela, unlocked the first cage, Ana and the two priests entered and Shiela followed, locking the cage door behind them. Ana walked by each child, peering into every face, searching desperately for her own Anita. Many children had the aluminum or scratchy wool blankets pulled over their heads to shield themselves from the light and noise. Ana lifted each cover carefully and gently, so as not to disturb the child more than she had to, and quickly gazed at the face of the child beneath it. Instead of seeing Anita, she found tear-streaked, dirty faces with frightened eyes, like wild animals caught in a trap.

Hot, salty tears welled up in her eyes again. Suddenly Ana remembered an incident from her childhood—she was probably four or five—that she hadn't recalled in many, many years. Her extended family had visited the *Zoológico de Chihuahua* not far from their home. It was the first time that she had been to a zoo, and everyone thought she would be excited about seeing the different, exotic animals. As they approached the first exhibit, she saw two regal, gold and black-striped cats lying on the dirty concrete floor of the cage. She had wrinkled her nose though from the stench emanating from the enclosure and had begun to frown and dislike the visit. Suddenly, one of tigers had looked up at her with its very sad eyes. Ana had begun to weep so hard that her mother had to take her out of the animal area to a park bench, where they waited until the rest of the family finished their visit. As she thought back on that previously hidden memory, Ana realized that the children she was seeing were being held in even more dire conditions; at least the tigers had more space in their cage and, possibly, were with a parent. She could not help but equate these children—and her own Anita—with that extremely doleful tiger.

Padre Manuel touched her arm, bringing her back to the present. They needed to continue their search. The adults wandered among the cages, and Ana looked at every child, asking some of the older children if they had seen a girl named Anita. Sometimes the confused children pointed to another child or to themselves, but never to her Anita.

Around nine in the morning, guards brought crates of small containers of apple juice and milk; dried, sugary cereal in diminutive boxes; along with bunches of overly ripe, bruised bananas. Some of the children devoured everything they could grab within minutes, while others just turned away and cried, as if repulsed or frightened by the so-called breakfast. As more of the children wakened, the noise level in the building increased dramatically, especially since the walls were made of wire fencing, instead of having normal rooms.

While Ana went from one child to the next, looking more and more desperately for her own, Padre Manuel and Father Bill spent their time talking and praying with the children. One little girl about four years old clung to Ana when Ana spoke to her and began crying and calling Ana *tía* when the guard tried to pry the small arms from around Ana's leg. Ana comforted her for several minutes, and some of the other older children also tried to help. It was obvious that Ana related well to the children. She peered into the faces that showed tired, hopeless expressions around the eyes, making the children look much older than they were. As she talked with them and tenderly touched or hugged them, however, they began to look more hopeful.

After about four and a half hours though, Ana hated to admit that she had probably seen every child of the hundreds in the compartmentalized cages in the facility and recognized the futility of returning to each cage. If Anita had been there, they would have found each other by now.

"I hate to give up here," Ana said, "but I have looked at each child, and Anita is not here."

"There are two other smaller facilities where we haven't looked yet, Ana," consoled Father Bill. "Do not despair. One is Tornillo, a tent camp, and the other is an even smaller facility with tent-like structures. We will grab a quick lunch and then continue looking at the other two centers for children."

Subsequent to checking out of the Clint facility, Father Bill drove to a nearby taco restaurant, where they ordered take-out food and drinks, and ate as they drove back toward the Tornillo tent camp in El Paso. Even Father Bill was more quiet and reserved after the emotionally exhausting experience of being with all those displaced children who had been forcibly separated from their parents. There was so much fear, depression, confusion, and loss of hope in such a concentrated group that even people full of faith and optimism, like both Padre Manuel and Father Bill, had to find their bearings. Before they entered the Tornillo tent camp, the two priests prayed with Ana, and she began to feel calmer again.

Despite their prayers and encouragement and their efforts to help Ana, the results at the next two facilities for children were just as futile as at the first. Father Bill tried to comfort Ana with what he had learned in the last several days about what was happening with the great numbers of children being separated from their parents.

"You know, Ana, some children were discharged to sponsors because the holding facilities for children were so overcrowded. I will investigate who the sponsors were that fostered immigrant children and see if I can find out where Anita might have been placed. Do not lose heart."

Even with the priests' assurances that they would not give up, Ana returned to Mexico that evening with a very heavy heart.

15

Anita

Late June 2018

I AM WATCHING TV WHEN Gek returns home one evening quite early. He starts yelling at me as soon as he hurries into the house and sends me up to my room. He continues yelling as he locks me inside; this is the first time he has locked me in the room in a long time.

"Shut up. Don't say one word," he warns me. "*Cállate.*"

At first I wonder what I have done to make him so mad at me but soon I realize that whatever has made him mad probably has nothing to do with me.

It was hot downstairs, but up in my room it is like an oven—especially with the door shut. I wonder how long he will confine me here. I go to the window and look out into the woods. The moon is shining and the trees are still. Not even the smallest breeze enters my window. I can hear the TV and the chirpy sound that fills the trees in the evenings. Gek tells me they are crickets or locusts. He doesn't know which. There are also little sparkly bugs that fly through the yard and flash their lights —lightning bugs, Gek says. I think they are really *hadas* though—fairies. I watch them and ask them to tell the *Virgen de Guadalupe* to help me.

After a while I hear a car in the drive and then another. Then someone knocks at the front door. Gek is talking to some men, but I can't tell what they are saying. At this moment I wish my window was on the front side of the house so I could hear and maybe even talk to the men. It doesn't sound like they are inside. Gek must be talking to them through the door. I wonder who they are. Gek never has visitors at the house. These men do not stay very long. I hear them open car doors and, after a while, more doors open and shut before they drive away. I think it is two cars. Gek keeps the TV on for a while but I also hear him banging cabinet doors in the kitchen, so I don't think he's watching TV. After a while he turns it off, and I hear him coming up the stairs.

"Gek, will you please open my door? Gek, I need the bathroom. Gek, will you unlock the door? *¡Por favor!*"

I yell to him, but he does not answer and does not open the door. Finally I climb onto my bed, even though I am thirsty, very hot, and sweaty and want to use the toilet. Apparently Gek is still angry about something and pretends he does not hear me or that I am not here. I decide to try to sleep. Maybe he will be nicer to me tomorrow.

But the next days and weeks are not much better. Gek does not go to work now but many nights he leaves and comes home drunk. After a couple of weeks he tells me I must work again.

"But Gek, I do work. I work here in the house. I cook. I clean the house for you," I tell him, knowing what he means though.

"That doesn't bring in money. I need some money if you want me to buy you food," he yells back at me with an angry face.

"If I call my *tía*, she will come for me. She will feed me."

"Great!" he yells. "Who will feed me? Come on," he says as he grabs me. "You have work tonight."

Gek drags me into his car and drives much farther than normal. We are driving through an area with very large, beautiful houses with lawns as big as parks, and he turns into the entry of one of these fancy places. Then we have to drive inside a tall fence and to the side of the building. A man in a black suit opens a door, and Gek tells me to get out of the van. I don't move, so he opens my door, grabs me, pulls me out, and picks me up to carry me inside. The place is gigantic—like a palace. The man in the black suit shows Gek the way up the stairs, and Gek still carries me. We go into a very big bedroom with a bed covered in a black, satiny cover. That bed is almost as big as my whole space in Gek's house, and there are also sofas and tables and elegant chairs in the room. A rather fat, mainly bald man in a satiny, red robe says hello to Gek and also to me. He hands Gek an envelope and Gek peers inside.

"This looks right," says Gek and nods.

Then Gek looks at me.

"See you tomorrow, Annie," he tells me and quickly leaves the room followed by the man in the black suit.

"Tomorrow?" I scream. Suddenly I am very scared and I even miss Gek.

At first the man is nice to me; he tells me to call him John. He fixes some drinks from a fancy table with bottles in a bucket with ice. John gives me a Coke in a fancy cup and also some snacks. He offers me wine too or some rum, but *Mamá* does not allow me to drink those. I wish she were here. I am so, so scared. The man sits down on one of the sofas and tells me to sit as well. He talks to me a little more and tells me I have pretty eyes and sits closer to me. His breath smells like liquor with another odor as well—like moldy leaves. Then he takes off his robe. I see his fat belly. He pulls me over to the bed and sits down. I must travel in my mind back to my home, to *México*, and my world of past and pretend dreams.

I am with my *prima* Luisa and we are walking together on the land around the house of my grandmother. There is a small area with *Nogales* and other trees where we have set up a pretend house. We bring our dolls there this afternoon, along with a basket with our lunch and some limeade to drink. We are laughing because Luisa has set up a funny chair made of stones for her dolly. The doll looks like a queen, so we make her a beautiful crown with some leaves from the trees. She looks so royal! We decide to make crowns for ourselves as well and we weave more and more leaves into the crowns, as well as some very small flowers that grow in the grasses to look like jewels. Luisa puts on her crown, but soon we decide to have a special ceremony to crown each other as queens.

After a while, we change our minds and decide to become *hadas*, fairies, instead. I remember my book *Historias de hadas*, with two fairies, some flowers, and a blue butterfly on the front cover. Since we are fairies, we can fly. We run around under the trees in the shady area, pretending first that we are flying like fairies, then like bees and butterflies. We go between the plants in my grandmother's garden touching the flowers. Once again though, despite my pleasant memories and imagination, I am interrupted by a painful image. This time I am running beneath a butterfly. I'm watching the butterfly and don't even notice that I am now running on a gravel road. Suddenly I trip and fall very hard and scrape my knees, hands, elbows, and chin—the whole front of my body. I cry out. I hear a pig snorting near me. Where am I? I don't remember anytime when a pig was bothering me after I fell down. I want to go back to the memory with the bees and butterflies. Let's see, Luisa pretended she was a bee, and I was a blue butterfly. But the pain is still with me, and I can't get completely back into the memory. I can still hear the pig.

Now I hear John snoring. I walk quickly and quietly to the door and open it, but the man in the black suit frowns at me and tells me to go back inside and pulls the door shut. I curl up on one of the *sofás* in the room and cry myself to sleep. That night on the fancy *sofá* I have nightmares again.

I am under the sea, and a big fish has invited me to tea. He sets up a table with a teapot and little almond cakes, like the ones my grandmother used to make. I start to eat a cake, but it turns into an angry, red scorpion. Soon all the cakes are scorpions and they start chasing me. I swim away from them but then I realize that the scorpions have turned into a very big fish, which I then recognize as a shark with very huge, sharp teeth. I swim faster and faster but now I cannot breathe. The shark can swim faster than me no matter how fast I go. He opens his jaws and starts to bite my leg. I scream and scream.

I wake up and I am still screaming. The man in the red robe is pulling on my leg.

"Wake up! Wake up! You are screaming in your sleep," he says gruffly.

16

Antoine Benet

July 2, 2018

GETTING PEOPLE TO CONVERT to solar power can be a challenging feat in a new area, especially when there is a preponderance of conservative people who view it as an unnecessary complication or a liberal plot to undermine gas companies. Antoine understood that many Kansans still had their doubts about what he had seen to be an amazing way to capture natural energy. There were so many benefits to solar energy, and it, too, was an industry that produced profit for companies, including gas companies that had expanded their horizons. Even so, he had all sorts of challenges cut out for him as he also helped to demonstrate to private customers, developers, and builders the advances Mid-Wester Energy had made in solar technology.

He met with groups of developers and city leaders about the state-of-the-art solar street lights that Mid-Wester had installed in the new demo development area where he lived. These solar powered street lights worked fantastically and required neither electrical lines nor buried cables. In addition to storing solar energy and turning on automatically with darkness and off in the daylight, the lights were also soft lights, meant to reduce light disruption cycles for both people and animals. Antoine always pointed out that bright, white lights had been shown to increase insomnia, for example, but these new soft lights did not adversely affect the sleep cycle. And the street lights were just one of the many new solar powered products and innovations that Antoine was demonstrating for customers, especially new home builders in the area.

Antoine met with hundreds of potential customers, both companies and individuals, to show them his new solar products and systems. During the second half of June—and even last night, July 1—he had

Sandra J. Schumm

worked late many evenings, depending upon whether he needed to promote lighting or other appliances and electrical features which could not be appreciated during daylight hours. On more than one occasion, he had to rearrange his personal life to fit an erratic work schedule. His opportunities to spend time with Cheryl had been more limited lately than he liked, he thought. He remembered how she had cared for his cut—and his erratic emotions—after the encounter in the Score Sports Bar that evening. He also pictured her with her legs curled up on the sofa, looking so calm and chic at the same time. He thought the way she pushed back the lock of dark blonde hair that framed her high cheek bones. But he really hadn't had any free nights or even weekends to spend with her. Also, on some evenings, the only time he could run was after darkness fell, even though sunset wasn't until about 8:45 PM. So he was very pleased when he learned that the Fourth of July celebration would give him a day off and some extra free time.

"Hello, Antoine," Cheryl texted on July 2. "Do you have plans for the July 4th holiday? Call me when you can. Hugs, Cheryl."

Antoine was at work at his desk catching up with the paperwork for new orders of solar powered products when Cheryl's text arrived. He was delighted to receive her message, and his first impulse was to call her immediately; they hadn't really been together socially since the night of that incident at the bar and had only talked occasionally about work-related topics. He was also surprised that she didn't just come by his desk. But then he hesitated; maybe he should wait until after work. Subsequently he began to ask himself if he was avoiding Cheryl—or perhaps if she was avoiding him—and, if so, why? Maybe she was afraid to see him as well—or maybe she was just busy. He slowly began to recall the pain he had felt after his breakup with Elodie. That hurt seeped deeply through his body again; his chest actually ached.

He pushed away the mediocre pizza he was eating for lunch as he worked, also amazed that he had stooped so low as to eat from a box. The French prided themselves on truly enjoying high quality food along with the social ambiance that accompanied a good meal. Yet here he was, eating from cardboard, scarcely tasting the equally cardboard-like flavor, and alone! How had he come to this? He then wondered if he was subconsciously afraid to get too emotionally attached to Cheryl—afraid of being hurt again—afraid of feeling the fear that might manifest as anger.

114

"Ah, Antoine," he muttered to himself, "*Qu'est que c'est?* What is all this? What are you doing to yourself? Don't you know that hiding yourself away hurts too?"

Antoine half-heartedly continued with his reports during the afternoon. More intently, he was stopping every few minutes to sift and measure his thoughts and emotions, as if he were preparing a meticulously made soufflé, gently folding his self-revelations together and revealing any unexposed materials. Yes, he owed it to himself—and to Cheryl—to call her back, but he preferred to do it from home. The office atmosphere did not foster the more personal conversation he hoped to have with her. He began to think of a plan for a short holiday there in Kansas with her.

As soon as he returned home that evening, Antoine called Cheryl, and she answered almost immediately.

"Hi, Antoine. How are you? I know you've been super busy lately."

"Yes. It has been quite busy. But I realized after receiving your message that I would like some personal time with you," he replied, as he looked out the window of his kitchen and then wandered momentarily onto the too hot sunporch. "I'm happy you have this holiday in your country; I'm ready for a break. Did you have something in mind that we could do together? I have some good ideas. We have the whole day and, perhaps we could do something on the weekend too."

"I'd love that, Antoine. I have a few suggestions, but what did you have in mind?"

"I don't know if this sounds like something you want to do, but one guy in my running group, Dave, has offered me his sailboat that he keeps on Shawnee Mission Lake. Do you sail?" he asked, thinking again of how good he had felt in her company.

Cheryl explained that she had never had the opportunity but that she was willing to try and also eager to see Antoine again.

"My *maman* often took us to Capri for holiday, and we sailed around those islands. Sailing in a small lake may not be so very exciting, but the weather is good for it, I think."

"I think sailing with you would be lovely," Cheryl reassured him. "Of course, Capri sounds much more enticing, but I'll gladly settle for Shawnee Mission Lake, considering our time constraints."

Antoine and Cheryl planned the morning for sailing, followed by a picnic lunch there in the park, the Kemper Museum in the afternoon, with dinner there, and then a fireworks display after dark. If all that was too much for one day, they could always save the museum for the weekend and adapt their plans. Antoine felt rejuvenated just talking with Cheryl again. He knew he really needed to reinitiate his private life once more. His world had been empty for far too long.

Before Antoine and Cheryl ended their conversation, they planned to finalize the time the next day after Antoine confirmed the sailing jaunt with his friend. Even though it was already getting dark, Antoine decided he'd love to stretch his legs and have a run. He rapidly changed, took a few sips from a bottle of seltzer water, and headed out the door. The night air was still hot and heavy from the humid summer day, but Antoine didn't care—his mood was lighter, and he felt almost like he could fly now that he actually had plans to see Cheryl again. Cicadas serenaded him from the trees as his feet drummed an accompanying rhythm along the roadway. Sweat poured from him but it felt purifying. His thoughts went back to his conversation with Cheryl and their plans for the approaching holiday as he gazed into the starry sky. He would love to be with her beneath these stars—would love to hold her hand and then to kiss her again. Perhaps he would call her again after his run—just to hear her voice again. Maybe it wasn't too late to still see her tonight. Why not ask? Why wait?

Abruptly Antoine recognized, with a flash of apprehension, that he was running on the road where Jack lived. He had not intended to go there; it was as if he had been attracted there by some unexplainable force. That house was still ahead of him—should he turn around? He really had not meant to even get near the man's house after that night at the bar. Then he then heard a vehicle approaching behind him. The motor was getting louder, drawing closer. The gravel spattered as the car or truck picked up speed. He sensed its energy rapidly approaching. Suddenly—with a thud—he felt propelled into the heavy, humid air. And then he felt pain—extreme pain—as he fell.

How odd! *Papa* was also hit by a vehicle. Is this the way he felt before he died? Was he thinking of *maman* and me?

In that moment, he remembered the time he fell from his bicycle as a child and his mother running toward him to help him. It hurt so much! He had looked down at his leg, and his knee was bleeding. He was terrified to see all that blood streaming from his leg, but his mother simply wiped it away with her feathery, lavender scarf and told him he would be fine very soon. The dark, cherry-red blood seeped into the feathers and stained them. He felt horrible that she had ruined her pretty clothes, but she didn't seem to mind that—even though it was her favorite new scarf. She was only worried about him. He desperately wished he could see her again and tell her good-bye and how much he loved her. But he never would have the opportunity to return to France, he now realized with a pang of homesickness.

Then he thought of Cheryl and their plans for the holiday and felt an acute sadness. His heart ached, and he also wished he could explain to her both his fascination and his fear of initiating a relationship with her. Falling in love with her would have been such a joy. Why hadn't he tried harder to see her? How could he contact her? Who would tell her what had happened to him and why he would not see her for their holiday plans? He would never get to see her again—never have the chance to develop the budding romance with her that he had so foolishly avoided so far. Did she know that her cool sophistication and beauty had truly beguiled him? Maybe not; he had hardly let himself perceive it so far. And now that he realized he was truly entranced with her it was too late. But perhaps it was best that she was not yet too attached to him. Wouldn't a deeper intimacy with her only have hurt her more? Cheryl, can you feel my love for you?

Et mon dieu—what about that little girl? His concern returned to her plight. There truly was something disturbing about what he had observed in Jack's behavior with regard to her—that child who remained nameless to Antoine and whom he had seen only once. But it appeared very clear to him in this moment that she was in danger—he could feel it. Here he was so close to where Jack lived and he could feel her aura. How could he help her? Could he even move? The pain shot through him as he tried to get up and as he realized that he had left truly important matters unfinished.

Then he felt himself drifting up from the road, leaving his body, and merging with the stars. This celestial energy pulsed so distinctly from solar energy—perhaps that was the way to go. Perhaps he needed to work with star power. A coolness and lightness lifted him, and he completely comprehended in that moment that he was no longer running in the world he knew.

17

Black Jack

July 3, 2018

JACK WOKE TO A MIDDAY sun-bright room, dripping in sweat, with a pounding headache. His mouth tasted as dry and gritty as a sand box; his whole body screamed for water. An empty Jack Daniels bottle was lying on his bed. Now he remembered why he drank it after an afternoon of quite heavy drinking at his new regular hangout, The Place. He recalled driving home yesterday evening and seeing the jogger on his county road. Even as drunk as he was while driving home, it wasn't hard for Jack to identify the runner lit up by his headlights as the French guy who'd been asking about his little girl at the Score Bar. A wave of anger had swept through him.

"You cost me my job, dude!" he had yelled as he accelerated.

He had headed his van right toward him but then seemed shocked when he actually heard the thud and felt the jolt as he hit him.

"God damn! I hit the guy," Jack recalled now through his fuzzy brain.

Even in the moment of impact, Jack realized he had probably killed him. Where should he go now? Wherever he went, he probably needed to take Annie with him or he would be in even more trouble. So he returned home and, because of his dilemma about what to do next, he had drunk all the remaining bourbon from the bottle in his house to try to escape the whole problem.

"Now what do I do?" he asked himself now in the morning or afternoon or whatever time it was. "This may be the end. I guess I'd better go look at my van."

Jack stumbled down the stairs, where he caught sight of Annie seated at the table in the kitchen. She appeared to be reading a book. It was hot and steamy inside and even hotter outside in the sun, as well as being extremely humid. It had obviously rained heavily late last night, and there were big, muddy puddles all over the drive. Jack looked nervously at his van, especially the front, where he remembered hitting the guy. His old clunker already had so many bangs and dents that he couldn't find any new telltale imprint or divot. Also, the heavy rain had washed the vehicle sparkling clean—well, as close to sparkling as an old, beat up van can be. At least he didn't have any big crushed area with blood all over the front.

Jack went back inside to grab his keys and told Annie to stay put; he'd be right back. Then he started up his vehicle and drove down county road LL to see if he could find the body. He drove up and down the road several times but didn't see anything. Perhaps he hadn't hit him after all. Maybe he'd imagined or dreamed it. Could he have been so drunk that he'd hallucinated it all? Or had the guy not been hurt and just walked away? Jack was pretty sure he'd really felt a thud, but maybe even that wasn't real. On the other hand, if he'd hit him, and the dude had walked away, he'd probably report it to the police. Jack's head throbbed and the bright sun was making his headache worse. Also, people were starting to shoot fireworks already, and those explosions were adding ammunition to his pounding head. He drove home, dragged himself inside and took three Advil with a glass of water.

"Don't bother me; I don't feel so good. You'd better stay in this house or I'll take you back to stay with that John," he muttered to Annie before he climbed upstairs and fell onto to his bed.

Despite his hangover, fatigue, and the three Advil he took, Jack could not fall asleep again. He was in both physical and moral agony. He kept wondering if he was now a murderer—in addition to being a child's pimp. Had he only imagined the whole scene of hitting the French guy? Or had someone already found his body? Would the police be coming to his door any minute to question him? Would they also find out about Annie? Or maybe come to the door when only she was at the house?

Finally Jack decided he should get up, lock the girl in her room, and go back to The Place, where he had spent the better part of last week gambling in the back room with the money he'd gleaned from Annie's overnight stint with that John in the mansion. The back room gambling sessions had become quite the event at The Place and, even though he hadn't exactly been winning, they were the highlight of Jack's life at the moment. Trying to win at cards and having a few drinks were the only things that had any meaning for him now. Soon he'd have to be setting Annie up for another job to get some more cash, but maybe he'd win big today anyway and he could avoid that chore for a while. And what was he going to do with her anyway? The longer he hung onto her, the more chance there would be of getting caught. Maybe he should get rid of her too, he thought, as he visualized hitting that dude again. Jack jumped up out of bed, groaning at the way his head responded. He needed a little hair of the dog to feel better. In addition to his hangover, his thoughts were swirling in vicious circles.

"Hey, Annie, get in your room. You've gotta spend the rest of the day there," he yelled at her.

"But why, Gek? It's so hot in my room—more hot upstairs. Please, can I stay down here?" she pleaded.

"It's either your room or down in the cellar! Get the pan and some water and something to eat later. Hurry up, or ya'll have to do without them things!"

Jack locked Annie in her room. He couldn't risk having her go to the door if the police came. Well, maybe they would hear her anyway, but it just seemed safer to have her more confined there. Perhaps the cellar would be a safer place to hide her away, but he'd need to put locks on that too and he didn't have another padlock at the moment. Right now he just needed to get out of the house. He headed straight toward The Place.

"Hey, Black Jack! Nice to have you back. You're getting to be a permanent fixture here," greeted Sam. "What'll you have to whet your tongue this afternoon?"

"How 'bout a strong Bloody Mary? I need sumthin' to get me going today, Sam—a little hangover helper."

"Ah, stayed a little too late last night, eh?" rejoined Sam as he started pouring tomato juice over the healthy portion of vodka.

Jack really hadn't stayed late at all; he'd left quite early, before nine o'clock. But having guys at the bar remember that he'd stayed late, like he normally did, would be a good alibi if he needed it.

"Yeah, I shouldn't have stayed so late," muttered Jack.

"Well, this fortified celery and tomato smoothie should help revive you," joked Sam. "My daughter is always drinking smoothies out of spinach and stuff. I keep telling her I make 'em out of tomato juice."

Jack stayed as late as he could that night; he was afraid to go home—fearful that the police would be waiting for him there. He drank and gambled and he didn't win. The bartenders finally suggested he might want to go home, and did he want a ride? He didn't want a ride and he felt he could still drive so he headed home. But the only person waiting for him there was Annie, eager to get out of the hot, stuffy, locked upstairs room.

18

Ana López de Domínguez

May–June 2018

AFTER LEAVING THE LAST DETENTION center, Ana was barely aware of any of the drive back to Ciudad Juárez—everything was a blur. Seeing all those caged children, so frightened and so removed from their families, made Ana feel like she'd returned from a war zone or a concentration camp. Yes, it had to be an area of unreality—something from a former time perhaps—but this really couldn't be happening now, could it? And yet, this was only a minor part of the situations of all those children. Even worse for her was that they had not found Anita. Not one clue to her whereabouts. It was so devastating! Father Bill got out of the car when they reached his vehicle parked at the border. Ana barely remembered telling him good-bye. Then Padre Manuel brought Ana back through the border crossing and returned her to the *Casa del Migrante*, since she had no other place to go.

"Ana, I'll be in touch with you as soon as I hear from Father Bill," assured Padre Manuel, clearing his throat again after he stopped in front of the migrant center. "He will continue to search for your daughter."

Ana nodded and took a deep breath, trying to fortify herself.

"In the meantime, you should talk some more with Rafael Gómez or one of the other volunteer lawyers at the Casa to see if they have any more suggestions or options for you. I think you do have some legal recourse in all this. In the meantime, I'll be praying for you and your daughter Anita. But remember—*confía en Dios*," he said as he held Ana's hand.

"*Muchísimas gracias, Padre Manuel.* I appreciate all your help today. I'll try to keep my faith strong," Ana said as she wiped the escaped tears from her eyes.

In the days that followed, Ana arranged with the *Casa del Migrante* to stay for a few days in exchange for her helping in the kitchen and cleaning. After she volunteered her time, they also permitted her to call her sister Elena back home in Luis Aldama to tell her what had happened on her journey and that she had been deported back to Ciudad Juárez—also that Anita had been taken from her.

"*¡No, Ana, no! No puede ser.* Please tell me this isn't true. How can *Estados Unidos* take your child from you?"

"Elena, I don't know. I'm working with a lawyer at the *Casa del Migrante* here in Ciudad Juárez. As you can imagine, I am nearly crazy with anguish. The priests here and one in the US are also helping me though."

Ana updated Elena about everything that had happened to her and Anita after the *coyote* had helped them cross the border. It was painful for Ana and for her sister to think about the whole event. In fact, Ana had still not let herself think about what had happened that night in her own home before she arrived at Elena's house. Then Ana related what had occurred a few days ago when she crossed the border again with Padre Manuel. They had to keep their words to a minimum because there was so much to catch up on, both in Ciudad Juárez and in Luis Aldama, and so little time to talk. Elena also had a lot to tell her about what was happening there.

"Ana, you should not come back here now. Those gang members have taken over your house, and there is a whole pack of people in and out of it all the time," Elena told her nearly hysterically. "I've seen them entering and leaving, and they aren't the kind of people we want to have around us, but you already know that."

As she spoke to her sister, Ana looked around her where dozens of migrants were also trying to resolve their own problems. It was disconcerting, but she also felt a sense of community with them and with the volunteers trying to help them. Was this her family now?

"*Sí*, Elena, I know. But you need to be careful of them as well. They could connect you with Diego and me and try to get something from you as well. Or perhaps they suspect you know what they did," Ana cautioned, worried also about her sister and the rest of the family.

"Evidently they either do not know that I am your sister, Ana, or they know we have no money or anything valuable to give them, because they have just ignored me when I pass by on the street. But if you come back they will not only want to get you out of the way, but it could endanger the rest of the family here as well. I miss you so much though!" Elena cried.

"Oh, Elena, *no te preocupes*; do not worry! I could not come back now anyway; I must stay here until I find Anita. Soon I'll have to find a place to live here because I can only reside at the *Casa del Migrante* for a short time; it's too crowded, so busy with hundreds of deported migrants. It feels so strange to be this unsettled—not to be able to go where I intended to go and not to be able to return either."

Ana told Elena how much she missed the rest of the family and that she would be in touch again soon. She would also let Elena know as soon as she acquired another residence, a phone, and definitely when she heard anything new about Anita. Her next task though was to find work that would also pay her a wage, she told her sister. She'd have to support herself there while she worked with the lawyer and priests to try to find Anita.

"*Besos, Ana, y muy buena suerte*," Elena wished her.

"*Besos a ti, querida Elena. Hasta pronto.*"

After the end of the conversation with her sister, Ana felt so strange. Not only was she alone and far from home, but she did not have a place to call her own, and nothing in her life was the same. If only she could find Anita! And, for the first time, she did not have the rest of her family close by to assist her. She could, however, still feel their love supporting her and she hoped Anita could feel it as well.

The next day Rafael Gómez was working at the *Casa del Migrante* again, and again he had a nearly endless line of people waiting to see him. Ana asked the man behind her in line to hold her place, offering to let him go before her if he would save her turn. She wanted to continue helping out at the center while she waited to talk with the lawyer. Padre Manuel did not have any news for her yet, but she knew he had also talked with Rafael Gómez after their visit to the holding centers for immigrant children in the US. Hopefully, Rafael would have news for her about Anita.

"*Buena tardes, Ana*," Rafael rose and greeted her after her turn arrived. "I'm so sorry that I don't have any positive information for you yet. That idiot US president has a policy called 'zero tolerance' and he's being ridiculous and cruel about any immigrants who arrive without papers at the border with Mexico. As you have seen, he's been regularly separating children from their parents."

"*¿Por qué? Es tan cruel.* How can he be so unfeeling? These are children!"

"Well, a group called the American Civil Liberties Union agrees with you and has challenged President Trump in court regarding the mandatory separation of parents and children at the border. We should hear something soon about that. In the meantime, we're still searching for Anita with the help of other groups in the US that are opposed to his policy. I'm preparing a court case for you as well," Rafael explained.

So Ana had to wait longer. The *Casa del Migrante* helped her to find a job in a nearby restaurant. Despite the fact that she was extremely overqualified, and the job didn't take advantage of her excellent credentials in education, Ana was very glad to have the work. The staff at the migrant center told her that perhaps a teaching related job would come up later, but Ana knew she needed something right away. Everyone promised to help keep her informed about better possibilities if they should come up, perhaps after the end of this school year. In the meantime, her wages and meager tips at the restaurant allowed her to rent a furnished room from an older, widow lady who lived fairly near to the *Calle Neptuno.* She lived close enough that Ana could continue to volunteer regularly at the *Casa del Migrante.*

On June 29, Rafael Gómez sought her out to tell her that the day before a federal judge in San Diego had ordered the government to stop separating immigrant parents and children. The judge's decision also specified that the already separated families had to be reunited.

"I hope this helps," Rafael told her, smiling and showing his dimples momentarily. "The current problem though seems to be that they didn't keep very good records about where they put all the children and parents, and now it's hard to match them up again. Also, many children were placed in foster homes, and the department of Health and Human Services didn't document that well either. We think Anita possibly was placed in foster care and we're still looking for her. At least we know where you are."

Ana's eyes filled with tears.

"Are you telling me that nobody knows where she is, even after you have checked with the agency about the sponsor families? Could this mean she has died?"

"Well, Ana, I have to admit that they don't seem to track that very well either, but I think that with all the people protesting the treatment of immigrant children in the US it would be unlikely that a child's death would go unnoticed."

"This news does not bring me much hope, Señor Gómez."

"Ana, please continue to call me Rafael. At the moment no one knows where she is, but we have not given up. You should not either," he reassured her. "*Sea fuerte*, Ana. Stay strong."

"*Lo intentaré, Rafael, lo intentaré.*"

19

Antoine Benet

July 3–6, 2018

WHERE WAS HE? AFTER HE FELT that initial amazing weight-lessness and incandescence, Antoine felt himself tumbling, groping almost, through a vacuous, murky space, not knowing where he was headed. It felt quite cool, as if he were in a cloud. Suddenly he felt a thud, and the vague, foggy expanse slowly began to clear. As the rheumy atmosphere receded, Antoine recognized he was in his own house in Olathe and he bumped rather clumsily through the rooms, unused to maneuvering his new weightless essence. He was quite sure now though that he was no longer propelling his physical body. As he wandered aimlessly there in his old space, he saw the clothes he had worn to work—was it the day before? They were lying on the bed, and his unfinished bottle of bubbly water was there in the kitchen. The morning sun was shining in through screens of his porch and the windows of his kitchen—promising another bright, hot day.

But his ability to transport both himself and other objects worked so differently now—he felt extremely clumsy. He practiced ineptly how to move around and was not very successful at first. And transposing another object to a different place was even more challenging. His cognizance of himself and other things, including memories was also altered. He felt as if he'd been hit in the head and was suffering from a concussion. Had that happened? Or was it just because he was no longer in his body? How could he organize his memories in that fog that still existed in his awareness? Pulling in his powers of recall was like walking through sticky mud. Soon though, images of his not-long-ago past life began to trickle in. His perception was then rapidly pulled toward Cheryl and their recent conversation and decision to spend the July 4th holiday together.

Then, however, he found himself back in that foggy, cool, undefined space, but not for too long. Soon he was back in his house again. Apparently he did not have much control over his location between worlds either. What had he been trying to recover? Ah, yes, a memory of Cheryl! He felt a strong desire to communicate with her but did not yet know how to do that. And as his recognition of that need to connect with her increased, he suddenly felt himself pulled toward what had happened with her just a short time ago.

He began to recall memories of her. The stimulating and encouraging conversation with Cheryl on the evening of July 2nd had heartened Antoine. Despite his flirtatious nature, until then Antoine had been very elusive with Cheryl; even after their intimate retreat to her house following the incident at the sport's bar he had basically avoided her, working on site with clients at the times she would be in the office. He had begun to worry that anything between them would not work out, and that he would only be hurt again. It seemed that she was fearful of that as well. She had told him after the bar incident that intimate relationships acted somewhat like lemons for her—bright, sunny, and welcoming on the outside with an enticing, seductive scent. He remembered that now. But, she said, when she really bit into them she ended up with a bitter, acrid taste. She had indicated that her marriage to Allen was like that—so promising at first, but then she was left with a completely sour situation that not only required thousands of dollars to resolve the legal ties but, also, had left her doubtful and even critical of herself. Allen had sued her for alimony, even though he was the one who had been cheating on her and he had asked for the divorce. Obviously, Cheryl had told Antoine, she should never have trusted Allen. But she said she was tempted to trust Antoine—partially because he had proven himself so reliable in the workplace and because he seemed so caring and responsible. Also, because they had so many things in common. So after their conversation about what to do for July 4th—was it yesterday evening?—he had yearned to see her the next day at work.

Now Antoine suddenly was pulled there to where she was at their offices at Mid-Wester. He was with Cheryl in her office but, despite his efforts to make himself present to her, Cheryl did not seem to be able to see or hear him. He himself was still unsteady in his new form without a physical body. What could he do as a spirit? He wasn't sure. His attraction to Cheryl brought him to where she was, but somehow he could not make his presence known to her. He could hear her muttering about where he might be and why he hadn't come in to see her. Obviously she was not pleased with him. And he could read the text she was writing and re-writing to him.

"Hi Antoine! I expected to see you this morning but you must have had appointments. Stop by later this afternoon when you have time! See you soon! Cheryl."

He noticed that twice she had inserted then deleted an emoji blowing kisses, but finally put it in again, perhaps to disguise her irritation. Did she think he was trying to avoid her? The very idea of that made his spirit-self ache.

By very late afternoon, however, he could tell she embodied even more impatience and annoyance. He could hear her under her breath asking why he hadn't contacted her. Although he tried to attract her attention to let her know why, she did not respond. She said out loud that she needed to know about the finalized the time that they were getting together for the sailing jaunt the next morning, but his efforts to make himself audible or visible to her were still evidently ineffective. She indignantly called his cell phone trying to contact him, but he could hear that the ring went to his voicemail.

"The subscriber you have called is not available; please leave a message after the beep," the automated voice unfeelingly intoned, while Antoine himself was bleeding with sorrow—if a spirit can bleed.

He saw her hit her cell phone in disgust as she began closing up in her office for the day and upcoming holiday.

"Okay, be that way," she bleated. "Don't even call me until the very last minute!"

Antoine continued trying to communicate with her in his new form, but it wasn't working; she was banging drawers in her desk as she put away papers. Then he was drawn with her after work to her condo and saw her fretfully attempt to sleep that night. The next morning—the 4th—she was even more upset when he hadn't called or come by on the day of their date. He saw that she waited around all morning distractedly dressing and putting her condo in order.

"Did I misunderstand him? Why doesn't he at least call and tell me he has changed his mind?" he heard her say, exasperated, into her mirror.

"Here I am! Let me explain," he tried to voice to her but to no avail.

Finally around 1:00 PM on the 4th she tried calling him again. But again, the call went directly to his voicemail.

"What a jerk," she recorded on his messaging. "It's been a very long time since anyone stood me up so completely. I hope you're having a wonderful holiday! Too bad I already wasted half of mine waiting around for you. I don't know about France, but here most people have the decency to back out of something with some sort of message!"

Antoine was devastated. What could he do? How could he communicate with her. He tried whispering in her ear, but she didn't hear. He finally succeeded in knocking a few things over in her house to get her attention, but Cheryl was oblivious in her anger.

She spent the rest of the day going through her closets and vigorously throwing anything away that didn't please her at the moment. She called her sister, and Antoine heard her say that she had decided that she hated it here in Kansas and was moving back to Denver and could she stay with her until she found a place and a job. She was crying as she told her sister she would be there soon—within the month or sooner. She vowed that she had no desire to be in this backward place.

"It doesn't matter that I won't have a job. I'll find something there," she sobbed as she told her sister she had to get away from where she was.

Antoine also trailed Cheryl in his spirit form on Thursday the 5th, when she went directly to Fred Woodward's office and resigned, effective in two weeks. Antoine still could not get her attention. Fred pleaded for her to stay, but Cheryl was resolved to leave.

"By the way, have you seen Antoine?" Fred asked her.

"No! I have not, and I hope I never see him again!" Cheryl yelled to a perplexed Fred as she turned and left his office.

Since Antoine, uncharacteristically, had not showed up for work by noon on Friday, Fred and some other coworkers questioned her again about whether she knew his whereabouts. But she did not. Nobody could contact him by phone either. Fred grabbed the master key to Antoine's Mid-Wester demonstration house and asked Dan, one of Antoine's colleagues who ran with him, to come along. They drove by Antoine's house to see if they could see any sign of him. They found his car parked in the drive, but, of course, Antoine did not respond when they rang the doorbell and knocked on all the doors. After they exhausted all other options, Fred opened the door with his key, and they cautiously went inside. Everything looked as if Antoine had just stepped out for a moment. There was a half-empty bottle of seltzer water on the counter, and the clothes he had worn to work on Monday were lying across the bed. But Antoine wasn't there, and no one had seen him since that previous Monday—July 2nd. Fred then called the police and started a missing person's report.

Later that afternoon, the police stopped by Woodward's office to report that a body that they suspected was Antoine Benet's had been discovered. Some media company employees had found the body in the brush alongside County Road LL while they were repairing faulty Ethernet cables. The police also wanted to speak with Cheryl Atkins since Woodward had explained that she worked rather closely with Benet. Fred's secretary went to fetch Cheryl. Right after hearing that the police would like her to help identify a body they believed was Antoine's, Cheryl fainted. Antoine again felt a very deep pain in his soul as he saw her collapse.

20

Ana López de Domínguez

Early June 2018

THREE LOUD BLASTS WOKE ANA in the night. Her eyes flew open, she sat up in bed, and her heart leapt into her throat. The noise immediately wrenched her back to the night in May when gunshots sounded in her own home. At first she couldn't remember where she was but, as she became more aware, she realized that she was in the widow Lupe's house in Ciudad Juárez where she had been renting a room as she waited to hear more about the search for Anita. She listened carefully, dreading any alarming noises to follow: shouts, screams, someone trying to rush away, sirens. But, no, she heard nothing abnormal. There was an occasional car, a dog that barked briefly in the distance, some faint music from a disco perhaps, but nothing frightening. She could even hear Lupe softly snoring in the other room. Had she simply dreamed that she heard noises that sounded like shots? Or were gunshots so common that no one paid any attention? At any rate, the sounds had overcome her ability to push that last horrific night at her own home back in Luis Aldama out of her mind.

Ana's thoughts gushed back to the tragic evening when those men had entered their home in Luis Aldama, the pueblo where she had lived all her life. Her mind was thrown into the scene she hadn't let herself view since she and Anita had run away that night. She had had too many other things to do instead of thinking about something she didn't want to remember. First, they had had to get out of their house, then out of Mexico, then she was too frantic after being separated from Anita. Lately she had continued to avoid thinking about it all so she could find living accommodations and a job in Ciudad Juárez. But now there was no more escaping that episode. It was like a wound she had covered over weeks ago, but now she had to look at that laceration. Now it was oozing through the cover.

That night—about a month ago now—there had been a knock at their door. Ana and Diego were reading in their living room; Anita had already gone to bed. Diego got up from his chair, looking at Ana inquisitively. No, she shook her head, eyes wide open, she didn't know who it was; she wasn't expecting anyone either. As Diego headed toward the door, it suddenly burst open, and three men rushed inside.

The men who had entered their house that night had known Diego from his insurance business and had once been his clients. Ana knew two of them. However, when the economy in their area took a sharp downturn, almost everyone had run into hard times; but those men got involved in the drug trade with some gang members from Sinaloa. And within that drug circle, they were pressured into extorting money from people they knew. Diego and Ana were better off than most people in their pueblo so, most likely, were obvious targets. Diego had talked with Ana several times about these ex-clients, worried because one of them was the brother of the head of police in Luis Aldama.

"If those guys ever decide to pick on me, there will be no one to turn to," Diego had worried. "The police are on their side."

Diego had resisted their more subtle demands in the past and had successfully evaded them until the night they showed up—right inside their house—with knives and a gun. Diego really didn't have any cash on hand to give them, so they shot him. Ana rushed toward her dying husband, his lifeblood flowing all over their living room floor. Stop blood! Stop! Please don't die, Diego—please don't leave us!

"We know you have a child," one of the hoodlums told her as he kicked at Diego's body. "*Anita, ¿no?* Well, if you want Anita to grow up, you need cash for us when we come back. You need 200,000 pesos by tomorrow night."

Then the men left, slamming the door behind them. Diego's blood was pouring all over the tile floor like red ink. The small carpet in front of their sofa was wicking up the ink, gradually turning a deep granite color. The only tragic moment of his life story was writing itself there in their home. She could not let Anita read it—she needed to get her out of here, not only because of her father but because Anita was threatened as well. Ana could *not* let them take her child too.

Anita had been asleep when it happened, but Ana could hear her calling out, frightened after hearing the loud gunshots. Ana ran into Anita's bedroom and hurried her into some clothes and shoes and out of the house before she could see what had befallen her beloved *Papá*. Then they literally ran to her sister Elena's home several blocks away.

After they got to Elena and Juan Pablo's house, Juan Pablo had answered the door and then woke Elena; the two of them put a plan into action. Elena made several phone calls that took nearly twenty minutes but, when she was done, she had made arrangements with a *"coyote"* named Jesuito, who would help them cross the border river into Texas. The plan was them for meet up with Rosa, another sister of Ana and Elena, who lived and worked in Arizona. Rosa would meet them in two days.

"I know the sister of Jesuito," explained Elena, "and I am certain he can be trusted. We need to drive north to Ahumada tonight to the Motel El Camino. The owner will be waiting to check us in—he's a friend of Jesuito. The ride should take us about 3 hours. Tomorrow afternoon at 1:00, Jesuito will meet us just north of town; then he will bring you to the river and take you across."

Elena had helped Ana and Anita quickly gather a few items of her clothing they could wear on the journey—they didn't dare go back to Ana's house to get anything. Juan Pablo packed up some *carne seca* and tortillas that would last several days and filled some bottles with water. Luckily Ana had grabbed her purse on the way out the door—she did have a little cash and a credit card, but she was afraid to use her credit card while still in Mexico, in case her location could be traced. Juan Pablo also told her she needed to get rid of her phone—which they did by smashing it and throwing it into a trash dumpster as they drove out of town. The drive to Ahumada was so tense that Ana barely remembered it—only that, again, she kept looking behind them to see if anyone was following. No one was.

When they arrived at the Motel El Camino at about 3:00 AM, the owner let them into a room where they had all three laid down on the bed, but neither Ana nor Elena had slept. Anita seemed to nod off after a while, just as she had in the car. Ana, however, was trying to breathe deeply to calm her still throbbing heartbeat in that motel bed in Ahumada.

Just like that night weeks ago when Diego had been killed, tonight, too, Ana's heart throbbed violently. How could all of that have happened? She missed him so much; tears flooded her eyes and slipped down her face and even onto her lips, covering them with salty wetness. Until now she had not allowed herself to mourn him. She had lost her beloved husband Diego. And now she did not know how to find her treasured only child, Anita. But Anita had also lost her father and now, even weeks later, she was still removed from her mother as well. Had Anita known or guessed that her father had been murdered? Ana regretted deeply that she had not been able to talk with Anita about this. Perhaps she could have consoled her a little about the death. Maybe Anita was completely bereft after losing her father and then being separated from her mother. Or perhaps Anita had been slain as well, and that was why no one had been able to find her. NO! It could not be—if both Anita and Diego were dead, Ana did not want to remain in this world. She wanted to die as well; she wanted to join them. How could she do that? It was so much against her faith. *Jesús*, how could you forsake them? How could you forsake me? Please take me to them! Please take me from this world!

For the first time in her life, Ana wondered how she might end her own life. A knife? Too messy, and she would surely faint before killing herself. Strangulation? What would she use? There was not really anything high she could use to hang herself in this room. Besides, it would destroy Lupe to have a suicide in her house! That would never do. Could she leave and then poison herself with something or overdose on a drug? Where would she go to do that? And what if Anita were found? Then she would have no father and no mother either. No, she could not take her own life; she had to wait and find out for certain whether her daughter was dead or alive. How could she be so selfish to think of taking her own life before she knew for sure? She had been praying but she wondered if God was listening to her prayers.

Her own *mamá* always seemed to have so much faith. Had she ever doubted the way Ana was doubting now? *Mamá* had encouraged the faith of her five children with special prayer and rosaries, lighting candles in Church, and by giving them *milagro* charms that corresponded to any problems they were having. Once, when Ana had a fight with her cousin Pati that dragged on for weeks, *Mamá* had given both her and Pati heart-shaped *milagros* to help them learn to love and forgive.

Ana and Pati were so touched by *Mamá* bestowing them with beautiful amulets meant to dissipate their conflict that they made an extra effort to resolve their dispute. They had never really fought again.

Ana then put her hand to her chest, where she wore the *milagro* charm Anita and Diego had given her for her birthday years ago. Diego had helped Anita make it from silver foil at a silversmith shop. It now hung from a silver chain between her throat and her heart. She had never taken it off since the day they gave it to her. She thought of them and then realized that this small ornament they had made for her was now a talisman in every sense and that it had a strong message for her, truly representing the power of faith and miracles, like its name—*milagro*.

Her amulet was shaped like a small foot, which Anita had always told her was a *pie de hada*, a fairy's foot. Anita had always loved fairies and the magic they represented, so when her *papá* took her to the silversmith shop so she could personally make a *milagro* charm for Ana's birthday, she had made a magic fairy's foot. Anita had been nine at that time, and Ana had always treasured this special gift from Anita and Diego. The toe of the tiny foot turned up—like a fairy's foot, Anita had told her—and the foot was decorated with small indentations that the silversmith had shown Anita how to make with his tools. In the same shop, Diego had purchased a delicate silver chain to carry the charm, and the jeweler had packaged it in a small box with a sparkly, silver seal. Anita had wrapped the box in pink tissue paper and tied it with a white ribbon. Diego and Anita were both so excited to tell her about the whole process after she opened the gift that Ana couldn't help smiling now just thinking about it.

How very amazing, thought Ana now, that Anita had chosen to make a foot for her. There probably was not a single symbol that better represented the situation they were in. They had embarked on a crossing from one life to another. The foot *milagro*, of course, represented a pilgrimage, a journey, a different path, putting one foot in front of the other, and recognizing the delights in each step, in each moment. Then, because of what had befallen them, she had taken Anita on a journey to a different world. So far it was not working out well, but all pilgrimages and journeys can be difficult—and even dangerous—but are meant to show us our strengths as well. Ana considered all of this as she thought about the symbolic significance of her *milagro*. Even onerous, treacherous, or frightening travels can also lead to faith and happiness. She definitely needed to remember that now, Ana told herself.

A glance at her phone told her that it was 3:00 AM. She could still hear Lupe lightly snoring in the other room. A warm breeze entered the window, calming her and belying any disturbance that might have awakened her. No other sounds warned her of danger. Surely the sounds she thought she heard were from her own past—something that had happened months ago. She wished she could revive the faith and calm that she had held before that time and for most of her life.

Ana remembered now when she had gone on a pilgrimage with her own *mamá* in the 1980s when she was a teenager slightly older than Anita was now. Was she 16 or 17? *Mamá* had wanted to make a pilgrimage to the *Basilica de Nuestra Señora de Guadalupe* in the northern part of Mexico City at the base of the hill of Tepeyac for Easter. *Mamá* had once made a pilgrimage to the shrine with her own mother when she was a girl, but she wanted to visit the new basilica, completed in 1976, with Ana. They had traveled on several buses during 2 or 3 days to get there, and it had been a tiring and exhausting journey, Ana remembered. The buses were crowded with people, chickens in cages, and crying babies, and they had had little to eat and drink on their way to Mexico City. It was both frightening and uncomfortable; one night they even had to sleep on benches in the bus station when a bus did not arrive on time. Ana had secretly wished many times during that journey that she had not even gone.

But after they arrived at the basilica—so stupendous and so awe inspiring—they had attended mass there. The huge, round building held the sanctuary which was filled with thousands of people who could all see the framed image of *Nuestra Señora* that hung on the enormously tall, gold wall behind the altar. She had felt filled with the Holy Spirit and the grace of *Nuestra Señora de Guadalupe* just by being in that holy place. She still remembered what the priest had said about a pilgrimage. He had told the travelers there that a pilgrimage meant stepping out of your comfort zone for a higher purpose. He said all had to make some kind of sacrifice to do it—whether physical or mental or spiritual—but that the whole journey was a period for growth and an affirmation of faith. Despite the difficulties on their return journey from that demanding trip with her *mamá*, Ana had felt a sense of peace.

She needed to implement that feeling of peace now. Yes, she was definitely out of her comfort zone on this journey and, yes, she and Anita both had made sacrifices, but this voyage was for a higher purpose. Ana hoped for the growth that would result and also the affirmation of her faith in the grace of God and for the safety of her beautiful daughter. She had to find her. She held onto her charm and repeated a prayer in a soft whisper: "*Cuídanos, Dios, en este viaje.* Take care of Anita and of me on this journey. Help me to completely trust in You. *Nuestra Señora, ayúdanos.*"

Finally Ana fell asleep again.

21

Black Jack

Late July–early August 2018

JACK ROLLED OVER IN HIS BED—his head ached again—and he was hot and sweaty. What day was it anyway? He groaned and rubbed his head—he must have drunk a lot again last night. His nervousness and vague pangs of conscience about hitting that French dude on the same road as his house did not help his mental state. Now he was positive that the guy really had died because there had been a newspaper article about a hit-and-run death that everybody in the bar was talking about. That story was especially of interest at The Place, since the locale was so near to where the guy was hit. Luckily, no one at The Place even knew where Jack lived. When he finally got a chance to read from the paper someone had left on the bar, Jack was relieved that the article hadn't pointed toward any suspect. In fact, it suggested there might have been an accident because of the darkness on the road and that the driver might not have known he had hit someone. Nonetheless, Jack went back and forth between being so afraid that the police would show up at his door any minute and his desire to tell someone and get the whole problem off his chest, no matter what the consequences. Or perhaps he should simply end his own life, but he was even too afraid to do that. Now his only consolation was drinking so much that he numbed his feelings to it all. His present life was just a blurred, dark and heavy, ominous cloud, always threatening a storm.

Another problem that had come up again, now that he was spending so much time drinking and gambling at The Place, was his need for more bucks. Even though the last stint he had arranged for Annie with that rich John had raked in a heap of cash, Jack had now blown through almost all of it. But even *he* hated to set that all up again. If only she would be more cooperative, he wouldn't feel quite so reluctant to do it. It just wasn't fun for him at all, although he tried to avoid thinking about what she must think of the whole situation. He tried not to mull over that at all.

But he did need cash—and very soon. Jack looked up the website babychicks.com and saw that John had posted a request to have Annie visit at least a week ago. Jack now replied to his message, saying that she had been busy until now, and asked when he would like to set it up if she had free time. John wrote back within half an hour and requested the evening of August 4. He also asked that she wear something "more silky and sexy" to the occasion.

"Silky and sexy," repeated Jack out loud. "What the hell! Oh, well; it will cost ya more, buddy!"

Jack wrote back saying her rates had gone up, but that she definitely would wear a sexy outfit. They haggled a bit over the price, but Jack was pleased with the resulting number.

Now he had some structure for his day today—was it already August 3? He had to get up and get going to find the sexy, silky garment for Annie for the next evening. She wouldn't be pleased about the idea of getting the flashy garb, and even less about the prospect of going to John's house again, but he knew she did like to go to Walmart. He didn't have a lot of money left, so the purchase would pretty much have to be limited to the dress or whatever it was, at least until after he got the payment from John the next evening. He always collected in advance; he demanded the money be paid when he first brought her to the client's house or hotel or wherever it was—just in case. At least he would have the money if something unknown happened. Duke had given him that tip before he ever handed Annie over to him, and Jack had always seen how practical it was.

In the Walmart store, he wasn't used to looking for clothing for a chick, and there was nothing that seemed to fit the description of what he was looking for in the kid's area. Finally, in the area with women's underwear and things, he found an eye-catching red nightgown or slip or something that looked both sexy and silky to him. It looked pretty big compared to Annie's size, but maybe they could make it work. When he held it up to her though, she began to yell out and protest.

Oh, shit!, he thought. She's gonna get me in trouble!

Then he whispered loudly in Spanish for her to shut up and, as he looked around, a woman was watching them. Luckily the dame turned away though and maybe she hadn't really thought anything about it. Lots of times kids were uncooperative in Walmart—he'd seen that enough times—with parents yelling at them and even hitting the kids to shut them up. Annie seemed to obey his command, and the woman went on her way, so he felt a wave of relief. All the same, he was ready to get out of the store. He'd have to threaten Annie that she'd never be able to go there with him again if she was going to make a fuss like that. Annie was quiet the rest of the time in the store and as they checked out. He'd kept a close eye on her.

"Your aunt is really gonna like this," he said in the checkout line, turning to give Annie a threatening look as he spoke for the cashier's benefit. "She loves red."

Annie just nodded meekly.

22

Claire de lune

August 3, 2018

I KNEW I MUST BE DREAMING; I didn't really like to swim at all and was rather afraid of the water, but now I was swimming confidently and without effort. I maneuvered through the blue water, effortlessly lifted and drifting, even though my head was underwater and my lungs inhaled the crystalline liquid. After aiding me to glide through the natural pool for several moments, the flowing current then carried me to shallower water, sprinkled with green leaves, but still clear. As I approached the shore, I began to crawl toward land. The path I followed after I arrived at the shore headed towards a wooded grove. I crawled quite a distance on the path but then, finally, stood and walked. When I stood, I could see my own face—as if I were looking into a mirror. It grew fuller and brighter, like the moon. My moon face illuminated the path in front of me, which I followed into the increasingly thicker and darker woods. After walking some distance into this dense thicket, I saw a slight clearing that contained a cage built from the sturdy branches of trees. As I approached the cage, my moon-eye slits could perceive a young girl confined inside it. Upon seeing me, the girl silently screamed "Help me! Help me!" with her lips while her hands grabbed desperately onto the wooden bars that enclosed her. But when I neared and pulled at the bars, the girl's eyes grew larger and more terrified, and she stared at something behind me. I whirled around to see a darkly bearded man holding a gleaming, silver machete ready to strike me.

I woke with a start, bolting to sitting in my bed with my heart pounding.

"Oh my God! I must help her," I proclaimed out loud, as if I were still in part of the dream.

I immediately got up and prepared a cup of coffee before I sat down at the kitchen table with a pad of paper and a pencil. I needed to figure out what to do next. What should I do? Call the police? And tell them what? That a ghost had come to visit me and had warned me that a child might be in danger, so I'd been spying on a house and saw a little girl in the window? And that last night I had even dreamed that the girl was locked in a cage? No, that would not do. They might be tempted to detain me for harassing my neighbors, test me for drugs, or try to get me to talk with a psychiatrist. No one would believe this far-fetched tale. No, I needed more information. And my dream had given me the distinct impression that time was of the essence. That little girl needed help very soon.

It was already nearly 8:00 AM, so I couldn't get to the house to observe early like I did yesterday. But that was okay; there was nothing to see until later anyway. Evidently the bearded man I had assumed was Jack wasn't an early riser, even though the girl was. Perhaps he had been out until late the night before and that was why he slept so long. That probably meant that he had left the girl in the house alone, because if she had been with him she likely would have slept later as well. Since he rose so late yesterday, maybe he would also leave in the afternoon or evening today, and I could see if the child was still in the house. At any rate, it was worth checking the house at a different time to see if I could figure out his schedule, if he had one, or at least I could note the times he was likely to be home.

I decided to venture into the woods late in the afternoon, now that I knew more or less where I could observe the house without being seen. At least I could definitely discover whether or not the van was there and, hopefully, still catch sight of the girl in the house again. But before I went, I wanted to stop somewhere to buy myself a mosquito netting to go over my hat. Perhaps that was overkill, but the mosquitos and other bugs were driving me crazy yesterday when they buzzed around my head. I'd be able to hide myself better if I wasn't worried about screaming when a bug buzzed into my ear or dive-bombed at my head again.

So my plan began with going to Walmart, not that I would nor-mally shop there, but because it was the closest big store, according to my search online, that apparently would have mosquito netting to cover my hat. I got into my trusty Subaru and drove to Walmart. After parking, I was amazed to note that the weather was pleasantly cool—quite a change from the way it had been for weeks. Inside the store, I found an economically priced mosquito head-net in the sporting goods section that claimed it fit over most headgear, but the label recommended a wide-brimmed hat for the most comfortable fit. The picture on the package looked like it would work perfectly to keep any sort of insect away from my face. However, the hat I had used the day before was a baseball cap, and I could imagine how a brimmed hat would keep the netting—and bugs—farther away from my head. I found some hats in that same section, but they all were a bit too large and might dip down over my eyes or fall off.

"Why don't you check in the women's clothing area," suggested the middle-aged, female employee in sporting goods. "I know they also carry some women's hats for summer. Many women want brimmed hats for sun protection."

"Thanks, I will," I answered and headed in the direction the she indicated.

After I had browsed through the hats and happened to find one that would work just fine, I briefly surveyed the surrounding area in that unfamiliar store. As I passed the section of women's lingerie though I stopped in my tracks and stared. In front of me was a bearded man in a black t-shirt and jeans holding up a silky, bright red negligee to a young girl, as if to check the size. I couldn't believe my eyes: it was *them*!

"There isn't a littler one, but I think we could put knots in the straps to make it fit," he told the girl.

"No! I no want it," she replied.

"That's too bad. Ya need it for tomorrow night."

"No, no! I no want to go," she retorted louder, beginning to cry.

"*¡Cállate!*" he hissed as he looked up and around and right toward me.

I immediately lowered my gaze and then directed myself rapidly through the checkout area with my hat and mosquito netting, paid with my credit card, and left the store.

Driving home from Walmart, I was shaking with emotion. I couldn't believe what I had just witnessed. How amazing it was that I had been at Walmart at the very same time that they were there! And why was that creep trying to buy the little girl a red negligee? He had said they could make it fit her; I was positive I'd heard that. And the child obviously was not pleased about the prospect. The whole incident reminded me too much of what my child protagonist from Syria— Rima—in *Girl in a Cage* had to endure. This was truly metafictional; this time though my fiction was entering into the real world and was playing out before my own eyes. But no; if only it were fiction! Was this little child really being exploited and trafficked as well? I shuttered as I thought about the sexy trappings being purchased for her. Yes, I definitely needed to return to the woods today to get more information. However, I already knew well from my research for that novel that this abusive situation would undoubtedly cause the child psychological problems, even after she got rescued from her predicament. But first and foremost she most definitely needed to be rescued! I still didn't have anything definite enough to report to the police, but I would later to- day—I was sure of it. I consciously made myself calm down enough to be rational and think about my strategy and my options. By the time I arrived home I was determined to execute my plan.

Just after I walked into her house, however, my cellphone rang. I glanced at the screen and saw it was Jim.

"Hi, Jimbo," I answered, wondering how much I should tell him about what I was worried about. "How are you?"

"I'm fine, Claire, darling. I have a little break for lunch, so I just wanted to give you a call. I'm sorry we couldn't talk last night, but it was so late after the evening program I was afraid I would wake you, so I didn't call. Are you doing OK? What's been going on there? Do you miss me?"

I suddenly burst into tears; hearing Jim's voice made me realize how much I really did miss him. It was great to have a ghost friend who could practically anticipate my every thought, but Antoine was dead and gone, after all. A ghost is just a ghost, but Jim was here in this life with me—even though he was out of town.

"Claire, what's wrong?"

I could hear the empathy in his voice and wanted nothing more than to have his arms around me—reassuring me about what to do in this situation. I told him about seeing the man I thought was named Jack in the Walmart trying to purchase a negligee for that little girl. I didn't tell him, however, about my sojourn into the woods yesterday to spy on them or my plans to do that again today. That might make him worry too much.

"Claire, are you OK? I know you have an active imagination; I doubt if you could be such an excellent writer without it, but are you sure you aren't exaggerating the situation because you empathized so much with that little girl you saw? She's not the girl in your novel, after all."

Not quite, but more alike than you know, I thought but did not say. In fact, I nearly had to bite my tongue in order not to say it, but I realized where this conversation was going. Jim definitely thought I was imagining the whole thing. Talking about it now wasn't going to resolve anything, and he would just worry about my mental health. Even relaying my dream to him now probably wouldn't be a good idea. I decided to change the subject.

"No, you are right. I'm fine. I'm just missing you. You wouldn't believe how nice the weather is here today though. The high is only supposed to be 82 degrees. I'm planning on taking a little hike today— to enjoy the weather. I've been writing and cooped up inside too much lately."

"Oh, good. I'm glad you're going to take advantage of the cooler weather. Be careful of the chiggers though. I'd hate to have you all spotted up with bites and nail polish again," he joked. "I am surprised you are going for a hike though. How's your writing going?"

I chatted for a while longer with Jim, but he needed to get some lunch before his meetings started again, and I needed to get ready for my "hike"—my spy and rescue journey into the woods—so we said goodbye.

"I can't wait to see you Sunday afternoon, darling. I really long to be with you!" he said.

"Oh, and I do so want to see you again!" I added truthfully, regretting that I was essentially lying by omission to him about the rest of my day.

I disconnected then, feeling rather remorseful that I hadn't confided more in him, but I had too much to do to spend time dwelling on that. After eating some lunch to fortify myself for my endeavor, I started preparing for the trek into the undergrowth—sulfur powder, bug repellant, mosquito-net covered hat, and all. I needed to observe as much as I could. I filled my water pouch so I'd have plenty to drink, grabbed a couple of chocolate almond protein bars, just in case I needed some supplemental energy, and drove to the same spot where I had left my car the day before. I remembered to turn my cell phone to silent mode and stuck it in my front pocket before I got out of the car and headed toward the thicket of trees.

The wooded area at the back of Jack's house looked more inviting today, now that I knew the way and had my hat with mosquito netting. Also, the cooler weather made the walk much more comfortable—it was quite pleasant just being outside in Nature. The sun was bright, but there was a cool breeze, and even the trees seemed more animated— showing off their green leaves and swaying their smaller branches in the light wind. Cardinals chirped enthusiastically, and several small yellow butterflies fluttered back and forth around some plants that I did not recognize. Despite these positive elements, I was exceedingly nervous about what might happen. I just had to accomplish something toward rescuing that child today!

"Antoine, are you here with me?" I quietly asked.

"*Bonjour*, Claire. I am here," he replied with a soft caress of cool air to my cheek that I felt even through the mosquito netting that covered my face.

"Oh, Antoine. I'm so glad you are here," I sighed with relief. "I really need your help today I think. Did you go to the Walmart store? Were you there when I saw Jack and the girl?"

"*Non*, I was not with you then. What did you see?" he asked as I tramped through the thicket of growth.

I briefly explained exactly what I had seen to Antoine and my conviction that his fears for the girl were exceedingly correct. I also told him about my dream from the night before and my resulting angst about the imminent danger for the child—reconfirmed by what I had seen this morning—which had convinced me that she needed to be extricated from that house without any further delay.

"I know you are right about that, Claire. She is in an extremely dangerous situation. You should trust your dream—trust your intuition," Antoine replied, even though I could not see him.

"I'm going to observe what is happening first—to see if he is there, to see what the situation is—, then I don't know at all what I will do .... I suppose it will depend," I added hesitantly.

"*Bien sûr*, yes, wait to see."

As I approached the house, I saw the old van parked in the driveway. Apparently Jack was still there, which meant I needed to be extra cautious. I shielded myself behind a large tree with scrubby bushes surrounding it and pulled out my binoculars. Looking through the netting around my face was a bit challenging, but I was so much more comfortable separated from the insects that buzzed around me. As I looked at the house, I could see the girl passing back and forth in front of the window I had assumed was in the kitchen. She seemed to be preparing a meal. From time to time, she gazed out toward the woods, as if she were expecting to see someone or something there. I also saw Jack pass before the window several times, then I couldn't see either of them for a while. Soon though, the girl was back in front of the window, evidently doing something at what was probably the sink.

Moments later, I saw Jack upstairs, passing in front of the bathroom window and then facing what I had determined was his bedroom window. Soon, the girl was upstairs too, in front of the window where I had seen her yesterday, looking directly out into the woods again, moving her lips and evidently saying something continuously. Eventually, I heard a door close loudly at the front of the house and saw Jack saunter over to his van. I shrank back more cautiously behind the tree. I could not let him see me now! Jack opened the van door, climbed in, and started the motor. Soon he pulled away from the house and headed down the road, dust gradually dissipating in the air behind him. I waited several minutes to be sure he was gone and not coming back for any reason, then I cautiously headed closer to the house.

Even with my binoculars hanging down in front of my chest, I could see the child standing in front of the second-story window; she definitely was watching me and still appeared to be saying something.

23

Anita

August 3, 2018

I'M LOCKED IN MY ROOM now waiting for Gek to leave. It's mid-afternoon, but—not like the weeks and weeks before now—this day is cool and there is some wind. It feels so, so good compared to most days this summer when I have been so hot in this room that I thought I would die. I had to put water on my face and neck to make me cooler, but it didn't help much. Today though the air is very, very nice. I look out the window, hoping and praying to see the *Virgen* again. I know—I'm almost positive—that I saw her there yesterday and maybe, maybe it was her that I saw earlier today at Walmart. I want her to be there in the woods again, looking toward my window. Maybe she will appear to me again after Gek leaves; I truly need her help before tomorrow night.

For almost a month, Gek has locked me in my room most of almost every day, and definitely every night. Ever since he lost his job he has been a different person. For a while I thought that maybe, maybe he would help me find my family but, the way he is now, I know that will not happen. Now I am up here whenever he leaves the house. I know he comes back very late in the night—sometimes I hear him bumping into things when he goes up to his room. And, even when the sun has been up for a long while, Gek sleeps, and I am still locked in. That is normal now. Now I am also used to that awful pan. Besides that pan, that I have to empty every afternoon and return to my room, I also bring food for my dinner—sometimes my lunch also. And I carry up some things that I can eat for breakfast too and two big bottles that I fill with water every day.

Living locked in this room, except for a few hours in the afternoon when I cook for Gek and me, reminds me of when I was locked in the cage right after they took me from *Mamá*. Only there—in that cage—

there were other girls that I could have talked to. There were bathrooms I could use. But it's very lonely here, even with the books I have read many, many times. Gek bought them for me when he was a nicer person—before he changed so much. Now he stinks like stale alcohol and dirty man smell all the time and he does not act normal. Gek seems very lost. He looks confused and almost scared or something. I'm not really sure where he goes every night—somewhere to drink I know. Maybe sleeping helps him not to feel so scared either because he also sleeps a lot every day. So I am here in this hot, hot room for a very long time—the cage in Texas was also much cooler. Well, maybe too cold.

Yesterday morning I heard Gek snoring, so I knew it would be a while before he got up and unlocked my door. I went to the window and looked out towards the woods and prayed again to the *Virgen de Guadelupe*. Until yesterday it didn't seem like she had answered me. I wondered if I was losing faith or if I wasn't praying the right way. Why wouldn't the *Virgen* answer even a tiny bit? I've had so many questions. How could *Dios* let me stay here locked in? Did I do something wrong? And how could He let them take me from *Mamá*? Why would He let me stay with those shifty-eyed men? I cry when I think about this because I hate to think of my own *papá* as a man. But he never acted like these others.

I wondered at first if all men in the US are like the ones I see, but now I don't think they are. Whenever Gek would take me to Walmart or to get something I would look at the other men—I did that again today in Walmart too. Some of the men have families with them and others seem very nice to the rest of the people in the store. Once when I was staring at a man in a blue shirt with blonde hair and glasses, he looked up and saw me. Then he nodded his head and smiled at me in a nice way—in a way that would let me trust him. I try to look into men's eyes in the store to see what they are like, and most don't seem shifty. Perhaps there were also men in *México* that were that bad. I remember that *Abuela* told Luisa and me not to go and talk to the old men sitting on the benches in the *plaza* or near the park. We asked her why, but she didn't say very clearly. She said they could be *viejos verdes*, and we might get hurt. Luisa and I didn't think the old men looked green, but maybe she was mad at them or something. We didn't really want to talk to them anyway so we stayed away. Could they have been bad too? But I was mainly around my *abuelos* and *tíos* and my own *papá*. And they were all very nice and good and loving.

Sometimes I think Gek could have been a nice person—sometimes it used to feel like he was trying to take care of me and sometimes we almost had fun together—but other times he would get very mean. I don't always think he's mad at me—maybe he's mad at himself. I wonder what made him that way? Perhaps a lot of bad things happened to him. Sometimes I even pray for Gek and I pray that he will be a nicer person again. Those prayers do not seem to be helping either though.

But yesterday morning, as I stared into the wood and prayed, I thought I saw something move. I stared harder. Could it be true? I believed I saw the *Virgen* in the woods. I was sure I saw her! She was standing there in the woods, partly hidden by the trees. I kept looking at her and praying as I stood there in the window. I whispered all the prayers that *Mamá* and *Abuela* taught me. I prayed the *Rosario*, repeating the prayers over and over, holding a string that I had knotted to be like the beads and moving my fingers from one knot to the next.

"Santa María, madre de Dios, pray for us." I added, "Pray for me, Holy Mother. Help me. Help me leave this place and find my family."

Again and again yesterday, I recited the familiar prayers, feeling blessed that the *Virgen* had let me see her. She was wearing pants and a baseball cap and watched me with binoculars, but I could still tell she was Holy. I stood in front of the window for a very long time, looking toward her and silently mouthing "Help me!" But I was also praying that something would happen, that she would get me out of here.

And now, as I look out again and pray, I know I need her help even more.

But while I was looking out at the *Virgen* yesterday, I heard Gek waking up and I knew that he would finally release me from this room for a bit. I left the window to put away my *Rosario* and to get dressed and ready to confront Gek for the day. I remember that I wondered if he would be nice or nasty to me—but at least I had seen the *Virgen*. After I put on shorts and a pink t-shirt, I went back to the window and checked to see if she was still there waiting for me. She was! But I heard Gek unlocking my door, so I turned away.

Then, after I went downstairs, I looked into the woods from the kitchen window to see if I could still see her by the trees. She was there still! Gek came to the sink in front of the window and looked outside too. I held my breath, hoping he didn't see her in the wood. The next time I could look outside without being too obvious though, she was gone. After that I kept looking out the window whenever Gek wasn't watching me, but I didn't see her again all afternoon. Even after Gek locked me in my room and left yesterday night, I gazed out until dark hoping to see her again but I didn't. On my bed cushions, as I tried to fall asleep, I prayed with all my heart that she would come again the next day.

This morning, again, I kept watch again out of my window while Gek was sleeping, but the *Virgen* did not appear. I wished she would. I prayed that she would. But she still hadn't appeared when Gek got up —a lot earlier than he has lately—and let me out of my room.

"Hey Annie, do ya want to go down and make us somethin' to eat?" Gek asked me after he unlocked the door. He was already dressed in jeans and seemed nicer than he had lately.

I went downstairs and looked again out of the window. No *Virgen.* Had I just imagined her there yesterday? It made me feel so sad that I could not see her again. Perhaps it had only been my imagination—but why would I imagine her with binoculars? That was strange.

"We need to go to Walmart today," Gek announced as I made toast for breakfast.

I was elated to hear this: a chance to leave this house, a chance to see other people, perhaps a chance to ask someone for help. But then Gek explained that we needed to get something silky for me. I didn't know this word, but he explained it to me—cloth that is so smooth it feels like glass. It's shiny like glass too, but soft, he said, and elegant. I think he meant *sedosa.*

"Why I need something silky?" I asked him, nervous about what he had planned for me.

"John wants ya to wear something silky tomorrow night," he explained as he ate a piece of toast, looking down and away from me.

"No, no!" I screamed; that was what I was afraid of. "I no want to see him tomorrow. I no want to see him never."

"It's all arranged. Come on," he said, standing up and ignoring my protest. "Let's get goin' to Walmart."

I decided I did want to go to Walmart, even though we were going to buy something silky for me to wear for that creepy John, and now I'm glad that I did. I cannot believe what happened there. Now I have faith again. I agreed to go because I thought maybe something good might come up. Maybe I would have a chance to escape before he brought me to see that John. Besides, I was too tired of staying by myself all the time at Gek's house. At least I finally had a chance to leave again, especially because Gek won't let me stay in other parts of the house now—not to watch TV or read or not even to clean and cook for him except when he is there. Without TV or new books it's hard to learn more English. I don't think I did anything to make him mad at me. I was still trying to work hard while he was at home, but he doesn't trust me now. Also, since he lost his job, I knew that I would probably have to start "working" at the other places where he takes me. And he likes to take me to that John's house because he pays more money. But I also have to stay there longer—the whole night.

I'm so glad that I went with him to Walmart earlier today though. Even the drive felt good. I could see the leaves of the trees blowing in the breeze. It felt so much cooler outside today. I held my fingers outside the window as we rode—they felt free and happy. It gave me hope to be outside again. It also gave me hope to see other people driving different places and to see them outside the Walmart store—something could happen here, something could happen, something *had* to happen.

We walked into the store, and the air inside was even colder. We went to the part with clothes for children and looked around. Gek couldn't find anything silky—and red; he was looking for red—in my size. I was so glad there was nothing there. But then we went to the area with women's underwear, and Gek found a red, silky slip. It was too big for me, but he held it up to me and said we could fix it. I didn't want it. I didn't want to wear that or to go to see that John, so I started to cry and yell a little bit. Maybe someone would hear me, I thought. Maybe someone would rescue me, like that girl I heard about on the news— back when I could watch TV—who said "Help me!" when she went to Walmart and then got rescued. Maybe someone would hear me too. I think Gek thought so too, because he told me to shut up. Then I saw Gek's face change to an even more mad look—maybe a worried look— so I also looked to see what he saw. A lady with a hat in her hand was looking at us.

Could this be the *Virgen?* Or could she help me at least?

"Okay, Gek, I take it," I said to distract his attention.

We went to buy the red slip, but I didn't see the lady again. I hoped I didn't miss my chance to have her help me. Gek was furious with me on the way to his van. He pushed me hard to get me inside it. All the way home he yelled at me. And I was also feeling sad and depressed that we were just heading back to his house again.

"What a stupid, little creep! Ya don't appreciate anything I do for ya. I'm just trying to feed ya and take care of ya," he shouted out in the car.

While he was driving he was jerking to stop and starting too fast, jerking as well. I knew he was mad.

"You're gonna get me in trouble. Then who'd take care of ya?" he said as he turned around to look at me. His face was red.

When I told him my aunt would if he would let me call her, he hit the steering wheel and swung around like he was going to hit me. He ran into the curb a little bit and yelled out a bunch of bad words. I was lucky to be in the back seat.

"I sorry," I told him after he got the van under control. "I no yell in Walmart again."

"Damn right ya won't. Ya'll be lucky if I EVER take ya there again," he responded, but he did get quieter then.

By the time we got back to his house he was not yelling but he still acted mad at me because he slammed the doors of the van and the door to the house too. After we went inside he told me to make some lunch fast because he had to leave soon. I was glad to hear he was leaving. Maybe there was a chance he would forget to lock me in or something. Anyway, even though I would have to spend the rest of the day and all night locked in my room, he had not been nice to be around lately. And he still stank like whisky today.

While I was making lunch I looked out into the woods. I was looking for the *Virgen* once more. I just knew she would come again. I could feel it. While Gek was in the kitchen I only took quick peeks so he wouldn't know I was looking for her, but after Gek went upstairs I looked harder. Maybe I saw her—I'm not sure.

"OK," Gek said after he came back down, "ya gotta get in your room now. I'm leavin' for a while."

I went up the stairs with my supplies for later. He let me use the bathroom and then he carefully locked the door behind me after I went inside the room. Why did he have to remember that? I set my things down and hurried to the window—where I am still standing.

I think she is there, but I'm still not sure. She could be behind that big tree or maybe it is only my wish that she is. I use part of the Rosary prayers and repeat those parts again and again, making the prayer fit my need and changing some of the words. *Mamá* told me a long time ago that when I am by myself—not when I am saying the Rosary in Church, but when I'm alone—it's okay to change the prayers to say what I want to say.

"*Santa María, Madre de Dios, ruega por mí… Santísima María, querida Madre, ayúdame, ayúdame…* Help me. Help me, dear Mother," I whisper. Then I add "Let me see you. Let me see you. Let me see you."

I hear Gek drive away and continue to say my prayers, louder now. The window is open, so I hope she can hear me and that she lets me see her. I even say some of it in English in case she understands me better in English here in the US. I keep watching out the window into the woods, looking for her and praying.

"*Santa María*, let me see you. *Santa María*, help me. *Santa María*, let my *mamá* be safe. *Santa María* let my *papá* be safe. *Santa María*, help us. *Santísima María*, let me see you."

I see her! I think I see her. I see her! She is coming out of the woods toward the house. I think it is her. Her head and face are covered, but I think it is her.

"Help me! Help me! Please, please help me, *Santa María*! Help me, *¡por favor!* Please, help me!"

24

Claire de lune

August 3, 2018

AS I APPROACHED THE HOUSE, I could see the girl standing in front of the upstairs window, leaning down toward the open part of the window and definitely speaking. The closer I got the better I could hear, and now I was positive she was saying, "Help me! Help me!" After I began running toward the house, I stopped just below the window and looked up, at the same time removing my hat and mosquito netting so as not to scare her.

"Are you okay? I heard you calling for help and I'd like to help you. What is your name?"

"*Soy Anita*. Are you the *Virgen María*?"

"No, I'm Claire," I replied, surprised at the question. "Are you locked inside?"

"Yes, locked inside, and Gek nailed the windows. They no open much."

"Who is Jack? Is he your father?"

"No! No is my father!" said Anita emphatically and beginning to cry.

"Don't worry, Anita. I'm going to help you."

I ran around the house trying to open doors and windows without success. After I returned to the back window I asked Anita if the door to her room was also locked. Of course it was—with a big lock outside the door, she told me. Then I asked her more about why she was living with Jack. Although Anita's answer was long and complicated, I understood that she had crossed the border from Mexico and had been detained there. Also, she started sobbing when she began to talk about her mother. At that point, I decided that I'd better call the police and let them know an immigrant child was being detained and that I was trying to get her out of a house where she was being held against her will. I dialed 911 and explained the situation and where the house was located. The assistant on duty said that most of the officers were already engaged with an emergency on I-435 near Olathe, but that a patrol car would be there shortly.

"Shortly? What does that mean?" I asked myself as I hung up. "Ten minutes? Half an hour? Or more? I'd better continue to work to get her out of this place."

In the meantime, I discovered a very old ladder lying near one side of the house. The ladder rungs were rounded dowels of wood inserted into the wooden side bars. Some of the rungs felt rather loose in their sockets, but I didn't see any other options to get up to the second story window to try to get her out. Even if I broke a lower-level window I wouldn't be able to get inside her room if the door was padlocked from the outside.

"Antoine, I hope you can help me with this ladder; it looks heavy and quite rickety," I said, hoping that Antoine had good telekinetic skills like so many ghosts I had seen in movies and read about in novels. Did spirits really have super strengths? I hoped so and, also, that my own adrenalin could help.

"*Bien sûr, ma chérie,*" he intoned.

The ladder then practically walked itself up to the house and lined itself up underneath Anita's window. Antoine had developed some amazing powers despite what he had told me about when he first returned as a spirit.

"Antoine, if you can move a ladder that easily I wonder if you could just enter and teleport Anita to the ground out here," I whispered.

"I do not know if she would be very scared by that," he answered in a very muted tone. I could see him fading in and out a bit with the breeze at that moment. "I have never tried to move a person before. I would rather not practice on her if we can get her out in a more normal way."

"Ah, yes, that could be quite frightening," I conceded. "Let's stick with the ladder plan."

At that point I heard a car approaching on the gravel road and stopped right there in my tracks. Could Jack be coming back to the house? Surely not, but I peeked around the corner to observe the vehicle I heard. Oh, NO! He was returning! It was definitely his van pulling back toward the house.

"Antoine, please help me move the ladder again. We can lie it down near the house here in back," I pleaded, now shaking like a leaf.

Again, the ladder moved without much help at all from me. Antoine set it on its side up against the back of the house. It was on a different side of the house than before, but perhaps that would not be noticed if Jack happened to walk around outside. I crouched down at the side edge of the back steps and prayed that Jack would not go behind the house. He opened and then slammed the door to his van, and then I heard him unlock the front door and bang it closed behind him after he went inside.

"Annie, Annie, where's my damn phone? Ya'd better not have my phone or ya'll be in big trouble," Jack yelled as I heard him storm up the stairs.

"He'd better not hurt her," I whispered to Antoine. "What can we do?"

"Let's wait a moment," Antoine advised. "I can always try to intervene if it is necessary. I'd still rather not scare her if I don't have to."

We listened outside as Jack approached and unlocked the door to Anita's room. The birds were still chirping in the trees bestowing an element of natural beauty on the scene that seemed terrifyingly unreal. The sun and breeze made this a perfect day to enjoy the outdoors, but I was frozen with fright—afraid that even my breath could be heard.

"Do ya have my phone?" he yelled, but not as loudly as before.

"No, Gek, I no have your phone."

"Then come help me find it if ya don't have it," his voice commanded, but not as forcefully.

We could hear both of them descend the stairs. I exhaled with partial relief; at least they probably would not be venturing outside if he had only returned for his phone. It would be unlikely that he would wander around to the back; I hoped, at least. I also wondered what would happen if the police showed up at this moment. But soon they apparently had found the phone because Jack was ushering her back up the stairs into her room.

"Okay, I'm leavin' now," he announced before he shut and bolted her door again.

Soon I heard him trudge down the stairs and out the front door, where he apparently spent time carefully locking it. Then he climbed into the van and, within several minutes, pulled away from the house. His vehicle traveled down the gravel road, again leaving a trail of dust, and finally was out of earshot, but neither Anita nor I said anything for quite some time. Finally I decided it was safe to get up off the ground near the back stoop.

"Anita, are you still there?"

"Yes, I still here," she answered quietly.

"Then I'm going to move the ladder back and we will try this again. He surely won't come back another time," I tried to assure her— and myself.

Antoine helped me return the ladder to Anita's window again. Then I gingerly began to ascend it, but a wave of uncertainty—almost like nausea—overwhelmed me. I suddenly stopped. Was this really happening? Was I truly about to climb a ladder at someone's house— someone I didn't even know—to try to rescue a child I envisioned was being trafficked? And with the help of a ghost? With the advice from my dreams? Was my refuge into fiction writing overcoming my sense of reality? Perhaps I was trying to avoid something in my own material life that had sent me over the edge of veracity. This surge of biliousness felt as if I unexpectedly need to rid myself of something I had held inside me for too long. Was I going to vomit? Or perhaps I really was Claire de lune in the most negative sense: crazed, looney, unhinged.

"Claire, what is the matter?" whispered Antoine into my ear.

And, from above, Anita was also speaking.

"Thank you, thank you for help me. What I should do?"

I had to continue. Crazy or not, I had to trust myself and help this child if she needed help. Slowly I repositioned my foot on the first rung of the ladder and held on with both hands as I began to hoist myself up. The treads beneath me seemed solid and grounded, but I could tell that the support I was feeling was not from the ladder alone. Antoine's ghost truly was holding me securely to the ladder. With help, I was able to remove the old screen on Anita's window, which seemed to magically unhinge itself at the top. However, the window itself would not budge and was not open enough for the girl to climb through. I thought about how dreadfully hot it must have been in that room most days and nights this summer.

"She needs to back away from the window. I'm going to have to break it," Antoine whispered to me.

"Anita, go away from the window. We're going to have to break it," I told her. "I mean I'll break it."

Anita stepped back, and I ducked down as the window burst open, glass falling mainly inside the room. I used my binoculars to break off some remaining shards of glass at the base of the window frame to clear the way for Anita to climb through. When I was sure that the broken area had no big protruding segments of glass, I surveyed Anita's room and asked her to bring the sheet from her bedding to cover the remaining slightly uneven broken glass areas on the window sill. We positioned the cloth carefully, then I instructed Anita to climb out backwards, helping her to place her feet on the ladder rungs. A force unknown to Anita helped to steady her on the ladder, and both she and I began to descend one rung at a time. Suddenly though, one side of the ladder began to separate from all the rungs, and we both started to fall. I let out the beginning of a scream. But then a comforting force—known to me, but not to Anita—gently scooped us up and lowered us down to the earth so that we both landed on our feet. The ladder and all its rungs, however, crashed into the tall grass at the edge of the house.

Upon reaching the ground, Anita began to shake and sob hysterically. I helped her to sit down on the grass and then seated myself beside her, enveloping her in my arms. I tried my best to calm her, even though I was trembling considerably myself.

"Don't worry, Anita. You are safe now. I'm going to help you get away from this danger and back to where you belong."

With my arms still encircling Anita, the tremors and tears that had engulfed her slowly began to subside. I could feel the tension in her body began to drain away and, as it did, my own anxiety eased as well. We sat there for at least a quarter of an hour, and then I also felt a special energy embracing me.

"Claire," Antoine murmured into my ear, "I'm so proud of you and so grateful to you! Because of you I have completed my *entente* here; I know you will help this child to be safe. That means I must leave this realm now, but I will always stay with you in a certain way. I think someday we will meet again; I truly believe we will. For the present, *au revoir, ma chérie.*"

"*Au revoir*, Antoine," I could scarcely mouth the words with my lips as tears slipped rapidly from my eyes.

Suddenly then, like a dream that dissolves upon waking, his presence was gone. I knew that I did not have time now to mourn his leaving, to feel depressed, or even question how he had come to me or why he had to leave. Nor could I take the time now to explore the doubts I experienced about my own perceptions of reality when I began to climb the ladder. First and foremost, I needed to get this child to safety, to help her find her family, and to support her so she could get over whatever had happened to her. I still had so many questions, but even those needed to wait until we were in a more protected place.

The police had not arrived yet, but I could not risk staying any longer in the vicinity of that house. It would be a disaster if Jack were to reappear. And even our being near the structure that had encaged her seemed perilous for the child. I stood up, took Anita by the hand, and lead her through the woods towards my car. Inside the car, I called 911 again and told the dispatcher that I had taken the girl from the house where she had been held, and that we were going to my home nearby. I gave the dispatcher my address and requested that the police officers meet us there.

25

Black Jack

August 3, 2018

JACK WAS LEANING ON THE BAR at The Place—he'd been there almost every night for a month now, drinking and gambling and drinking some more, trying to forget his problems. The Place—with its concrete floors, rough plywood walls, and stale smell of beer and grimy restrooms—wasn't nearly as nice as the Score bar. But since Jack couldn't go back there now—and because the drinks were cheaper here —he'd begun to make this his go-to. Now, however, he was out of cash and out of credit at the bar—he'd been asking for drinks on credit almost all evening, but they'd decided to put a limit on him. And the night was still fairly young—too early at least to go back home—and he hadn't drunk enough yet. He could still feel and think and he didn't want to. He'd asked a couple of men at the bar to lend him enough for another drink, but they'd had enough of him too lately, he guessed. Well, some of them had even told him that. He tried the bartender again.

"Jack, I can't serve you another drink without charging you for it," the bartender admonished, shaking his head furiously and walking away from Jack.

"I'll pay ya, Fred. I get paid tomorrow. It's just a little advance for one night," Jack pleaded, thinking of Annie's stint for tomorrow evening.

"We ain't a bank, Jack. We ain't in the loan business. I'll get fired if I don't collect from you tonight," Fred yelled back at him as he wiped sweat from his balding forehead.

"You jerk," Jack shouted. "I've been in here payin' every night. This makes me really mad! I'm just askin' for one day."

"Okay. You need to leave, Jack! That's enough! I said I can't do it. Get out NOW! You can come back when you can pay for what you drink."

Jack lurched over the bar and grabbed Fred by his navy and white striped polo shirt, ready to hit him in the face. Fred's brown eyes bulged in surprise and horror, and his face went pale. He looked around the room for help. At that moment though, other loyal patrons of the bar pounced on Jack and pushed him down and then out the door. When Jack tried to rush back inside, one large, burly man in a dirt-streaked, white t-shirt pulled back his fist and smashed it into Jack's face. A struggle ensued, but Jack was three sheets to the wind from the liquor he had already consumed, and the ogre, with his exaggerated biceps, laughed at Jack as he punched him. The other patrons seemed ready to witness a little scuffle and egged them on with whistles and boos. Finally the manager emerged, looking official and competent in his dark rimmed glasses and equally dark shirt and pants, and broke up the brawl. The robust giant dropped Jack onto the gravel of the parking lot, and—now that the entertainment was over—the crowd that had gathered from inside filed back into the bar. Jack rolled over to his side on the gravel and moaned, not willing or able to get up yet. After the door was shut, there was hardly any light in the parking lot. He lay there in the darkness, not even thinking about his next move. Then, when he heard someone crunching across the gravel, he wondered if one of the guys was coming back out to finish him off.

"Here," said a female's voice, "just hold this bag of ice on your eye and forehead for a few minutes. It'll help keep the swelling down. I think you're going to have a real shiner."

She squatted down and placed the ice pack on his head.

"I'm Gina, one of the waitresses in the bar. I've noticed you in there a lot the last few weeks. You're quite a regular now."

She said she'd heard his name was Black Jack and wondered how he got that name. Jack just moaned again; then he tried to push himself up onto his elbow to get a better look at her. At first he only saw her tennis shoes, her shapely ankles, and tight blue jeans. When he had righted himself a bit more, he looked her over entirely. She had long, dark, straight hair with shorter hair across the forehead and a pretty face with lots of eye makeup. In addition to the skintight jeans, she worn a sexy, red halter top and a dark green tip apron with straws sticking out of one pocket. How had he not noticed her in there before?

"Thanks. I guess I pushed my luck in there," Jack murmured as he tried to sit up better to take her all in. "Maybe I should've eaten somethin' before I had so much whiskey. I seem to have my father's temper when I drink."

"Just sit here with the ice for a few minutes. I'm on my break now. I'll bring my food out to you—I'm not really very hungry tonight," Gina remarked.

The gravel on the lot gritted against his hands, but Jack leaned up against a car, resting his elbows on his bent knees, and applied the ice bag to his throbbing head. There were cars parked all over the lot in a disorganized mess, and Jack gazed over to his van on the far side of the lot, wondering if he should just get out of there in case the manager called the police, even though they probably wanted to avoid bringing in the cops. But he stayed right where he was while Gina went back inside through the rear door to the kitchen. He wondered if she would really come back but he hurt too much to move yet. After a bit, she returned with a styrofoam box filled with a hamburger and fries and a gigantic, icy Coke in a waxed paper cup with a clear lid and straw. She handed him the drink and he took a long slurp.

"Why're ya doin' this for me?" he queried looking up at her. "I don't deserve it."

"I just think you're sort of interesting," Gina answered as she sat down on the gravel next to him.

She broke off a bit of the hamburger and handed it to him.

"Go ahead and eat something. Maybe you'll feel better."

"I'm a loser, Gina. Don't waste ya'r time on me."

"Well, I'll decide what I think of you later," she said. "I'm just helping you out a bit tonight. Besides, I have to get back inside in a few minutes. You just looked like you could use a friend tonight. Do you think you can drive home?"

"Yeah—I do need a friend, but I think I can drive now that I'm eatin' somethin'—if my head just stops poundin'."

Gina sat and chattered on a bit about being a waitress as Jack gobbled down the food. She said she'd had better jobs than this one, but it was working okay for her for the time being. She also told him a funny story about a customer who thought she looked like his niece and kept calling her Beatrice. Jack watched her as she spoke and liked how her eyes crinkled at the corners when she smiled. She was obviously trying to make him feel better. After a while, she glanced at the time on her phone, stood up, and headed back toward the kitchen door.

"My break is over—I've gotta get back to work. Good luck, Jack," she said as she blew him a kiss.

Jack just sat there, incredulous. He couldn't believe someone had been that nice to him, especially a woman. And she was good looking too. Again he felt a guilty unworthiness though. After a while he gathered up the strength to get up and head toward his van. Once he climbed in he noticed that it was only 10:15, but it seemed like it was much later. His head and his whole body ached, and he felt incredibly tired.

As he drove home, he thought of Gina's smile and her amazing interest in him. It felt so good to have her care for him—even for a few moments. She didn't have to do that. She didn't have to give up her dinner either. Maybe not all women were as fickle as the ones he'd known—including his own mother. Maybe he could actually see one that wouldn't break away as soon as he began to get really interested in her. Maybe he could still salvage his life. Maybe….

Or maybe not. He didn't have a job, he didn't have any money, and his life was quite dependent now on a foreign kid who could get him in so much trouble—*so* much trouble. Gina was just helping him out in the moment—not expressing an interest in continuing to see him. And—he'd almost forgotten about this—he had hit and killed a bloke. Even if the guy was a jerk, he'd still killed him. No, probably not; it was probably too late to make amends. No, most definitely not—this wasn't a new possibility. How could he even pretend to have possibilities? How was he going to get himself out of this situation?

As Jack's mind wandered through this thicket of prickly thoughts, as if he were in a convoluted maze with grasping brambles and no known exit, he barely noticed where he was while he automatically drove toward his house, without even paying much attention. He wished he could just drive off and never return to that dumpy, confining structure where he lived. And never return to the mess he'd made there. But where would he go? What would he do? Jack was so wrapped up in his thoughts and his pain that he didn't even notice the police car parked along the side of the road as he turned onto County Road LL.

And he could not have known that two more patrol cars were parked at other entrances to the route on the other side of his residence. Right after he pulled into the drive to the decrepit farmhouse, just as he was exiting his van, a cacophony of blaring sirens and flashing red lights screeched out into the formerly peaceful darkness of the night. Three police cars pulled into his yard and officers jumped out with pistols in their hands. Jack automatically fell to his knees.

"Oh, shit! I'm a goner now!"

26

Anita and Claire de lune

August 3, 2018

AT FIRST ANITA CANNOT STOP CRYING. She almost can't believe that the *Virgen* really did hear her—it's such a relief. She really did come. She says she is not the *Virgen*, but she helped Anita out of Gek's house. And it felt like magic—like a fairy from one of her books who had an enchanted wand and pulled her out—or like a miracle of the *Virgen de Guadalupe*. They had almost flown to the ground. Anita can hardly believe she is no longer in Gek's house, but she always knew the *Virgen* would help her. It feels like nearly everything bad has drained from her. Well, almost. But she definitely feels safe again.

Now they are riding in Claire's car. Her name is Claire, not María. But she is so beautiful. Claire says she lives close and she wants to leave before Gek comes back. Anita keeps staring at Claire and hopes she doesn't mind. Now they pull up to Claire's house, where the garage door magically opens, and she drives inside. She helps Anita out of the car and then into her kitchen. Anita's legs can hardly stand—they are so shaky. Claire takes Anita to a little *sofá* and asks her to sit down. Anita wants to cry again, but she's not sad.

"Let me get you a little snack and a drink. There is a bathroom just over here if you need it," Claire says, as she points to a door not far from the *sofá*. "Don't worry, you are just unsettled from that escape. I'm pretty shaky too. Just rest here a minute."

Anita just nods and sinks onto the *sofá*. She can't seem to say or do a thing—she feels so comfortable now that she can hardly move.

After Claire settled Anita on a couch in the living room to relax and so they could talk more about what had happened, she went to make Anita a snack to help to calm her, in case she hadn't eaten much in a while. Claire didn't know how much time they had before the police would come and disrupt the few peaceful moments they had together, but it probably wouldn't be long. She knew from research for her novel that the law enforcement officers would surely transport Anita into the custody of the state juvenile authorities. The police, as of now, had absolutely no reason to trust Claire, so they would have to assume that she, also, could be a danger to the child until proven otherwise. However, Claire wanted to reassure Anita before the authorities took her away that she would be safe and that they would help her find her mother; taking her to another confined place surely would be a traumatic action for her after all she had gone through. But the first order of business was to get her something to eat.

As Claire entered into the kitchen, she thought about how very charming Anita was. She really didn't want the police to take Anita away. And something about her large, brown eyes reminded Claire of someone she hadn't thought about in a long time. Claire felt, even after only a very few moments with the girl, a maternal caring that she hadn't experienced since her own little sister, Eva, had died. Eva was eight years younger than Claire and, because their mother was working, Claire had cared for Eva as if she were her own child instead of her younger sister. Claire fixed Eva's lunch every day during the summers and on weekends and holidays when school wasn't in session. She helped Eva get bathed and dressed, and read to her every time she could. She also taught Eva how to play games and, when they played pretend, Eva was always her own little girl. Eva even called her "Mimmi" most of the time. And Eva, too, had large brown eyes—like Anita's.

When Eva suddenly and unexpectedly died at the age of nine from a cerebral seizure, Claire, at seventeen, had spiraled into a grief so profound that her parents didn't know what to do with her. It was her last year in high school, and she missed so much school that she had to attend summer school classes in chemistry and citizenship in order to graduate. She had stayed in her room crying most of the time and didn't seem to have the energy to do anything at all—not even to shower or get dressed most days. Claire's parents had taken her to the doctor, who had given her a prescription that only seemed to make her sleep more. Then Claire's mother made an appointment for her with a psychiatrist—which her father totally opposed—but the psychiatrist just made Claire feel more lost and scared of what was happening to her. He even looked rather scary—with his skinny face and big, owl-like glasses—and the way he talked made Claire worry even more that she was not normal, not okay. The school counselor, Mrs. Winston, had even come to visit her. But, even though Claire thought that was nice of Mrs. Winston, she didn't seem to feel much better until late in the summer—after she had scraped through and just barely passed her chemistry and citizenship classes.

Following that traumatic year, Claire had vowed that she would never have children of her own for fear of losing them so, after attending and graduating from university, and working at a job that barely interested her, she absorbed herself in her writing and other interests, telling herself that she could have a very full life on her own. When she finally started seriously dating Jim about six years ago, at age twenty-nine, one of the discussions they had about their future relationship was about progeny. Jim had hoped to have children after he married, but Claire had an unbending angst of future pain and privation if they were to have a child and if, for some reason, that child would die. Perhaps she carried the gene that had allowed her beloved sister to die of that seizure. Perhaps her own child would suffer the same fate. She communicated all this to Jim—voicing out loud for the first time all the fears she held within herself. Then she had covered those fears over again with a thick, insulating blanket of isolation—not even thinking about them.

Now she clearly remembered Jim's words after they had been dating over a year, when he asked her to marry him.

"Claire, I love you so much that it doesn't matter to me whether we have children. If you change your mind about that, it's fine, but I will never pressure you to or wish you had. You yourself are more than enough for me to love."

Jim had respected his promise and had never brought up the subject of having children again, and Claire hadn't either. Her writing career, along with the trips and activities they did together, had filled Claire's life. She had even begun to estrange herself from the friends who had married and had children but—not until this moment—had she felt like she was missing anything. Maybe these covered-over fears were part of the angst and doubt that wanted to leave her body as she began to climb the ladder up to Anita in that window.

Now, thinking about the brown-eyed child in her living room, and of her sister Eva, she began to wonder if, indeed, there was a glaringly unfulfilled portion of her life. Was there some unconscious reason why she had recently written about a girl in a cage and, synchronistically, discovered one in real life? Was she herself also confined—trapped by her own fears and guilt? Were her own suppressed emotions holding her captive? Were they prostituting her as well, making her inauthentic? Recently she had felt more and more distant toward Jim; was that because she was being untrue to herself? How much had she hidden within her own emotions and body that she was unable to face?

"I will definitely think about this later," Claire told herself, truly meaning it. "Right now I've got to finish this snack and get back to Anita."

Claire assuredly needed to know more about Anita's situation in order to help her, and Anita was very helpful about telling what had happened to her and her mother when they entered the US. Her English was a bit limited, but Claire understood that something had happened to her father and that Anita and her mother had entered the US by crossing the river border, where they were apprehended by border control officers, detained, and separated. Anita told her about the foster family she lived with and that, after the wife left, the man, Bill, had given her and another girl to a man named Duke. Then Duke gave her to Jack. Claire shuttered to imagine how all of this had gone for Anita. She also learned more about Anita's immediate family.

"*Mi tía* Rosa live in Arizona. I know her phone number," Anita asserted, shaking her head affirmatively as she sat with her legs curled up on the sofa.

"You have an aunt who lives in the US? Have you ever tried to call her?" Claire asked, wide-eyed at this possibility.

"Gek no let me. He say his phone no call Arizona. I think he lie."

This girl is very observant, Claire thought. Claire also asked if Anita's aunt Rosa had legal papers to stay in the US, but Anita didn't know.

"We may need to be careful not to mention her to the authorities unless your aunt is here legally. We wouldn't want to accidentally get her deported. How about your mother; does she have a phone?"

"She broke her phone before we left *México*," Anita answered. "She put it in the *basura*. I think she no have one now."

Anita recited her aunt Rosa's number in Arizona, and Claire wrote it down on a pad of paper before dialing it. The phone rang several times and then went to Rosa's voicemail. In her voice message, Claire explained that she had found Anita and that Rosa should return the call as soon as possible.

"Well, I guess we'll just have to wait for now," Claire said as Anita's expression went from excitement to disappointment. "But don't worry; I'll try your aunt's number again later if she doesn't call us back soon. How did you learn to speak English, Anita? Did you study it before you came?"

"I study a little in my school in *México*. Also I watch TV and read here. It help me," Anita answered. "I tell Gek I want go to school."

"Well, you are speaking very well. You are a very smart girl and you have been very brave. You are still going to need to be brave and courageous though, but at least you will be safe now," Claire reassured as she patted Anita's hand.

Then she began to explain to Anita that when the police came they would take her to stay in another place but that she would be safe there, and that they would be in contact with her mother very soon.

"In a cage again? I want stay with you, *Virgen* Cler."

"Oh, Anita, I'm so sorry but I know they won't let you stay with me tonight—they don't know me yet. I definitely will still help you though, even when you are not with me. I'll help you to get back with your mother. I'll come to visit you as soon as they let me," explained Claire.

"I no want to leave," the girl pleaded.

Claire reassured her again and explained that the police needed to check to be sure that Claire was a good person and wouldn't hurt Anita. She reiterated several times that she would help to find Anita's mother and to reunite them again.

"I promise that I will do everything I can to help you, Anita. It will still be hard for you for a while, but you will be safe. And we will find your aunt and mother."

Claire and Anita ate the snack and kept talking. Anita ate with enthusiasm and good appetite, indicating to Claire that she truly had been hungry. But soon two cars with flashing lights pulled into the drive, and there was a knock on the door.

"Remember, Anita, they are here to help us," Claire encouraged her.

Both Claire and Anita went to the door, and Claire opened it to two police officers standing outside.

"Good evening, ma'am, I'm Officer Gerney, and this is Officer O'Connell with the Olathe Police Department," he said, showing his badge. "Are you Claire Schmidt?"

"Yes, I am."

"We totally apologize for the delay in answering your call," Gerney explained, "there was an eight car pileup on I-435 through Olathe, and all of our officers were helping with that emergency. We regret that we could not respond in a more timely manner to your emergency. Is this the young lady you rescued?"

"Yes, this is Anita," Claire said, looking with concern at her young charge. "Would you officers like to come inside?"

Gerney and O'Connell came into the living room and began to question Claire and Anita about what had happened. They took notes to the questions they posed regarding how Anita had come to be in Claire's house.

"How did you know that the child, Anita, was being held in the house, Ms. Schmidt?" asked O'Connell, as he poised his pen over a small notebook.

Claire paused briefly before answering—the ghost story probably would not help Anita's position, and the police were not as likely to have confidence in her if she brought up Antoine's visits at this point. As before, bringing up a ghost was not likely to bolster her credibility with them. She decided to recount what she had seen without involving him.

"Well, I drove by the house one day, to explore the area around my home, and I saw a bearded man in a black t-shirt forcefully push a young girl—Anita—out the door of the house and into the van. He glared at me so frightfully when he saw me looking at them that I was both alarmed and very concerned about the child."

"How long ago was that?" interjected Gerney.

"That was about a week ago. Then I saw them again today at Walmart. He was holding a red negligee up to Anita, and she screamed that she didn't want it. I heard him tell her that she needed it for tomorrow night. Then he looked up and saw me. Again, when he saw me, he looked at me so hatefully that I was concerned for my own welfare as well as that of the child," Claire rushed on and then stopped to take a deep breath.

"So, what did you do then, Ms. Schmidt?"

"I paid for my purchases and went home. After a bit, I went with binoculars through the field behind his house and watched to see if they were there. I could see them through the windows with my binoculars, so I called the police."

O'Connell asked if Jack was still there when she called the police, so Claire had to explain that she had watched until Jack left and then had approached the house, which was when she had heard Anita calling for help. She told them that before that she hadn't been sure if she was imagining the situation until she actually heard Anita calling for help out her window on the second floor.

"And after that?" asked O'Connell.

"That was when I called 911," Claire explained. "But the dispatcher told me it would probably be a while because of the accident you mentioned. So I decided to use a ladder to get her out of there in case her captor returned before you came."

"Yes, I want her help me," Anita interjected. "I no can wait."

"How long had you been living in that house?" Gerney asked Anita.

"I am there from May. I try to get away."

"Do you mean that you didn't want to be there with him?" asked O'Connor.

"No, I no want to be there with him," Anita said with furor, shaking her head and wrinkling her dark eyebrows in determination.

The officers questioned Anita more about how she had come to live with Jack, and Anita again relayed her story bit by bit. The officers and Claire interrupted her at times to ask for more information or to clarify what she had said. While they were gleaning all the details, O'-Connor's phone rang. The phone call obviously was related to Anita's case, and they heard O'Connor reply that Jack should be arrested when he arrived. After disconnecting from the call, O'Connor explained to them that his colleagues had found the broken window in the back of the house, but that Jack had not returned yet.

"There are three police cars positioned near his house, and they intend to arrest him when and if he reappears. We've had him on our radar for a while now but didn't realize he actually had a kidnapped child living with him," O'Connor said.

After more questions, the officers explained to Anita that they would have to take her with them since she was a UAC—an Unaccompanied Alien Child—until they found her parents or established a legal guardian ad litem for her—a guardian who they were sure would take good care of her and keep her safe.

"*Virgen* Cler will keep me safe," Anita pleaded. "I no want to leave here."

"I would keep her safe," Claire added, "but I am happy to cooperate with you in any way."

"Well, we can try to arrange that guardianship through the court, but for now it's our obligation to take Anita with us. There is also something called a T-Visa that we can get for her and for her mother, when we locate her, if they will help us with the prosecution in this case."

"Yes, I know about the T-Visa from researching for one of my novels."

"The Migrant center in Ciudad Juarez may know where she is. We'll put someone on that to try to find her," said O'Connor.

Then Gerney gave Claire his card and asked her to call him the next day, as he and O'Connor led Anita toward the door. Tears came into Claire's eyes as she said goodbye and then watched the officers open the police car door for Anita. After they pulled away, Claire began to sob uncontrollably—images of Eva, imaginings of Anita, memories of Anita's escape from Jack's house, thoughts of Antoine and Jim, and even notions of her own wounded self flooded into her awareness. She collapsed onto the sofa where Anita had sat and permitted a torrent of salty tears to escape. She hugged the sofa pillow to her chest as if it were one of those lost children at the border that were taken from their parents. After a time, the tears simply ceased, and she felt very empty. She realized that Jim would be coming home the next evening. As she reached for her phone to call him, it rang in her hand, but it was not his name or number that appeared on her screen.

"Hello," answered Claire.

"Yes, hello. Is this Claire Schmidt? I am Rosa, Anita's aunt …"

27

Black Jack

August 3–4, 2018

"STAND UP, SIR, AND RAISE your hands in the air."

Jack complied mutely. Even though he was standing just outside his rented house, he felt like a restrained dog being forced into its kennel. But he had already accepted his fate. In fact, he almost welcomed his own capture in contrast to the anxiety and guilt he had felt in the past few weeks about hitting that guy and even during the past few months with regard to Annie. He had always known it was a horrible thing to do to her, but it had seemed like the best and easiest option at the moment Duke had called him. And once he had agreed to it, there was no clear way out. He was caught in a maze that had got more enmeshed and difficult to maneuver the deeper he penetrated into it. He suddenly remembered a cornfield maze his dad had taken him to as a child. Jack was scared and lost walking among the tall, leafy cornstalks and pleaded to come out, but his father just laughed at his cries for help. He recalled as if it were yesterday: the intense heat of that day, the grasshoppers that kept jumping on him, and the feelings of fear and helplessness he had endured. However, this time he—and he alone—had ensnared himself into the absolute entanglement that had choked him into this corner. There was no escape now, but at least he didn't have to fight his way through it any more. Thinking of how his father had treated him as a child made him suddenly feel very regretful about how he had used Annie to earn money for him. He'd pushed her into something worse than a maze—for her there really wasn't a way out. He'd been even more rotten than his dad in that way. He thought for the first time how he would have felt in the situation she was in. It was way scarier than a cornfield. What a creep he was! And yet, Gina was so nice to him tonight. Maybe that was why he could finally recognize how unfair he had been to Annie.

"Are you Jack Collins?" asked the officer, with his hand on his revolver.

"Yes," Jack assented as he tried to pull himself out of both the negative maze of his childhood and the positive, captivating thoughts of Gina back into the melody of locust chirruping in this warm, but pleasant, night in August that signaled the end of his life as he knew it now. Now he would have to face up to everything he had done and he knew it wasn't pretty.

"Mr. Collins, you are under arrest for kidnapping. I'm going to read you your Miranda Rights. You have the right to remain silent. Anything you say can and will be used against you in a court of law. You have the right to an attorney. If you cannot afford an attorney, one will be appointed for you."

Jack wasn't sure what to say anyway, so he said nothing as another officer snapped handcuffs around his wrists and led him into the back of the patrol car. He knew he couldn't afford an attorney but he didn't even say that yet. As soon as he was shut in the back of the police vehicle though, Jack began to feel stressed out, despite the sense of relief that he previously experienced. His fear of entrapment returned with a wallop that left him nearly numb there in the car seat. This new realization that he was no longer a free man hit him as hard as the fist punched into his face earlier in the evening. Yes, he was both numb and aching—in true pain.

After arriving at the jail, he was processed in the entry area— searched, fingerprinted, photographed, and examined by medical staff —who gave him some medication for his head injury. He was also given prison attire and toiletries. His anxiety worsened as he was led into a cell with a cot hanging from the wall and a metal toilet and hand wash bowl mounted to another wall. The barred cell door had a horizontal slit for food trays but left one whole side of the cell open to the view of anyone that passed by. A waif of astringent floor cleaner overridden by a moldy, musty odor that permeated everything flooded over Jack and left him more than slightly nauseated.

It was now very late at night, and he felt exhausted but he couldn't fall sleep in that cell with all the noises, smells, and proximity of prisoners in other units. His head hurt, and the chorus of snoring from other cells really irritated him. He now appreciated the quiet and calm of that decrepit farm house he had rented. But his whole situation was the true culprit in his insomnia. How was this any worse than what he had done to Annie? It wasn't—he had locked her in too. And she didn't even have a throne or sink. And he didn't have anyone preying on him —at least not yet—but he had heard about what happened lots of times in jails, and he might become the same sort of victim that Annie had been. At least hers were of the opposite sex; if it happened to him that would not be the case. He shuddered; what would happen to him now? He wished he could just end it all but he certainly had nothing on him or in the cell to accomplish that feat. The Processor had told him that he would have an arraignment the next morning, and asked if he had a lawyer he wanted to contact. He didn't though and didn't have money for either a lawyer or bail and had no relatives or friends who might help him out or who he needed to contact.

"It's just me, and I'm dead broke," were the few words he had told the balding, male Processor at the Reception Center of the jail.

"Well, the court will appoint a public attorney for you tomorrow at the arraignment then," the official had explained. "I know you are charged with kidnapping, but there may be other charges as well. You'll find out tomorrow."

Jack must have fallen asleep in his cell for at least a little bit though because he woke with a jerk when a guard called out "Breakfast" and banged on the bars of his cell door with something made of metal. He asked Jack to get up and take the tray he was handing him through the slot. Jack retrieved the tray and drank the lukewarm coffee, but the sulfury smelling, scrambled eggs and limp toast didn't tempt him at all. He climbed back onto the cot and shut his eyes, but now he also had that eggy smell from his food tray irritating him. Later the guard returned to take the tray and told him his arraignment was scheduled for 1:00, so they would serve him lunch early about 11:45, and he should be ready to go to the courtroom by 12:30.

Judge Clarice Newman—an efficient-looking woman he thought —with her hair pulled back from her face, was presiding over Jack's arraignment and told him he was charged with kidnapping, commercial sexual exploitation of a child, and second-degree murder. She also named a public defender for Jack—a scrawny looking, young lawyer named Hugh Douglas.

"How do you plead to the charges against you?" Judge Newman asked.

The lawyer rapidly stood and addressed the judge before Jack could say anything regarding the charges.

"Your Honor, I request a chance to speak with the accused before he pleads to the charges."

The judge honored Douglas' request and granted 45 minutes before the court would reconvene, so Jack and Douglas stepped into a small side chamber with a wooden table and several chairs. Douglas indicated he should sit and explained that they needed to work fast. He asked if Jack was guilty of the crimes and was rather surprised that Jack admitted so readily that he was. He asked Jack to recount his version of what had happened. He also wanted to know if there were any complicating factors or anyone else that could also be implicated in the crimes.

"Yeah, I'm guilty of all those things and now I feel awful 'bout 'em. Maybe if I can work in prison to send money to that little girl, I wanna do it," Jack said. "And yeah, I can tell ya 'bout who I got her from and the creeps here that used her. There's a website for all that I can show ya. I know I'm a creep too though and I am guilty."

Douglas asked Jack to explain in more detail about how he had acquired the child and if he had ever tried to get money from anyone in exchange for her. When Jack told him how his ex-friend Duke gave her to him in exchange for a debt, but that he had tried to get money from customers for her sexual services, Douglas thought that wasn't technically kidnapping.

"What we're talking about sounds more like commercial sexual exploitation of a child—CSEC. You didn't really abduct her from anyone. Maybe we can nullify that kidnapping charge. Every little bit helps. What about the murder accusation? Were you responsible for that guy's death?"

"Yeah, I hit him. He was runnin' on my road when I came home dead drunk that evening. I hit him before I knew it. I hadn't planned to do it, but I did it anyway. I was afraid of him—afraid he was gonna tell the police I had the girl. He made me lose my temper one night at the bar where I worked and made me lose my job. But I really wish I hadn't killed him," Jack said, running his hands through his hair and shaking his still-aching head.

"Is there anything else you should plead innocent to?"

"Nah, I did it all. I'm guilty. I just wanna get it over with."

"Well, perhaps your willingness to cooperate with the prosecution will at least get you some leniency. The charges against you are very serious though. I think we're talking about at least a hard 25 years in prison, according to the grid—perhaps more—even with concessions," advised Douglas. "But dropping the kidnapping charge would help. We need to get the Prosecutor in here now to try to bargain with him before it's time to see the Judge again."

After returning to the courtroom, Hugh Douglas relayed to Judge Clarice Newman that Jack Collins was ready to plead guilty to all counts except for kidnapping and that the Prosecutor had agreed to drop that charge. But he stressed that Jack also wanted to cooperate with law officials to identify others who were involved in the CSEC charges, and that the Prosecutor was willing to make some considerations for the extra information Jack could supply about others implicated in the sexual exploitation crimes. Both he and Jack relayed what had happened and briefly described what additional information Jack could reveal.

The judge conferred with the Prosecutor and said she'd work with the prosecution about a downward departure from the grid after Jack's information was checked out. They explained to Jack that his cooperation might mean possibly shortening his sentence time in prison. Then she arranged to schedule another date to sentence him after all the investigation was complete. In the meantime, Judge Newman said she wanted Jack to undergo counseling in the jail for his alcohol abuse and also to participate in a program called *Yoga 4 Change* that met several times a week both in the jail and in the area prisons. She advised him that strict cooperation in those two programs could shorten his prison sentence and recommended that he take those opportunities seriously.

"Yoga, what the hell?" Jack muttered to himself as he left the courtroom with the jail guard. "I don't know what the hell that has to do with me—stretching and skinny tights. Stupid, I'd say. I guess I could use the booze counseling though."

28

Anita

August 4–5, 2018

I AM IN VERY DARK, DEEP WATER. There are dirty, disposable cups and pieces of paper and plastic that float by me. I am scared. I know there is something near me, looking for me, but the water is so dark that I cannot see it. I look all around me. I want to escape, but I'm not sure which way to go. The murky water hides whatever is looking for me, and it also is very hard to breathe. My heart is beating fast. I can hear my chest thumping loud and fast and I know that the thing looking for me can hear it too. Suddenly something very big swims past me. It swims all around me. I turn around struggling to see what it is and what it will do, trying at the same time to get away. As I look back in the other direction, I see it. It is looking right at me—a gigantic shark with sharp, bloody, dirty teeth. It swims to me and opens its mouth. The teeth are long and jagged—like knives of different sizes—and they are dripping with blood. I open my mouth too and bare my teeth and growl at it, but the shark isn't scared of me, and its teeth are much bigger than mine. The shark comes nearer, opening its mouth even wider. I know this shark will hurt me and make me bleed; I scream and scream, but the dirty water comes into my mouth and makes me gag and cough.

"Gross! That is soooo disgusting! Phew! It stinks! You little creep; you just vomited all over your bed."

I hear a girl yelling about vomit and I open my eyes. A light is on next to one of the beds near the door, and she is standing near the bed. The girls in the other beds are awake and sitting up as well. It is true— it stinks horribly, and I have vomited all over myself and the bed.

"Yuck," says another girl in the bunk next to mine. "This is really gross! Ms. Nelson! Ms. Nelson," she yells, "we need help!"

Within a few minutes, the overhead lights in the room turn on, and the assistant to Ms. Nelson, Sarah, hurries into our room.

"What's going on?" Sarah demands.

"The new girl just puked," one girl reports.

Everyone begins talking at once, saying it smells and asking Sarah to take me out of their room.

"Okay. That's enough!" says Sarah. "I think I'd better get Ms. Nelson."

Sarah leaves, and both she and Ms. Nelson return within a few minutes. Ms. Nelson, wearing blue pajamas with her hair all tangled, heads over to me and feels my forehead with her cool, rough hand.

"Oh, my! You are burning up with fever. We need to get you to the clinic. Are you okay to walk into the other room, Anita?"

"No. Not okay…dizzy," I say before I vomit again.

There is another chorus of oohs and yucks and grosses, but I don't even care; I am sooo dizzy.

I hear Ms. Nelson tell Sarah to have the staff clean up the room right away. She also said that they probably should have put me in the clinic from the beginning since I am scheduled to go there in the morning for physical and mental evaluations.

"Now the others have another reason to pick on her—in addition to being from a different culture. I think we'd better find a foster care situation as soon as possible," Ms. Nelson comments quietly to Sarah as they stand near my bed.

I know where I could go to be safe—*Virgen* Cler would keep me safe.

29

Ana López de Domínguez

August 3, 2018

ANA NEARLY DRAGGED HERSELF back toward where she had been living at the widow Lupe's house. It had been a very exhausting and disheartening day at work. Nothing had seemed to go right; all the orders came out slowly, and everyone was decidedly impatient to get their food—much like her own life of tedious waiting with no news about Anita to nourish her. But at least her customers had received what they had wanted in the end, while that was not happening in her own life. Essentially nothing had happened. It was as if Anita had dissolved into thin air. After all, it had been nearly three whole months since she had been waiting here to get any news at all of Anita. And there had been nothing—not one word, not one hint. As Ana walked along the streets of Ciudad Juárez, even the beautiful *palo verde* trees, with their yellow-green canopy of soft leaves did not cheer her. The day was hot, but the high desert climate was not unbearable. Ana, however, felt distinctly uncomfortable and irritable. Even her own odor, her clothes and hair saturated with the smells of tamales and grease and peppers, repulsed her today even more than it did most days. The restaurant where she worked, like several others in Ciudad Juárez, definitely catered to the tourists' expectation of Mexican food, and smelling those same strong odors of fried food everyday cloyed her sensibilities.

She used her key to enter the gated plaster wall surrounding Lupe's small beige house. It was obvious that the walled entry and house had seen better days, but it was nothing that could not be fixed with a little maintenance. Since Lupe's husband had died though, she had told Ana that she hadn't had the energy or funds to make many repairs. Lupe was in her late sixties and, understandably, rather consistently pessimistic about her future life and life in general—a fact that didn't help Ana's attitude about her own problem. Lupe always comported herself in a very kindhearted way toward Ana though and frequently told Ana that she not only appreciated the funds she was contributing with her rent but, also, Ana's companionship in her home.

"*Muy buenas tardes, Ana,*" greeted Lupe exuberantly as Ana entered.

"*Muy buenas,*" replied Ana with less enthusiasm than normal.

She told Lupe that she was really exhausted and wanted to take a quick shower and stretch out on her bed for a moment. She went into her room to get clean clothes and then hurried into the bathroom to shower, wanting nothing but to rinse off the odors of food and then to lie down. Subsequently, clean, with her wet hair wrapped in a towel, she went into her room and collapsed onto the bed. Only moments later her phone rang.

"*¿Hola? ¿Eres tú, Rosa?*" answered Ana as she quickly sat up after seeing her sister Rosa's phone number flash across the screen of her ringing phone.

"*Sí, Ana, soy yo, Rosa.* Ana, listen, there was a caller earlier who left a message for me while I was at work. I just called her back—she's a woman named Claire here in the US who says she has found Anita."

"*Rosa, ay Dios, gracias a Dios.* I thought this day would never come! Is Anita okay? She is still alive and ...? Oh, I can't believe it. At last! Where is she? How did this lady find her? Is she a policewoman?"

"Slow down, Ana. I think Anita's fine, but... I don't know if I can tell you," Rosa began to sob into her phone.

"Tell me what, Rosa? I'm imagining the very worst now even though you have said she is fine. What can't you tell me? You need to tell me no matter what it is. I have waited too long and must know." Ana held onto the foot *milagro* dangling from her neck and said a silent prayer.

"Yes," sputtered Rosa, "but she is so young."

"Rosa, calm yourself! You must tell me what has happened!" Ana nearly screamed with hysteria herself before rubbing her fairy foot charm again.

"Perhaps you should be seated to hear this. Claire said the police took Anita into a facility for juveniles to protect her until they could get in touch with you, but that she seemed fine," Rosa sniffed and paused for a moment, stopping to blow her nose. "However, Ana, Claire said she rescued Anita from a house where a man had her locked inside."

"What? How did he get her and why was she locked in his house? *Ay, Dios,* my poor baby girl!" Ana was already sitting on her bed, but her knees and arms still went weak when she heard Anita had been a captive. "Did… did he hurt her?"

Rosa went on to explain everything that Claire had told her, but added that Claire really didn't know all the details yet either.

"I'm not sure… I don't know if he hurt her physically himself but, Ana, I don't know how to tell you this… but I do need to tell you. Apparently he… he was using her for *el tráfico sexual de niños.*"

"*¡No!*" screamed Ana. "*¡No, no, no! ¡No puede ser!*" Ana continued to scream and wail.

"*Ana, tranquílate*; you too must calm yourself so we can help Anita. You are right; neither of us is any good at all to her like this, and we won't be able to make a plan if we are hysterical."

Ana agreed and sobered herself even though she had tears streaming from her eyes; her hands and knees and whole body were shaking. Rosa proceeded to tell Ana that Claire was concerned about Rosa's status in the US and didn't want to cause her problems as well. She had also told Rosa that she had considered calling the migration center in Ciudad Juárez—she assumed that Ana would have been deported there. Claire could then tell the police she had been able to contact Ana through the migration center. That way she would not have to involve Rosa when she talked to the police. Claire had already looked up the Juárez *Casa del Migrante* online, Rosa told Ana.

"*Sí, es verdad*. They definitely know how to contact me; in fact, I am in the *Casa del Migrante* nearly every day, helping out, because they have assisted me and so many others so much. I live just two blocks away from it," Ana said as she looked for her shoes and begin to prepare to leave.

"*Excelente*. Can you go there now? I will call Claire back and tell her to contact you there in a short while. Also it might help to have them there to interpret anything you might not understand in English when Claire calls you."

Ana agreed, and they said good-bye, promising to call each other again as soon as either had any new information. Pulling the towel off her still damp hair and grabbing her purse, Ana told Lupe she had an emergency and would be back later. She headed out the door with renewed vigor and energy, even though she had previously been exhausted after waitressing the whole day. She nearly ran to *Casa del Migrante* and headed to the main office there, hastily greeting everyone as she rushed inside. She explained that she was awaiting a call from a woman in the US who was going to call her through their office about her lost child. Ana told them that the woman needed to contact her there so as not to implicate Ana's undocumented sister in the US. Pacing through the hallway and then finding small jobs she could help with as she hopefully anticipated a call, Ana waited. She did not have to wait long; she absolutely knew when the phone rang next in the *Casa del Migrante* that a woman named Claire was calling to talk to her. The volunteer who answered the phone, Ignacia, talked with Claire for quite some time in English, but it was evident that it was in regard to Ana. After writing some things down, Ignacia turned to Ana with a smile.

"*Ana, es para ti,*" Ignacia said as she held the telephone out toward Ana.

Ana answered expectantly, and Claire told her in slow, clear English that she had found her daughter and had talked with her sister Rosa. Claire also told Ana that she could help to arrange for Ana to come to the US to get Anita. Ana was more than welcome to stay in her home for as long as she needed to during the process, Claire invited.

"Ana, I know that there is a special visa called a T-Visa that the center there is going to help you get so you can come here. Then, if you and your daughter will help to testify about what happened to her," Claire told her, "I believe you can stay and even work in the US for four years. You could also even apply for citizenship during that time if you decide you want to stay here. Anita told me a little about why you had come to the US, but I don't think she even understood that completely."

"No, she no understands everything. I never tell her that her *papá* was killed," Ana relayed and then paused. "Rosa just tells me some of what happens to her. I am so worried about her."

"I plan to go to visit her tomorrow and tell her you are coming, Ana. She will be so happy. The lady at your center there, Ignacia, I think, told me they could arrange for you to come to the US on a T-Visa after they talk with the police here. I will speak to the policeman again and tell them I have found you and that you want to arrange to come," said Claire. "Is it okay for you to leave and come here as soon as they can arrange everything?"

"Yes, of course," replied Ana. "I only wait here to find my Anita. I come as soon as they let me."

In the next few days, Ana had several meetings with Rafael and also with the administrators of the *Casa del Migrante*, with whom the detectives at the Olathe Police Department had been communicating. Together they were arranging for the T-Visas for both Ana and Anita. Ana was also in constant communication with Claire about Anita. Claire was visiting Anita regularly, and Ana learned that Anita had been in the clinic of the facility recuperating from a bad case of influenza. The Olathe Police had also checked Claire's records and spoke with Ana's lawyer, Rafael, about making Claire a guardian ad litem for Anita so she could get out of the juvenile facility. Within less than two weeks, the police had procured a T-Visa for Ana, hoping to get her there as soon as possible to help Anita testify about the perpetrators of the crimes against her.

30

Claire de lune

August 3–5, 2018

AFTER SAYING GOODBYE to Anita's mother I set down my phone, feeling weak with emotion. I literally sensed the energy vibrations from Ana as I talked with her briefly about how I had found her daughter. Then I had suggested to her that she should make arrangements with her lawyer there to come to the US. I also informed her that I would be calling the police officer who helped us and that I was relatively sure he would be contacting her there soon.

As soon as I had recovered a bit from the intensity of that conversation, I drank a big glass of water and ate a few cashews to tide over my hunger and calm down my shakiness. Then I got out Officer Gerney's card and picked up my phone to call him. I still had to be careful; I didn't want to reveal anything about Anita's aunt, who was even now an illegal immigrant. The way things were now with regard to immigration, I really did not want to risk endangering Rosa. Anita's family had suffered enough lately without getting Rosa into trouble as well. So I would only tell Gerney about calling the *Casa del Migrante* and talking with Ana there.

Apparently the number I dialed went directly to him, because he immediately answered the phone.

"Officer Gerney, this is Claire Schmidt. I'm calling to let you know that I have spoken with Anita's mother and have a number for you to call her."

"How did you find her so quickly?" Gerney asked after he cleared his throat.

I wondered if he suspected something fishy about the speed with which I had contacted her but I tried to simply keep myself calm.

"Because you mentioned the migrant center for Ciudad Juárez, I looked that up, called there, and asked if they knew Ana López de Domínguez, like Anita told us. Her mother, Ana, was actually right there in the facility when I called. Evidently she has done a lot of volunteering there while she's been waiting for word about her daughter." I glanced out at the darkening sky, thinking both of how hungry I was and the fact that Jim would be arriving home tomorrow evening.

"So her mother is staying at that center?" Gerney asked. I could imagine him annotating that in his little notebook.

"Actually, she rents a room from someone else, but she goes to the center very frequently to volunteer, she told me. Ana gave me the number of her cell phone too, so I have that as well as the number of the center. And she gave me her lawyer's number. He volunteers at the *Casa del Migrante* as well, but she said he has his own private practice in Ciudad Juárez," I explained to Gerney.

I also told him that her lawyer, Rafael Gómez, according to what Ana had said, had been working with an attorney at the American Immigration Council who had filed a suit against the US government on behalf of a group of immigrant parents seeking asylum who were separated from their children. They were suing the government for abuse and cruel treatment. In addition, I explained that she told me her lawyer was also suing individually on her behalf regarding the ongoing separation from her child. Gerney, in turn, told me he would try to contact both Ana and Rafael Gómez right away, despite the late hour.

After I hung up, I found some leftovers in the refrigerator to eat. Now I felt more tired than hungry but I knew I needed to eat something. Jim called while I was consuming my snack to let me know he would be home the next evening in time for dinner. I was so emotionally exhausted that I didn't feel like telling him about my whole adventure over the phone. Tomorrow evening would be soon enough.

"Are you upset with me?" he asked in a worried tone.

"No, I'm just very tired. I can't wait to see you tomorrow though; I've truly missed you in so many ways." And I definitely meant all of that.

After saying good-bye, I drew myself a warm bath and poured some lavender Epsom salt bubble bath into the water. The bubbles, meager at first, continued to foam and filled the tub with their fragrant effervescence, which thickened and mounted up the sides of the tub as I undressed and slipped into the water. The foam edged over the top of the tub. Perhaps I put in too much bubble bath! But it felt so relaxing as well as vitalizing. Suddenly though I burst into laughter as a thought came into my head. There were definitely advantages to having the ghost of Antoine return to his other realm: now, at least, I did not need to worry if either his visible or invisible form had floated into the room with me as I bathed or whatever. Sorry, Antoine, but I do need some privacy. I went to bed feeling more optimistic than I had in days. Sleep overtook me before I had finished even one page of the novel I was reading.

Just before seven the next morning, I woke feeling refreshed and quite relaxed. The sun was shining, and I knew deep in my bones that everything was going to be okay but that I needed to get in touch with Anita right away. I immediately called the Juvenile Detention Center where Officer Gerney told me they had taken Anita the night before. Someone named June answered, so I told her my name before I inquired about Anita and asked when I could visit her, adding that Officer Gerney had given me the information to call.

"Just one moment, please. Let me get her file," June answered curtly before she placed me on hold.

While I waited I used my laptop to look up the family law firm in Olathe that Officer Gerney had recommended to me. He said I should contact Devon Newton at Newton and Andrews Family Law, because they were also involved in migrant law. I found the phone number and wrote it down, as well as the address. Their office did not open until nine, but it seemed like they worked on Saturdays. Good!

"Ms. Schmidt," June returned to the line, "Anita has put you on her visitor list, so you can apply to visit her. You should schedule your visit at least a day in advance. If you go to pigeonly.com you can apply to be a visitor and also request a visitation slot. It's 'pigeon,' like the bird, with 'ly' on the end. Since you are on her visitation list, I can also tell you that Anita was admitted to our on-site clinic early this morning."

"Your clinic? Is she ill?" I asked, significantly alarmed. "Was she harmed?"

"I really don't know many details about her condition except that she was admitted with a fever around 4:00 AM. You might also apply on the Pigeonly site to call her there in the clinic."

After I thanked her and hung up, I immediately went to the Pigeonly site and applied as a visitor and requested an appointment for the next day, even though it would be Jim's first day home. I couldn't get the phone call portion to connect me though. I still wanted to see Anita as soon as possible and was extremely disappointed that I'd probably have to wait until tomorrow.

The nine o'clock opening of the law firm gave me time to dress and prepare myself some coffee and a smoothie before I called the firm. I took my liquid breakfast outside to the screened-in porch to drink. The day was going to be hot again, but it was nice to be outside in the fresh air, and it reminded me of the incredible adventure I had the day before as I ventured through the wooded area to find Anita. It still seemed unreal. And I felt strangely lonely knowing that Antoine would not be visiting me or aiding me anymore.

At nine on the dot, I called the Newton and Andrews Family Law Firm to get an appointment with Devon Newton to talk with her about Anita and to apply to be the guardian ad litem. I could hardly believe my luck when the male receptionist informed me that—"of course"—Devon Newton was seeing clients and he said that there had been a cancellation; he wondered if I could be there by 9:30. I said I could and hurried to brush my teeth, apply some lipstick, and grab my purse before heading to my car.

I barely remember the drive over there, except that I amazingly found their office without any problem. The receptionist, a mustached, young man named Derek, showed me right into Devon Newton's office. Again, my mind was so occupied with the issue at hand, I barely noticed anything about the office except the shiny wooden desk and the gray upholstered chairs in front of it. A man and woman were standing behind the desk looking at some papers when I went in. I was totally surprised, however, when I realized that the attractive African-American woman behind the desk was Devon Newton, because I had assumed that Devon Newton would be a man. Even I, with my feminist bent, had a preconceived idea of who the lawyer would be.

Ms. Newton smiled as she greeted me and asked me to sit in one of the gray chairs in front of the desk. Newton was dressed in a classic, light gray suit with a blue blouse and her shiny, black hair spiraled out around her head in a chic, modified Afro style. When she flashed her beautiful smile again, I couldn't help but think of Michelle Obama—

they both were lawyers, after all. But Devon Newton was a much more petite woman than the former First Lady—perhaps only 5'2". Newton's diminutive size did not diminish her air of strength and power however; she radiated energy and confidence.

She introduced me to her associate, another family immigration lawyer, Scott Andrews, a man in his early forties, with thick, combed-back hair and a fair complexion with pinkish cheeks. He wore unobtrusive wire-rimmed glasses and an amazing, lime green striped tie with his white shirt and dark suit.

"It's so nice to meet you, Ms. Schmidt," said Andrews as he elegantly nodded and motioned for me to sit down. "Well, I'll give these clients a call," he said, turning back to Newton, and then excused himself.

"Scott and I like to both be present when we first meet to a new client, if possible, so that someone familiar with a new case is always available in case the other is not for some reason," Newton explained as we sat down.

"So tell me about what is going on. Derek mentioned that you wanted ad litem status for an immigrant child," she said as she grabbed her laptop from the desktop to take notes.

After I explained the whole situation to her, Newton asked if I could call Ana's number in Mexico.

"Since she already knows your number she will be more likely to answer," Newton said. "You can talk with her for a moment and see if she wants to speak with me."

After greeting Ana, I told her I was in the lawyer Devon Newton's office and that she wanted to talk with her. As it happened, Ana was already in the *Casa del Migrante* volunteering, and Rafael Gómez was also working there that day. Ana was able to have the attendant at the desk buzz Rafael to see if she could interrupt his appointments to talk briefly with her and with Newton. I told her Newton would call her right back on the law firm phone in the meantime.

Newton began speaking in what sounded to me like very fluent Spanish as soon as she called Ana back. After turning her phone to speaker mode, Newton let me hear the conversation too, briefly translating for me from time to time. After a few minutes, Ana was admitted to Rafael's office, and he joined in on the conversation. Ana and Rafael then agreed to engage Newton's services to represent both Anita and

Ana in the US. Newton then emailed a document to the *Casa del Migrante*, which Ana and Rafael both signed and emailed back shortly after we hung up. Throughout the entire phone conversation though, I was impressed by Newton's ability to speak so fluently and professionally. I understood the general tone of what was happening, but Newton kept summarizing the important parts for me. She also asked me to contribute information or ideas at times and told me how helpful it was to have the acquiescence of Ana and her lawyer with regard to my guardian ad litem request. After we finished speaking with Ana and Rafael, Newton called the Juvenile Detention Center as Anita's lawyer and found out that Anita had been admitted to the clinic with the flu and was also being examined and treated for sexual abuse. Anita was scheduled to visit with a counselor later that morning. My knees felt weak again when I heard about her condition. But Newton arranged for both of us to visit her at the clinic at 2:00.

"I believe I can cancel some other things today," she added as she looked over her appointment schedule, "because I think it is very important that we go there together as soon as possible. That way, you can reassure Anita that her mother will be arriving soon. I'll also push to get your guardian ad litem status expedited. It will be very helpful for her to be staying with someone she trusts until her mother arrives. By the way, please call me Devon."

"Okay, Devon it is," I concurred. "And please call me Claire. I agree that we should see her ASAP, and I really appreciate the changes to your schedule to make that possible. By the way, I'm absolutely envious of your fluency in Spanish, Devon. How did you learn to speak it so well?"

"Well, I studied it in high school and university, but then I went to Spain for a study abroad program on a scholarship when I was a senior at KU. I knew I loved speaking it while I was there and I loved being in Barcelona but I couldn't even imagine at that point that it would be so essential in my career. At least half of my clients hire me for my ability to speak Spanish," Devon said as she touched a small, colorful, ceramic lizard on her desk. "This is a lizard from Antoni Gaudí's *Parque Güell* in Barcelona. He's my lucky totem."

After discussing more of the details of the case and Devon's strategy for dealing with it, we agreed to meet at 1:35 to go together to the Juvenile Detention Center. Devon had her assistant, Derek, re-schedule a few appointments that she had that afternoon—one of them Scott would handle, and the other was going to work out better for Monday anyway, she said. Then we shook hands, and I left to let her see her next client. It was just after 11:00 when I walked out the door and decided to go to buy Anita a few articles of clothing before we went to visit her. I stopped in a Gap store for kids and bought her underwear, pink striped pajamas, a couple of tops, and a pair of shorts. I also bought a pair of leather flip-flops, hoping I had the right size. Luckily, I had a protein bar in my purse, which I ate on the way back to the law office to meet up with Devon. She met me in the parking lot, and I drove to the Detention Center while Devon gave me directions. Soon we were walking into the clinic of the Detention Center, and I saw Anita, small and curled up in a clinic bed. She woke as soon as we approached her bed.

"*Virgen* Cler," she said with a sigh and a smile as she weakly tried to push herself to sitting.

"Hi, Anita. How are you feeling?" I asked. Then I introduced her to Devon and told her that we had both just talked with her mother and had arranged for Devon to be their lawyer.

"*Encantada, Anita. ¿Cómo estás?*" Devon said and then continued to explain in Spanish, pausing and briefly telling me in English to be sure I understood too, that she would be helping to bring Anita's mother here and that she was arranging for Anita to stay with me instead of at the Detention Center.

It was obvious that just hearing the lawyer speak so confidently in Spanish was reassuring to Anita.

"Anita, I spoke with your mother last night, and Devon—Ms. Newton—and I talked to her this morning," I told her as I held her feverish hand. "She is coming here as soon as we get some travel papers and arrangements completed. She says she loves you and can't wait to see you."

Anita smiled the most beautiful smile and murmured something to herself that I didn't understand. She looked very relieved though. Among other things, Devon also explained to Anita that, as soon as she could arrange the legal matters, Anita could stay with me. When we left her, she looked so much happier and was enchanted with her new clothing. Devon promised Anita she would be working to get my guardian ad litem status quickly confirmed, and I told Anita good-bye.

"Rest and get well," I told her, giving her a little hug. "I'll be back to see you tomorrow. Don't worry, Anita, things will get better now."

Anita rested back on her pillow and closed her eyes. She did look more peaceful. As Devon and I checked out of the Center and walked to her car, she explained more of the details about what would happen next with Anita. It would take until at least Monday or, more likely, Tuesday or Wednesday to get the guardian ad litem status confirmed. I dropped her off at her office, and she said she'd be in touch with me soon.

By 4:30 I was on my way home and as I drove I thought again of Jim and the fact that he was arriving that evening. I realized how very eager I was to see him. Now that I had actually found Anita, Jim could not possibly doubt my sanity or intuition. Besides that, finding Anita had made me realize some things about myself that I had been denying or covering up. The grief and guilt that I felt about my sister's death had been like a giant boulder in my life, preventing me from feeling almost everything—including my love for Jim. Perhaps I was too worried that even his love would be taken from me. I heard my phone ping, signaling a text message, but had to wait until I pulled into our driveway to dig it out of my purse.

"My plane arrived. Waiting on the runway for a gate. Should be home in 1 1/2 hrs. Love you!!" Jim wrote.

What could I make quickly for dinner? I started to prepare a salad and decided to fix a tuna pasta dish with zucchini, sun-dried tomatoes, and onions sautéed in olive oil and some tomato paste and goat cheese to complete the sauce. I wanted to have plenty of time to talk with Jim, so I worked quickly and stuck a bottle of Chardonnay into a wine cooler with ice water before quickly freshening up my lipstick and hair. I was just finishing the sauce and had the water boiling for the pasta when I heard Jim open the garage and pull inside. He came in, looking a little travel weary with a slight growth of beard—he obviously hadn't shaved or had any meetings today. But he still looked great in his casual blue shirt with the collar open. He dropped his suitcase by the door as he entered and smiled broadly at me.

"Hi, Claire, darling. You look beautiful, and, boy, have I ever missed you!" he said as he pulled me toward him and gave me a lingering kiss.

I kissed him back and felt so relieved to see him. I realized that my own lack of awareness of my feelings had been an obstacle for a long time—like a heavy backpack that I wasn't aware that I was carrying until I took it off. I sensed a lightness and hopefulness that I hadn't felt in months. And I was absolutely confident that once I began to confide in him I'd feel even more joyful and optimistic.

"Wow! Whatever you're making smells fantastic," he said as he looked into the saucepan where the pasta sauce was simmering. "And I'm really starved—all I've had since my skimpy breakfast is a very small sandwich on the plane."

I poured us both a glass of wine.

"To us," Jim toasted as he looked into my eyes.

"Yes, to us! I'm so glad to have you home again. And do I ever have some interesting things to tell you! And some important things about us too," I said while I began to finish up the dinner.

"Hmmm. I can't wait to hear. You seem more animated than I've seen you in a while," he whispered into my ear while he stood behind me and gave me a quick, but suggestive, hug.

During dinner I told him the story about rescuing Anita, about her being taken into custody, and about talking with her aunt and mother. Also I explained how I had contacted the lawyer and our visit to the detention center clinic today. Jim sat there wide-eyed, interjecting a few questions when I went too fast.

"I don't understand how you knew about all of this just by driving by that house," Jim said with his bottom jaw dropped a bit in amazement. "I know you are pretty intuitive and that you've done research on this subject for your last novel, but I can't believe you ventured into that rescue all on your own. I'm—well—incredulous."

I hesitated again before telling him about Antoine. Again I wondered if he'd think I was just crazy, but I really needed to confide in him. It was really important to me—as if I had given myself permission to free myself—to trust. So I took a deep breath and looked out toward the night sky. The moon now was waning in almost its last quarter. It seemed incredible that just over a week ago all this began with Antoine's other-worldly visit. Was it all really real? I inhaled deeply again and then began to relate the whole story, bit by bit, about Antoine. The part of the rescue when Antoine had helped us off the collapsing ladder must have sounded especially fantastical.

"I'm sorry I couldn't tell you this before but I was afraid you'd think I was losing it, going crazy, or maybe just totally nuts. I also didn't want you to worry about me while you were gone," I entreated, thinking how maybe I should have explained at least part of my experience earlier.

"From the sound of all this, I guess I should have been worried," Jim said as he took my hand. "You were living an Isabel Allende moment. I feel a bit hurt though that you didn't trust me enough to tell me."

"Could you have gone on your trip knowing what I just told you?"

"No, probably not," Jim rubbed his hand on his forehead and shook his head, looking down into his lap.

"Don't worry, Jim," I said, rising from my chair to rub the back of his neck. "I think it all was supposed to happen this way. Not until all this took place did I realize some important things about myself that were keeping me from connecting with you better in our marriage. It was like I was caged too—by my fear of what had happened to my sister."

Jim looked at me quizzically and then I proceeded to tell him about what I had realized after rescuing Anita. Never, before my strong feeling of tenderness toward that immigrant child, had I realized how much my own sister's death was affecting my present life. I had been afraid to let myself become too attached to anyone.

"That fear of losing someone I loved made me afraid to have a child of my own. It was also preventing me from being too close to you," I explained to him. "I guess I thought that if I kept everything at a distance I could prevent being hurt again if something bad happened."

"And you figured all that out after you found Anita?" he asked in a rather dubious tone.

"Yes, it all hit me sort of like a bombshell when I realized that I really didn't want the police to take Anita. She reminded me a lot of my sister when she was younger. Then everything started falling into place. I really hope we can be foster parents for Anita, at least until her mother arrives."

"Well, of course," Jim replied, looking confused.

"But I also really hope we can have our own."

"Our own?" he asked, even more perplexed.

"Our own child. I hope we can have a child like you always wanted."

"Wow! This really is an evening of surprises. You have just made me an even happier man. I'll understand though," he added quickly, "if you need to change your mind."

Then he took me into his arms. I've written about people who felt like I did in that moment, but I couldn't remember the last time, if ever, when I felt so totally secure and happy, but also liberated. It truly seemed like an episode taken from fiction.

31

Ana López de Domínguez

Late August 2018

ANA BUCKLED HER SEAT BELT and sat back with a partial sigh of relief as the last few passengers got on the plane. Even though she had finally made it this far, her breath was still short, her heart felt like it was beating in her throat, and her nerves were on edge. She really couldn't believe she was sitting on a jet in El Paso, Texas where, after a plane change in Dallas, she would be headed for Kansas City. The *Casa del Migrante* and her lawyer there, Rafael Gómez, had made all the arrangements for her to get to her flight, including a very early morning car ride to cross the border and then to the airport. Rafael, with his dimpled smile, tried to calm and reassure her the entire way, and even accompanied her until she cleared security and headed toward her plane. At last she had all the papers she needed to get into the US, including a passport, a T-Visa, and other legal documents that proved she had every right in the world to be there. Soon she would see Anita! At last she would be with her darling daughter again! Claire had told her that she and Anita would be parked outside her gate at the airport in Kansas City to pick her up, which was so reassuring and yet so hard to believe after all this time. Ana glanced out at the tarmac, where airport personnel and carts of luggage were moving like large insects around the planes. The sun was high in the sky now, and Ana was glad she brought some tortillas with cheese in her purse to eat on the plane. She was hungry but too nervous to eat earlier—or even now.

"Madame, would you please put your bag under the seat for take off?" demanded the flight attendant in the aisle next to Ana's seat.

"*¿Cómo?* My bag? She… it is up there," responded Ana, a bit confused, and pointing toward the luggage compartment above.

"I mean the one in your lap—your purse—it needs to go under the seat in front of you. You can take it out again after we're in the air," the gray-haired attendant responded automatically. How many times did she have to remind passengers of this simple request?

"Oh, of course," Ana answered, a bit embarrassed—as if she should have known this basic rule—and quickly stuck her purse under the seat.

Within minutes, the plane began to move and head toward the runway. Not only was Ana nervous and excited to be headed to Kansas to see her daughter, but she also was extremely apprehensive because she had never flown before. As the plane taxied, she thought of the time when she and Diego had planned to take Anita to Florida to Disney World to celebrate her eighth birthday. They had saved up for the trip and had even made an appointment at the consulate to apply for their passports, for which Diego had filed all the necessary documents and paperwork. Together they investigated flights and hotels online after Anita went to bed at night. But when Ana mentioned the proposed trip to her brother Miguel, he looked affronted.

"Anita will be too fancy afterwards to play with her cousins," Miguel had complained.

At first Ana dismissed his words as pure sibling jealousy and even told him so, enflaming his anger. But later she thought about how impossibly expensive a trip like that would be for Miguel and Teresita and their five children. Since Teresita did not have an outside job, like Ana did, they had only one income, and seven family members would be much more expensive than three. They would even need more hotel rooms—it would be a crazy idea for them. In the end, Ana decided that her family ties were much more important to all of them than taking a trip to a fantasy world with cartoon characters. She apologized to Miguel, and he to her. She and Diego canceled their passport appointment at the consulate and gave up their searches for flights.

Instead, for Anita's birthday they took all her cousins, aunts, uncles, and grandparents to a street fair in a village near Chihuahua that featured many different varieties of *mole*: *mole poblano*, *pipián*, and almond *mole*, among others. For the kids there was a ferris-wheel, a merry-go-round, bumper cars, and scores of other activities. Anita and her cousins had such a joyous time together that Ana and Diego had never really regretted their decision not to go to Disney's theme park.

Now though, Ana realized that she and Anita would have had passports to at least enter the US after Diego was murdered. Perhaps she and Anita would never have been separated at the border; Anita wouldn't have been.... No, no, she wouldn't, *couldn't* think like that! But now Ana nervously did wish she had some experience flying and traveling in the US. Suddenly the plane dipped, and Ana's stomach rose up to her throat. They were on the edge of a thunderstorm, the pilot explained, and the flight would be a little bumpy for a while.

Ana held onto her *milagro* necklace again and chided herself for her regrets, cowardice, and what-ifs; she needed to be brave and optimistic. The foot charm again reminded her of their pilgrimage—she and Anita had embarked on what had turned out to be a treacherous journey. But the goal was for their safety and well-being; she needed to remember that and trust that God would guide her. She recalled again when she had accompanied her mother on her pilgrimage to the *Basilica de Nuestra Señora de Guadalupe* on that seemingly endless bus trip. Ana hadn't been able to imagine how her mother could stay so cheerful on such a tiresome journey, but she had. Ana thought again of listening to the homily at the mass in the basilica, when she finally had felt comforted. She brought back the priest's words again about how a pilgrimage meant stepping out of your comfort zone for a higher purpose. To do that, he said, we all have to make some kind of sacrifice, but that contributes to our growth. Ana had felt the sacrifice that took her out of her comfort zone then, and she most certainly felt it on their original journey and even now. But it all was definitely for a higher purpose, and she thanked God and also thanked Anita and Diego for this charm that reminded her once more of that.

But how could she help her daughter get over this horrible ordeal? That would not be a simple process. Nonetheless, she was so grateful for Claire and how she had helped both of them. Ana had asked Claire to be frank with her about Anita's condition, and Claire told her that Anita was seeing a therapist that Claire trusted and Anita liked very much. At first Anita was having nightmares that left her screaming in the night, but the frequency of those upsetting dreams had diminished. Claire had also been texting her photos of Anita and she had helped Anita call Ana every day since Anita had gone to stay with Claire and Jim. On those phone calls, Anita had been very quiet at first but was beginning to sound more normal. Surely everything would work out—

wouldn't it? Just last week when Anita called, she was so excited about a kitten that Jim had adopted for her. Claire told her that Jim thought Anita needed a friend she could hug whenever she wanted to. Anita had named the kitten Mía and couldn't say enough about her soft, sweet *gatita*. And now Anita was all excited about the beginning of school—and, of course, more than anything, that Ana was coming to be with her.

Yes, Anita would be okay; Ana trusted in that as she held onto her *milagro* charm.

32

Black Jack

September 2025

JACK NEATLY REROLLED AND REPLACED a yoga mat that one of the new prisoners had wadded up and stuffed onto the shelf. He totally understood why some of the men were uncooperative in the yoga class; he'd been there and done that himself. It had been six years now that he'd been in the pen and six years since he'd first been required to take the yoga classes. He had hated them at first—had thought they were stupid, queer, and ridiculous. All the *oms* and *namastes*—why didn't they just speak English? Jack had felt like a f-ing weirdo. So now he truly understood the rebellious attitude of the newbies. What he had a hard time understanding was how he himself had changed so much. How had he changed from an angry, lawbreaking, drunk to what he was now? And how was he so different? Well, he just didn't get so upset now; he felt peaceful and purposeful—which was quite a feat for a guy in prison. He'd even started teaching a lot of the yoga classes. *Yoga 4 Change* they called it, and lots of the judges were starting to require prisoners to participate in the classes. He was glad now that his judge had made him do it; he never would've done it on his own, but now he couldn't get enough of it. He'd not been a good student when he was in school; he'd thought that was stupid too. But now he was reading all the yoga books he could get his hands on through the interlibrary program the prison had. And every time an outside yoga instructor came to the prison, Jack was in the class and trying to learn all he could about the poses and what they did for people. He even learned that most of the poses—*asanas*—were designed for men and even Indian wrestlers. Who'd have known? He'd thought they were all stretches for skinny girls.

"Hey, Jack, we've got another new yogi-bogey for ya," said Gene, one of the prison guards. "He's gonna start tomorrow."

"Okay, Gene. Bring 'im to me," replied Jack as he finished organizing the equipment so Gene could lock the room and escort Jack back to his cell.

"It sure has made you a different bloke," said Gene, rubbing his steel gray crew-cut head with one hand before he locked the door. "Maybe I should start doin' it too," he laughed.

"Maybe ya should," Jack responded quietly.

Jack thought back to when he had first started to feel the peaceful effects of the yoga he was doing. One of the first things he arranged after he started teaching classes and doing other physical labor in the prison was to start sending checks to Anita. Now he couldn't believe he had used her like he had. He knew he could never really make it up to her, but he wanted her to know he was sorry about it and that he was trying. He'd even written her a letter to tell her that, and after a few months he had received a card from her addressed to Jack Collins on the envelope. Inside, in very neat script, it read:

Jack,
Thank you for your apology. You don't need to send me more money though.
Sincerely,
Anita.

He had saved that letter. It had made him feel so good that she had taken the time to answer him. He'd continued to send her as much money as he could though. He wrote back that he wanted her to have the money for school—that she was a very smart girl and needed to go to as much school as she could. Besides, continuing to send that to her helped him not to feel so guilty about what he had done to her. She deserved to have whatever he could earn for her. Yes, she was more like a kitten than a dog, as he had observed once back then when she was asleep. He himself was the dog—a nasty dog that is—but he was getting better now.

Also, he had written a letter to Gina and sent it to The Place Bar where she was working the night he had been beat up and then arrested. He'd wanted to thank her for being so nice to him that night. She had made him feel worthy and important for perhaps the first time in his life—at least that night she had thought he was worth giving up her dinner for him and that he was worth talking to like a friend. He was amazed when she wrote him back several months later—especially since the newspapers had published several stories about him being arrested—and then convicted—for second degree murder and commercial sexual exploitation of a child. Didn't she know what he had done? She did. In her second letter to him she asked him to explain in detail what he had done and why.

He wrote back—cautiously at first—explaining bits of what had happened. She continued to question him through the letters, but also revealed some things about herself. So they began a conversation through their letters about how he had ended up where he was, and how she had completed her GED and finally started classes two years ago in Criminal Justice at the community college. When he read that, at first he was taken aback.

"Why do you want to know all this stuff about me?" he wrote— the only words in the next communication he had written to her. Was she just trying to use him for a case study for her Criminal Justice or something? Maybe he didn't really want to tell her anything more about what he had done.

In her next letter, Gina explained that her dad had been in prison for while she was in jr. high and high school for embezzling money from the company he worked for. Neither he nor Gina had gotten along well with her mom, and Gina had missed him terribly while he was in prison. Her parents had separated even before he went to prison, and Gina had dropped out of high school. When her dad was finally released, Gina stayed with him more than with her mother. While she was living with him, her dad had explained a lot about why he had done what he did. Being in prison had taught him a lot about himself and the world, but he also needed to tell her about what he had done. During those conversations, he had realized that money was really the least important thing to him. Gina said that her dad's experience had intrigued her; and she had begun to understand herself better too as she talked with him. Also, what he had told her made her decide to get her GED so she could start studying Criminal Justice.

"For some reason, when I saw you coming in to The Place so often, you reminded me of how my dad was—so confused and lost before he was arrested and went to prison. You obviously hadn't even noticed me. But that night you got hurt I just wondered if I could be a helpful friend to you," she had explained. "My dad and I really helped each other just by talking things out. I thought maybe you might need someone to talk through whatever was bothering you."

Did she want another father figure? She was looking in the wrong place if that was what she wanted. But she had been both helpful and a friend. Maybe he was just being too suspicious. So he began to write to her about Anita—cautiously at first. He did want her to know about it though and he also needed her to know he was changing. After that he really began to enjoy writing to her—it was a relief to be able to tell someone how he felt. He told her about the yoga—she hadn't tried it yet but she wanted to. After they had been writing about a year—old-fashioned letter writing—she had asked if she could come to visit. Jack put her on his list of visitors—not that he had much of a list—but she was on it, and they talked about days that she might come.

It was late January of 2020 when the guard on his floor informed him that he had a visitor. As Ollie, in his long-sleeved blue-gray uniform shirt and dark pants, led him into the visitation area, Jack looked out at the cold, barren landscape. There was just a scattering of snow blowing across the prison yard; the sky was gray. The visitation area contained a bunch of compartments with glass windows that looked into the visitors' area. It was noisy with so many people talking, and the fluorescent lights overhead made a slight buzzing sound. Jack looked back at the officer, with his short brown hair and mainly grayish-white beard, as he led Jack into one of the booth-like compartments with beige painted walls and a single, round aluminum stool attached to the floor. There was a desk-height, Formica-covered shelf, above which was the glass window that looked into the visitors area, and a black phone receiver hung on the wall. When Jack looked through the window, he saw Gina sitting there, with her longish hair framing her face and wearing a lavender sweater; he momentarily held his breath. Was she really here to see him? It must be a mistake. Then she smiled at him and held her hand up to the glass. He sat and held his hand up to hers and picked up his phone. She did likewise, but neither of them said a word for a long several moments.

"Hi Gina, thanks for coming," he finally said and smiled back at her.

"Jack, how are you doing?" she asked, slowly getting back her composure and her normally talkative manner.

She said she hoped today was a good day to visit. Jack nodded. Then she asked him all sorts of questions about his meals there, his state of mind, his accommodations, and other things too. In between questions she brought in funny little stories about things that had happened in her life—like the lady in the grocery store who was convinced that she knew her. She even wanted to give Gina a bar of vanilla scented soap she was buying.

"Vanilla soap? Did she want ya to taste it too?" Jack laughed.

Gina began to laugh out loud and shook her head "no." Man, she was even prettier when she laughed. He began to feel more relaxed and, despite his initial discomfort, he really began to enjoy her visit—which ended all too quickly because of the time limitations for visitors.

That was the first of Gina's visits; she came once more in February, but then visitors were banned for months and months because of the COVID-19 virus. Some prisoners with sentences that were nearly over and those convicted for minor crimes were released early in order to separate everyone more. Jack didn't qualify for either of those, of course. They tried to isolate or put fewer prisoners to a cell, and everyone had to eat their meals there too for a while after an outbreak. Then they tried having everyone wears masks. Even mail had to be treated with ultra-violet light to kill germs, but he and Gina both kept writing.

Gina had started taking yoga classes before the pandemic, but she wrote to tell him that all the classes were canceled now—she could only do yoga by Zoom. In the prison, the classes were no longer available either, and all the prisoners were isolated as much as possible. Jack began to do yoga in his cell, partially because it calmed him so much, and it kept his muscles strong and stretched in that confinement. Gina also told him that she'd stopped working at the bar because it was closed too. She said she had a lot more time to dedicate to her studies, even though most classes were on-line. She was short of money, but she said it was a lot better than working in a crummy bar with drunk men slobbering over her all the time, and she would get her degree more quickly. They communicated about their situation in common of being isolated and confined—it wasn't all negative.

Jack kept telling himself not to get too interested in her; he would still be in prison for a long time. She had told him she did have a boyfriend—she'd even tried living with him, but he was so messy that she had moved out. Besides, she told him, she wasn't ready to marry or commit herself. Was she just a friend to Jack? Or could it be something more? No, he would be here too long. But even if she stopped writing, even if she… well, she'd still been good for him. It felt so different to be able to tell somebody his thoughts—even though having her as a friend probably wouldn't last. Why would she want to wait around for an ex-con? But she had been loyal for a long time and she had begun to visit him again occasionally after the vaccine was developed for the virus and all the prisoners had been vaccinated—after things slowly got back to more normal.

In the meantime, Jack had shortened the time he was required to serve in prison. Except for the beginning—when he had been rather rebellious at times—he had been earning good-time credit that was slowing mounting up to shorten his prison stay—54 days off for each year of good behavior. Volunteering for things, like teaching the yoga classes, for instance, also earned him more credit. And paying Annie back some money not only had helped to relieve his own conscience but, also, had shortened his stay. The biggest boost to reducing his sentence though had to do with cooperating with the police and courts to charge other people in juvenile sex trafficking cases. He had not only helped the police identify his customers, like Romeo and John, for instance, but he had also ratted on his old buddy Duke. In court, Duke had glared at him like he couldn't believe that Jack would stab him in the back that way. But Jack didn't owe Duke a thing. In fact, Duke had gotten him into this whole mess by trying to repay a loan with what turned out to be a baited trap for Jack. And Jack definitely felt more compassion for Anita at this point than he did for Duke. Additionally, the whole babychicks.com website got torn apart, and many other promoters and users were apprehended. Jack's cooperation on all of that had definitely helped to cut his time.

So maybe someday he would get out of here. Maybe, by the time he got out, Gina might be interested in him—maybe as even more than a friend—just maybe—and maybe not. It wasn't something he could count on—not at all. But she'd helped him tons just by showing him he had some value, and she had told him that he had helped her too.

Jack was working on his GED now—Gina had challenged him to do it—and he was almost there. There was even a program to earn some college credit online in the prison, and he had plans to do that too. When he got out of the slammer he wanted to be able to do something other than hanging out in bars and gambling. He knew now that those kinds of places were not so good for him. There were other possibilities—even now he was giving encouragement talks to the other prisoners, as well as teaching the yoga classes. He was sure that he would find something that he really wanted to do by the time he qualified to be released. It was funny; now—even though he was in prison—he felt more hopeful, stronger, more confident, and FREER than he ever had in his life.

33

Anita

August 2026

I WHEEL MY CARRY-ON BAG out of the airport door—into the Midwest heat and humidity. It hits me with a jolt, but even this extreme weather feels oddly welcoming—like the summers I remember when I lived here—like home. Immediately I see Claire's blue Tesla with both her and *Mamá* in the front seat. Claire and Jim are so ecological—with their solar appliances and generator and now their electric car. Good for them! Claire pops the trunk open so I can put my suitcase inside, and I climb into the back seat with Claire's cute little boy, Andrew, with his straight brown hair, blue eyes, and freckles. He smiles at me. Suddenly everyone is talking at once.

"*Hola, mi hijita*. It's so good to see you! You look just beautiful, and I'm so proud of you!" says *Mamá* as she undoes her seatbelt and turns around to hold my face in her hands and to give me kisses. "How was your flight?"

"Congratulations, Anita, on passing the bar exam," says Claire excitedly while looking at me in the rear view mirror and getting ready to pull out into the line of traffic in front of the airport. "And on your new job! I'll give you hugs and kisses as soon as we get out of this airport mess."

"*Bonsoir*, Anita," adds Andrew shyly, leaning toward me to give me a quick kiss on the cheek. "*Ça va?*"

I laugh, "*Oui, ça va.* I can't believe you're speaking so much French all the time, Andrew," I praise him and give him a tight hug. "*¿Hablas español también?*"

"*Sí, un poco,*" he answers as he looks down toward his feet.

Claire pulls out of the space in the airport pick-up area and eases into the exiting traffic—accelerating rapidly then to blend into the flow of cars. We head south on the highway and soon exit onto I-35 to head south toward Olathe. I remember the very first time I did this with *Mamá* and Claire in the car—before Andrew was born—when *Mamá* first arrived from Mexico. This time I am just as happy—or even more so—to be all together with them. I'm so excited to see this family I love so much—*Mamá*, Claire, and Andrew. And soon I'll see Jim and my aunt Rosa too. They're all my family now.

My mother just turned fifty-nine, but she looks wonderful and healthy. Her curly, dark hair shines in the sunlight of the car, and she has no wrinkles that I can see on her face. I'm so proud of how she has adapted to her life in the US. She's been teaching Spanish at a high school here for about five years now and has wonderful stories about her students and their successes.

"*¿Cómo está Rosa?*" I ask, loving this moment of closeness in the car; smelling my mother's cinnamon-like scent I missed so much, not only when we were separated at the border but, also, while I was away at law school.

"Rosa is fine. She's at work now but she'll be home before our welcome dinner at Claire's house," *Mamá* responds, turning half-way around in her seat to look at me and smiling so deeply she glows.

Rosa and *Mamá* live in a small house about fifteen minutes from Claire's; the three of them are very close friends. Claire and Jim decided not to move away from Olathe after they took *Mamá* and me into their home. Now I think it was because they didn't want to move me from my school there, the friends I knew from the school, and perhaps the psychologist who was helping me get over all that had happened to me. They bought the house they had been renting from the electrical company—Claire said she couldn't bear to leave it—and it was easy for Jim's company to keep him on a more permanent basis in the Olathe office. He said he really liked it there anyway.

Mamá and I are both US citizens now after we applied through our T-visas, but Rosa is still technically undocumented, although she's recently applied for citizenship as well. I'm so glad she decided to move from Arizona to be here with *Mamá*. Luckily the situation for immigrants isn't as extreme now as it was when we crossed the border. That hostility toward immigrants back when we first came to the US is what led me to immigrant law though. I was so very certain that was what I wanted to do after all I had been through.

"How's your writing going, Claire?" I ask as I look out at the wide-open landscape I missed so much while at law school at Cornell. It's amazingly green for August.

"Oh, it's going well. I have a bit more time to write now that Andrew is in school and so grown up. I'm working on a historical novel about a French woman who immigrated to Canada, and it's been fun researching for it. My grandmother was of French-Canadian origin, so it's personally meaningful to me to learn more about that group of women. They also had a very tough situation," Claire says as she glances at me in the rear-view mirror, probably worried about how I will take this last statement.

"I can't wait to read it," I reassure her. "If you want some feedback from a fellow immigrant before it's published, just let me know. How's Jim doing?"

"Jim is fine and said to be sure to give you a big hug and tell you he'd see you tonight—but I haven't even had a chance to hug you yet at all! We've missed you tons but we're both so proud of you."

I smile and remember how Jim and Claire took care of me so wonderfully both before *Mamá* arrived and after. They were my second parents. Even after *Mamá* got here, they never let my birthday pass without a big celebration that included whatever type of cake I wanted that year, chocolate ice cream, and presents—especially lots of books, which I loved. They also let me invite as many of the new friends I had made at school as I wanted. They took us all to Worlds of Fun and the water park several times, as well as to museums and special celebrations. Jim even adopted my kitty Mía for me, I remember fondly. She had long, yellowish fur that reminded me of the color of the corn tortillas my *abuela* used to make, so I named her Mía Tortilla—because it sounded so cute and funny—but I usually only called her Mía. I take out my phone and show Andrew a picture of Mía sitting inside my carry-on bag when I was packing for this trip.

"Mía wanted to come with me to see you," I tell him.

"Did you bring her?" he asks, smiling widely and looking excited.

"No, they wouldn't let me. She's staying with a friend. You'll just have to come and see her soon—and me!"

"*Bien sûr*," he states so naturally I can't believe he's always lived in the US. Maybe Claire's French ancestry?

I continue thinking of Jim and Claire and how they always planned with *Mamá* about how to make me feel at home here. Jim is the only father I had after my own *papá* was killed back in Mexico. I still haven't even been able to see my *abuelos* or *tíos,* who were always so close. If it weren't for Jim, I'm not sure I would ever have been able to trust men again—especially US men. But Jim was so patient and understanding toward me—both in his actions and his words. He thoughtfully led me into some very deep conversations about all I went through. He specifically told me he didn't want me to think that all men in the US were like the ones I had met after I arrived. He also negotiated with the lawyers regarding the payments Jack made to me that assisted me with my tuition at university and law school.

And I am still perplexed about how Claire rescued me. When it happened, I thought she was the Virgin Mary and had supernatural powers. But after I got older I felt totally bewildered about how she climbed up that rickety ladder to pull me out of Jack's house. The ladder even broke apart, and we were plummeting through the air but didn't fall and both landed, amazingly, on our feet. I do remember that clearly. And I can't imagine how she even found me there. She's explained how she drove by the house and saw Jack pushing me into the van and then saw us again at Walmart. But, logically, it all doesn't quite make sense. In contrast to all the rationality and philosophical thought I was exposed to in law school, just being here in the car near Claire again is reigniting my sense of wonder and mystery, opening unused boundaries. I can sense the mystical again—like back when I commuted with fairies all the time. Claire is amazing! I'll have to ask her more about how she really found and rescued me. I'm sure there is more to it than I realize.

Both Jim and Claire truly freed me. Andrew is a very lucky boy to have a caring, communicative father like Jim and an imaginative, loving mother like Claire!

Speaking of Andrew, I turn to him now. He's rattling along to me in French again, as if that were his native tongue—or mine. Why is he so fluent in French? It's incredible, I think. Maybe Spanish, because my mother, aunt, and I were always speaking to him and around him in Spanish—even as a baby. But French?

Acknowledgements

My unending gratitude goes to everyone who encouraged me to write this novel. My artist brother-in-law, Bill Schumm, first suggested that a novel should be my next project after I wrote an unrelated short-story for him to thank him for a painting. Our writer's group—Ken Buch, Kim Condon, Sharon Condon, Joseph Rodriguez, David Strabala, and Lois Wilkins—animated and critiqued me throughout the entire process. I appreciate my granddaughter Mary Clare's desire for me to read each new chapter to her; she gave me valuable feedback about what she wanted to know about the characters and pointed out specific errors. Many thanks to Caryn Mirriam-Goldberg for her critique and her excellent advice about how to flesh out my story. Marge Banks read the manuscript several times and, thankfully, spotted many details I had overlooked. Carolyn and Madeline Lamphier helped me with the wording for my synopsis. Marguerite Schumm, in addition to designing the cover for my book, helped me perfect the layout. I also appreciate that so many of my dear friends and loved ones have asked continually about the progress of my book. And, without the loving support of my husband, Robert, my four amazing children, their wonderful spouses, and my fantastic grandchildren, I probably never would have completed the novel. Thank you to all of you!

Of course, since this is a work of fiction, all of the characters and events in the book are either my imaginative creations or are used fictitiously. Some places, such as the *Casa del Migrante* in Ciudad Juárez (whose director is *truly* Father Javier Calvillo) and the Clint, Texas Immigration Detention Center, actually exist but are used in a fictional

way. Others places, such as the town of Luis Aldama, which my character Ana claims as her hometown, do not exist. That town's name was
created by me to represent a place with a dangerous situation that could
possibly exist and might cause some of its citizens to need to migrate to
a different area or country. The friends and family that I have in Mexico actually live in safe areas and do not feel that threat, but there are
areas in many countries that pose dangerous hazards to their citizens.

The problem of separation of parents and children at the border
in recent years is a veritable tragedy that will have negative consequences for years. I am indebted to Vivian Van Vleet and her expertise
regarding immigrant children, T-Visas, and the guardian ad litem status; she helped me immensely in understanding the real process in these
situations. I also researched numerous books and news articles to make
my fictional situation regarding both immigration problems and child
trafficking as true to life as possible. Unfortunately, those issues are *not*
just fiction.

Of utmost importance is these acknowledgements is my gratitude
to my late aunt and uncle Ellen and Caleb Lipscomb for inspiring my
interest in the Spanish language, in Hispanic cultures, and in travel to
other countries. When I was ten or eleven years old, my uncle started a
business relationship with the Erosa family in Mérida, Yucatán, Mexico.
Their professional association developed into a close friendship that
extended throughout our families and throughout the years. Our families still maintain close ties; in essence, they are a wonderful part of my
family.

Made in the USA
Columbia, SC
09 September 2020

19999168R00136